Fighting Over You

'Sexy bitch,' said Josh. 'I've given you enough for the first date. I don't want you to think I'm too easy.' He yawned. 'The trouble with sex is it makes me want to go to sleep, and I guess we better get something done today.'

'After lunch. On me. Wherever you like,' said Yasmin.

Josh raised his eyebrows. 'Really? Wherever?'

'Sure. Damn the expense.'

He laughed. 'All right. A pint of Young's and a steak pie at the Rose and Crown – that all right with you? Or are you a vegetarian alcohol-free zone?'

'Like hell. I like food and drink almost as much as sex.'

'Good girl. I almost wish your errant husband would run off with his little violinist and leave you to me.'

'No you don't. You don't want a full-on relationship at the moment. You want a little playmate.'

He laughed and stood up, pulling on his disreputably creased jacket. Yasmin ruffled his hair affectionately. Really, to think she'd been cross at the prospect of working with him. Things really were looking up. A mate, a colleague, a good shag – well, from his performance with his mouth she guessed he would be. What more could a girl ask for?

Author's Other Titles:

Fire and Ice
On the Edge
Going Too Far

Fighting Over You
Laura Hamilton

BLACK LACE

Black Lace books contain sexual fantasies.
In real life, always practise safe sex.

First published in 2003 by
Black Lace
Thames Wharf Studios
Rainville Road
London W6 9HA

Design by Smith & Gilmour, London
Printed and bound by Mackays of Chatham PLC

ISBN 0 352 33795 8

1

Looking back on the night of the fateful dinner at Jalabert's, Yasmin realised that the main source of her anger was that she had absolutely *no idea* what was going on in U's mind. Obviously, otherwise she wouldn't have worn the new deep-violet velvet slip dress with nothing but a lilac satin thong and matching fishnet hold-ups, though as it went they proved their value in other ways. But she had put them on for U, for the energetic sex she had anticipated after dinner and maybe a few drinks at Juicy Lucy's, preferably on the huge divan in the low-lit meditation room on the top floor of their flat, overlooking Clapham Common but not overlooked by anyone else. She had even chosen the colour of the thong to match the throw on the divan, because U liked things to flow and she usually went with his flow.

Instead of the evening she'd planned, however, U chose the moment when the plates were cleared, pudding declined and coffee ordered – decaf for him, of course – to slide seamlessly into the conversation about the sudden relegation of world music to the ranks of the totally unhip in order to give way to the rise of contemporary serious music the fact that he was having an affair with Amelia.

'Who's Amelia?' Yasmin was so used to knowing who was who that she was more taken aback by the unfamiliar name than the fact that her partner was being unfaithful.

'When I say an affair, I don't mean I have technically fucked her.'

How do you fuck someone untechnically or, come to that, technically? Yasmin wondered. A split second behind her in conversation, he added, 'Pandora's niece, you've met her. The violinist. She's just come back from a year in New York.'

'Oh, that Amelia. Last time I met her she was about twelve. Is this a joke?' Of course it was pure coincidence that he was screwing a violin-playing Lolita and that avant-garde classical music was the next big thing – wasn't it?

'I'm obsessed with her. I can't work, I'm just not picking things up properly, my mind's stuck on her.'

She noticed that he didn't even look apologetic. It was as though he was explaining that he wasn't feeling up to going on to a club because he had a cold coming rather than anything relatively life-shattering.

'It's only a phase, of course, but I thought it was fair to let you know,' he continued in a reasonable tone.

'She's a child. You're forty-two years old.'

'What does age matter? She's nineteen. And she's changed.'

'She'd have to for any sane guy to obsess about her. She used to look like George out of the *Famous Five*.'

'I'm sorry?'

Yasmin had to concede that even an Englishman would probably be baffled by the reference to her mother's ancient Enid Blyton books she had treasured as a child, and a German obviously had no chance.

'A scruffy-haired tomboy.'

'Yes, maybe. But now she looks more like – I was going to say Courtney Love, but that's not right. Well, never mind. She's got attitude. And some. New York has matured her.'

Like Courtney Love? Attitude? Please. So Amelia – stupid name – had discovered sex and make-up and dyed her hair. When the waiter appeared with the coffee, Yasmin asked for a large Armagnac, sharp. She needed it.

'U, we've never discussed our little ... indiscretions, have we? What's going on here? Unless you're planning to move in with her, which I doubt, you could have just fucked her, technically or otherwise, and I wouldn't have known.'

He sighed and sipped his decaf. 'Because I can't work, because I can't keep this a secret, and because I thought it was fair to tell you. The other things, well, they were temporary, but this might not be.'

Yasmin kept to herself the fact that she'd screwed Rory O'Hagan senseless for three months when she was working on *Tinker's Curse* last year. Shame he'd moved to Hollywood and she'd moved on to writing scripts for the sensational soon-to-be-premiered adult-orientated soap *49 Madison Avenue*, set in an über-cool glossy town centre hotel whose employees were, basically, screwing each other as vigorously as she'd screwed Rory. But that wasn't the point. Anyway, how was he defining temporary?

'So what else? Do you want to split, is that it?'

U looked self-righteously shocked. 'No, of course not. I can't imagine ever leaving you, Yasmin. But this is ... big ... though not bigger than us. You might think I should just walk away, but I can't. I'm not going to.'

Thank God the drink arrived. Apart from the fact that she most definitely needed a large alcoholic boost, it provided an excuse for her to step outside the situation for a minute. The great thing about working in TV – well, Yasmin realised there were lots of great things about working in TV, but the valuable one in the particular situation she suddenly found herself in – was that in the odd moments of drama in one's own life, of which she found there were surprisingly few compared to those in the characters of the average soap, it was almost inevitable that you could stand back and assess the situation the way you would if you were writing the scene yourself.

So what did she see? The soap: a quality glossy set in the glamorous world of trendsetting magazines and television, where the main characters were an elegant German magazine editor in his early forties and his slightly younger, beautiful wife, English through and through despite the fact that her actual father, the one who provided the DNA but did a bunk after a couple of years, was Turkish. The scene: the couple have just finished dinner at a newly opened, blond wood and yellow walls, the usual that year, London restaurant. She is dressed dramatically in minimal velvet, he in his usual summer whites, or rather off-whites, trousers and collarless shirt handcrafted in Devon from unbleached organic cotton. The plot: he has just told her he's having an affair with a much younger woman. She reacts – how?

Should she shout at him, stand up and walk out? Discuss it rationally? Yasmin considered the options. Maybe walk over to the actor she knew two tables away and summon him into the ladies for a revenge fuck? But it wasn't *Sex in the City*, and anyway the guy he was with was more than just a friend. Apart from which, as the preceding dialogue had just indicated, and as the viewers would of course already know if they'd followed the series from the beginning, they had never set much store by fidelity.

She moved back inside her own life rather than looking at it objectively as a drama and decided that rationality was the only way forward. U hated scenes and she wasn't keen herself. Let the drama stay on the screen.

'Then let's get practical. You've got to be able to work. Will it be easier now you've told me?'

'I hope so. The problem is that over the last two weeks I've thought about her all the time. It's hard to pick up on other people's thoughts when you're obsessed with your own.'

U was acclaimed in the style world for his ability to predict trends by tuning into thoughts and desires that escaped from other people's unconsciousnesses; not exactly the collective unconscious, he always said, more the unexpressed collective wishes. He dismissed accusations that he used telepathy, rather asserting that it was an ability to latch on to what he described as ideas and possibilities vibrating in the dimension of thought waves. It was how he so successfully predicted trends, foresaw the next big thing and generally kept afloat the most influential style magazine ever. *Slice* was most definitely his magazine; the writers, photographers and production staff were all dispensable, but U was not. No one else had a gift like his. It was a miracle, a marvel, a phenomenon.

In essence, U himself was a phenomenon. Born in what was then West Berlin at the turn of the sixties, Urs Steinmann had at an early age started to sense what was going to happen. Not to predict events like a soothsayer, nothing so crass, but to tune into the *zeitgeist*, to realise the students were going to revolt before he was out of kindergarten, that it was going to dissolve into the summer of love and that love and peace weren't going to last. He knew that the strains of the sitar were going to give way to electronica even before Tangerine Dream had stopped reciting nursery rhymes.

From the age of ten he started to keep a diary predicting trends in music and clothes and realised he was eighty per cent successful. He went to university to study journalism and design, worked hard at English, dropped two letters from his name and got a job in London on *Black Box*, Pandora Fairchild's influential magazine. It was only a matter of time before he set up on his own, having by then moved in with Yasmin, who also wrote for *Black Box* before going into TV scriptwriting.

She looked across the table at him. His close-cropped blond hair, his tanned face, his penetrating blue eyes, his quintessentially Aryan good looks, were overshadowed by the worry etched on his features. He was as gorgeous to her as ever. She was certainly not going to let some little violin-playing slut related to that past-it old cow Pandora muscle in between them, but that wasn't going to be achieved by creating a scene here or anywhere else.

'Oh, Bear. What are we going to do?'

Bear was her intimate name for him; Urs meant bear, he had told her when they started seeing each other properly, which was why he had changed his name to U. She could understand it, because his blond good looks and immaculate appearance had nothing bearish about them; although in his whiteness and savagery as far as protecting the reputation of his magazine was concerned, he could be likened to the polar variety. It was a good name, though, to use when she desired the animal in him rather than the stylophile. Not that she was trying to raise the animal in him now, but she wanted to emphasise their own unique relationship.

'I knew something was coming. After all, I sensed

the new celibacy was coming years before it did, then I knew we were going into postmodern promiscuity. Obviously that's lasted a long time, but I knew something else was coming. I just didn't expect to find out about it like this.'

'What the hell are you talking about?'

'The new sex. I *knew* it! I *felt* it coming! But before I could articulate it I found myself caught up with Amelia!'

Yasmin was starting to feel a little irritable. She stared at U until he paid attention and realised that he wasn't making sense.

'It's a way of putting screwing on to an irrelevant plane of a relationship. Amelia will screw at random, but not me because we're in a relationship. She reserves sex for chance encounters.'

'So what are you, just another string to her bow?'

He managed the ghost of a smile and shrugged.

'So it's a mind fuck?'

'Yes – and no. I can't describe it, Yasmin.'

Yasmin was baffled and annoyed at the same time. 'Oh, sure, you don't think I even want to know the exact details, do you?'

'It's not so easy.'

'Can it, U. I thought she lived in the country when we met her, anyway. She's obviously moved to London.'

'She's staying with Pandora. While she studies at the Royal Academy of Music.'

Great, thought Yasmin. Not only is she living with a voracious old harpy who has seriously never forgiven U for moving in with me when she was screwing him from time to time, but what's more she's set to stay here for years scraping her bloody instrument.

A suspicion crossed her mind. 'Why are you telling me tonight? You're not planning on seeing her, are you?'

He had the grace to look ashamed. 'I don't know – I didn't know what you wanted to do after dinner. I just said that if we didn't have any plans I might call round later. She's at the opera seeing *La Traviata*.'

That was the last straw. Never mind the plans for energetic sex with her, he was planning to not technically fuck Amelia back at Pandora's. Yasmin contemptuously imagined Pandora unable to resist the urge to join in, niece or not. She shivered at the thought and picked up her bag.

'OK, have a nice night. I'll see you later. Or tomorrow. Whatever.'

U stood too. 'Yasmin, I didn't mean that you should leave me to –'

'Look, you can't describe your relationship with her. Maybe tomorrow you can tell me what you did tonight, and I'll try to understand.'

She was just about keeping her cool. U couldn't stand scenes.

'U, I'm seriously telling you to do what you like. I have a friend I said I might look in on, too, so it suits me fine.'

She even managed to plant a finger kiss on his cheek. '*Auf Wiedersehen*, pet.'

Soho's not the best place to wander alone wearing a skimpy dress, fishnets and stilettos, but Yasmin tried to look purposeful as she walked down Broadwick Street. Her mind was once again working on two levels. On one it was tearing itself into shreds with a mixture of outrage, fury, total despair and the desire to collapse in helpless tears. But the other was seeing Lisanne from *49 Madison Avenue* stalking the streets of Kings-down, a fictional area of London that bore an uncanny resemblance to Knightsbridge. Coincidentally the first trauma in the plot of the new series had been Johnny, Lisanne's husband, confessing to an affair. Tears streaming silently down her face, Lisanne had wandered the busy streets aimlessly, the neon-lit background shot out of focus, with the odd passer-by turning to look at the tear-stained face of the tragic heroine. The episode ended as she sobbed just once, stifled it with her hand, then, looking heart-brokenly into the window of a busy pizza restaurant, had muttered, 'Oh, Johnny . . .'

Get a grip, Yasmin told herself. This is real life, let's think of a real life solution. Unfortunately the *49* solution she relished was Lisanne distractedly walking under a bus, because she couldn't stand the little tart, but this was Yasmin in Soho, and she had to go somewhere because she sure wasn't going to be sitting meekly at home waiting for U to return later, or worse the next day, after not technically fucking his new babe.

No matter how wide a circle of acquaintances you've got, there's never one within spitting distance you can turn to in a moment of crisis. Yasmin was starting to get most definitely pissed off with Soho, betrayal and life in general when she remembered Wee Willie.

It wasn't his real name, of course, but the arrival of a six-foot-four redheaded Scotsman on the set of *Over the Border* who would only answer to the name of Willie, what's more, pronounced as 'Wullie', naturally led to the prefix. Wee Willie had been killed off when his lifeboat had capsized after successfully rescuing a family in distress in their yacht off the coast of Galloway a few years ago. The series itself died shortly afterwards and, having missed out on getting a part in *Braveheart*, thanks to another redheaded Scots giant getting in first, Willie had decided to abandon acting and bought a bar in Soho, proclaiming that Irish bars seemed to be spreading faster than shamrocks and it was time the Scots got in on the act.

They had got on really well, especially after she wrote his last words: 'Scotland, ma hame, ma heart ...' as the waves broke over the deck for the last time.

Not one to miss out on a PR coup, Wee Willie had named his wine bar 'Over the Border' after the TV series, which at the time was still fresh in the minds of the public. Yasmin had gone to the opening party but she hadn't seen him since, and it was with joy and an almost superstitious sense of coincidence that she realised it was in fact just round the corner.

With relief she pushed her way through the royal blue and white doorway and the crowd up to the bar. Both the bar and the dining tables were packed, and as it was getting to the end of the evening everyone seemed to be slightly dislocated by booze and having a damn sight better time than she was. Wee Willie was nowhere in sight, and as it obviously wasn't her night she backtracked on her optimism and started to bet with herself that this had not been a good idea. The barman, a smiling dark-haired Scotsman – of course – asked her what he could get her.

'Willie, if possible. I'm an old friend.'

He raised his eyebrows theatrically. 'Oh yes? And can I give him your name? If he's around?'

Gay, of course. Was there a barman in London who wasn't either gay, Antipodean or possibly both?

'Yasmin.'

The one advantage of having an unusual name was that she rarely needed to use another.

'Hang on.'

He went to the end of the bar, kilt swinging over his pert little behind, and picked up a phone. Yasmin wished she'd ordered a drink while she waited, but then if Willie wasn't in, or receiving, she wasn't going to hang around with all these jolly punters. But just as she'd decided she was out of luck and maybe she'd just check into a hotel for the night and order a bottle of Armagnac from room service, Willie appeared from the back of the room.

'Yasmin, pet! About bloody time, mind you! I'd almost given up hope of ever seeing you again.'

Enfolded in Willie's huge arms, her head barely reaching his shoulders, Yasmin felt safe and even, wonderfully, loved.

'You look absolutely terrific. That hairstyle's brilliant! I don't think I'd have recognised you.'

She'd almost forgotten the difference her hair made to her; when she had worked with Willie it had been its natural luxuriant black curls, cascading glossily halfway down her back. For the last couple of months though she had had it braided, enjoying the relative flatness against her scalp, and changed her make-up accordingly, from understated eyes but brilliant red lips, to smoky eyeshadow to match her soot dark eyes, and vibrant violet lipstick which matched the merest tint on her high cheekbones, not to mention her dress. With her slightly hooked, aristocratic, Arabic nose she did look stunning.

'Come on, pet, come through to the back. We're just having a wee drink before we go out to dinner.'

'Oh, shit, you're going out!' She realised she'd betrayed herself and tried to cover up. 'I mean, never mind, look, I was just on my way home, don't worry, I'll call in another time . . .'

'Darling girl, whatever's the matter?' Willie looked at her, concerned. 'God almighty, you need a friend and I'm due to go out for dinner with Isla's folks. Her wee sister's just graduated from St Andrews and they're all down for the weekend. Now just sit down and tell me what's wrong.'

He gestured at the barman who produced two bar stools and they sat close together at the bar in front of two glasses of whisky which also seemed to have materialised from nowhere. Despite having been on the brandy Yasmin took a swift gulp.

'I'm being a big baby, Willie. But U's just told me he's having an affair with some nineteen-year-old, not any nineteen-year-old actually, but Pandora Fairchild's niece ... she's staying with her.'

'Christ. The shit.' Willie looked as though he'd happily capsize U's lifeboat if he had half the chance. 'And Pandora, that old cow. I bet she introduced them on purpose.'

There was no love lost between Willie and Pandora. They had met when the cast of *Over the Border* had been featured in *Black Box*. Pandora's combination of *faux* innocence and arrogance had got straight up Willie's nose and he'd spent the whole interview taking the piss out of her.

'Yeah, I wondered. You know she and U were an item before I came on the scene – I wonder if this is like getting him back in some way.'

Willie choked on his whisky. 'Pandora and U? Sorry to say this, petal, but the man needs his head examining. Unless it was a career move?'

Yasmin shook her head. 'I don't think so, he was already well in with the magazine before he got well in with her, so I heard.'

Willie gazed at her. 'Jesus, if I wasn't a happily

cohabiting man I'd like to give you the chance of a bit of revenge, pet, that's for sure. In fact, even though I'm a happily cohabiting man and can't make it tonight, how about –'

'No way!' Yasmin laughed. 'You and Isla are a perfect couple. Anyway, a revenge fuck seems a bit childish, don't you think?' Not to mention that's exactly what Lisanne did after finding out about her unfaithful husband, she thought.

'What's wrong with being childish? I'll tell you what though, pet, come through the back and have a wee drink with us anyway.' His face took on a cunning look. 'It's just me and Isla, Gavin and Euan – you remember Euan, don't you?'

'Oh yes, I remember Euan.'

She could hardly forget the bar's chef. He had flirted heavily with her at the bar's opening party, much to her entertainment. Apart from being a flamboyant character with a wickedly amusing tongue he was drop-dead gorgeous, and she'd been flattered. Willie had obviously remembered it too.

Taking her by the hand he led her through to a small back room, where a table was littered with empty bottles of Scottish organic beer and half-full bottles of different types of whisky. Willie's partner, Isla, and his manager, Gavin, were smoking languidly, while Euan, still in chef's whites, was sitting well back from the table, his feet crossed on top of it, yawning ferociously.

'Here's something to wake you up, boy,' said Willie, slapping Euan's legs down off the table.

The chef looked up enquiringly and slowly a wide, joyous smile spread across his face. Without being conventionally handsome, with his wide, high forehead, snub nose and square jaw, Euan Beattie's attractiveness lay in the fact that he loved women and wasn't afraid to let it show, especially in his intimate smile. He had an enormous appetite for food and for sex; although he couldn't be described as fat, the appetite for food gave his build a stockiness that he only managed to control with strenuous workouts in the gym every morning; and the appetite for sex gave him an animal confidence and natural intimacy of manner that made women fall at his feet.

Unlike most men, it was true to say of him that he liked all women. But he especially liked attractive women, and even more especially attractive women in skimpy dresses who didn't seem to have a man in tow.

While greeting Isla and Gavin, Yasmin was aware of Euan's eyes on her – or maybe she was aware that if she were writing the scene, they would be appreciatively running over her caramel coloured shoulders and bare back, her fishnet-clad legs under the short skirt and her calves, their curves pronounced by the high heels. Willie poured her another whisky, she talked to Isla about her family, Isla quizzed her about *49 Madison Avenue* and, before she knew it, Gavin had excused himself to go back to work, Willie and Isla had regretfully left for their family dinner, and Euan was pouring her another drink. She didn't want it, but she knew that he was pouring it to indicate that he didn't expect her to leave just yet, which was fine with her because she didn't want to.

'So what are you doing alone in Soho on a Saturday night wearing fishnet tights and fuck-me shoes, Yasmin?'

Unlike the others who came from the cities of the Lowlands, Euan was from the Highlands and, rather than harshly accented, his voice was low and caressing, his soft accent sounding to Yasmin to have more in common with Irish than Scottish. The intimacy in his voice was emphasised by the way he twisted his whole body round to face her, making her feel protected from the rest of the world, which as far as she was concerned had suddenly turned remarkably shitty.

She decided she couldn't be bothered to pick up on his lead about her clothing and joke about just looking for business. Unfortunately she had to admit to herself that, scriptwriter or not, she wasn't able to come up with a fictional alternative to the truth. After all, just wandering around Soho looking for a friend sounded more than a bit sad.

'You remember U? My husband? Well, boringly, and in retrospect stupidly, I'd put on the fuck-me shoes for him. We were in Jalabert's –' she checked her watch '– just over half an hour ago, I was still licking the last drops of lamb jus from my lips, and he told me he's having a thing with an nineteen-year-old.'

'Bummer,' said Euan gravely. 'How was dinner?'

Yasmin burst out laughing. 'I knew that was coming! You bloody chefs are all the same. Very good, actually. Leg of new season's Welsh lamb, served pink, with a shallot, rosemary and green peppercorn jus on a bed of rösti potatoes served with a garlicky purée of broad beans.'

'Hey, you're good at this. Have you ever done any food writing?'

'In my early days on *What Women Want* – but you're missing the point, dear.'

Euan smiled archly. 'No I'm not, but you can't blame a cook for asking about food. You can tell me about the starter later. No, hang on, you don't have to, I bet you had asparagus. You look like the kind of woman who takes a hands-on approach to food, not to mention one who knows what's fresh and available and makes the most of it while she can.'

He was looking at Yasmin intently, his hazel eyes slightly hooded.

'You're right,' she admitted, raising one eyebrow to acknowledge his double entendre: she knew he wanted her to take a hands-on approach to him, and was signalling that he was only too available. She'd often worked in a pool of writers and was used to picking up on someone else's lead in a conversation.

'Did you have pudding?'

'Hey, can we skip the menu deconstruction?' She laughed. 'No, I didn't.'

He had drawn even closer to her and his eyes were probing hers insistently. 'Neither did I. I think I'd like my dessert now. And I think you deserve yours, too.'

'I get it,' she said, her voice faint as she suddenly felt short of breath. 'My just desserts, you mean.'

'Naturally. With a younger man, of course. Don't you think it's always best to balance the scales?'

Yasmin nodded slowly. Although she'd told Willie it would be childish to seek a revenge fuck, and although she didn't want her life to shadow the miserable Lisanne's, she couldn't pretend to herself that she wouldn't have been tempted by Euan anyway. Not only was the proximity of his muscled torso to her lightly clad body tantalisingly warming, but his word-play had amused her and his compelling light-brown eyes were penetrating hers almost as thoroughly as he was planning to penetrate her elsewhere.

'Where do you . . . eat dessert?'

'In the kitchen, of course. I have my little pudding preparation table at the back, out of the way.'

'Won't there be . . . other chefs in there?'

He shrugged, his eyes still on hers, part playful, part veiled in desire.

'We're almost finished now. Just a couple of lads

clearing up. The sous chefs'll be having an extended fag break at the back door. Anyway, if I tell them to mind their own business, they'll take no notice.'

For the first time he touched her, his big hands, scarred with cuts of kitchen knives and burns from searingly hot ovens, caressing her shoulders so that the straps of her dress fell down her arms. Yasmin realised that her breath was coming quickly and that her breasts were rising and falling fairly obviously under the deep-purple dress.

'Your body's so warm,' Euan murmured. 'Let me cool you down before I warm you up again.'

She didn't have the faintest idea what he was talking about and cared even less as he stood, his hands still on her shoulders. They were face to face and she knew the desire in his eyes was mirrored by that in her own. He let go of her shoulders after putting her straps decorously back in place and, taking her by the hand, led her through the side door of the kitchen. The first thing she noticed was the temperature in the room, even though there was no cooking going on any longer, as he walked purposefully through the long and narrow room to a small island at the rear where a stainless steel table was flanked by two large fridges.

He was right: the kitchen was almost empty. The washing-up was being tackled by a young lad at a massive double sink but that was at the other end of the kitchen, while another was emptying an industrial-sized dishwasher. An older man was whistling out of tune along with the music on the radio as he sliced cheese and put oatcakes on to plates. The swing door at the front of the room banged twice as a kilt-clad waiter came in for coffee and went out again, but that was just out of sight.

Euan put his arms around her shoulders and looked

her in the eyes. 'Are you ready for this?' he asked gravely, his voice a soft lilt.

'I don't know what you mean about cooling me down. It's like an oven in here.'

He nodded, still smiling at her, and moved his hands down to her legs and ran them up the back of her thighs, up to her buttocks. She held her breath as his hands were allowed almost unimpeded access to her arse thanks to the slenderness of the scrap of lilac satin, and then suddenly realised exactly what he'd meant as he lifted her hips and sat her down on the stainless steel.

'Christ, that's freezing!' She dare not move; she felt as though the metal had stuck to her arse and the back of her thighs, like an ice cube sticks to your fingers and you briefly worry that your skin will come off in strips.

Euan laughed unsympathetically as he pushed her down so that her bare back and shoulders also came joltingly into contact with the cold table. The beads at the end of her braids clattered against the metal and she wondered if the noise would arouse the attention of any of the workers.

'Once you get past the shock, you'll find there's something amazingly warming about coldness,' he offered, his smile wicked. 'Like a cold shower.'

'Not one of my usual habits,' said Yasmin faintly, unable to raise her voice any higher. But she could see what he meant. The cold metal was almost burning on her naked skin. Like ice, like fire, she thought to herself. Like when someone fingers your clit long and slow and it burns so much with desire that at the same time it almost feels icy cold.

'Put your arms up and hold on to the edge of the table,' Euan – asked her? Instructed her? – she didn't mind or care which as she snaked her arms above her head and found her fingers curled over the rim of the table. This time the shock of the cold steel on her arms was expected, or she might even say anticipated, and it was more pleasurable than painful.

'You gorgeous girl, you're a perfect fit,' he said admiringly. 'I've had a few women on this table – not that I'm trying to make you jealous, you understand – but you're the first one who's fitted so well.'

She saw his eyes travel over her body. She couldn't help but be aware that the short skirt of her dress was riding high as her arms stretched upwards, and that the top of her hold-ups would be exposed, and that he could probably see the bottom of her lilac satin thong. If he could see that he could almost certainly see the lush black curls escaping from it, because she hadn't had a beach holiday for a few months and U liked her unwaxed when possible. And he would see that her breasts, flattened by her prone position, pointed upwards and outwards, rounded and trying to escape from the velvet, and she had no doubt that he would also notice what she was pretty sure of, that her nipples were big and hard and straining against the material that held them. For the first time it occurred to her that she would like to work on an erotic film, where she could choreograph scenes such as this rather than churn out predictable slanging matches between dysfunctional families and downbeat neighbours.

Euan had disappeared from her range of vision; she had nothing but the stark white fluorescently lit ceiling to stare at.

'What do you feel like, Yasmin?' his disembodied voice asked.

She laughed with a catch in her voice, as at that moment he lifted the skirt of her dress and pushed it up around her waist. She imagined his eyes on her crotch and wondered if the heat she was feeling there was also showing wet on her thong, the pale lilac turning a darker and darker shade of mauve.

'Feel like? Well, sexy. Vulnerable. Like I could be – I could be on an operating table, with those bright lights. Or a sacrifice in some devil-worshipping cult.'

'Very kinky. Don't forget this is merely a dessert preparation table. Speaking of which –' his hands and then his head came into view as he leaned over her, his thumbs gently stroking her nipples through the velvet '– I think there are a couple of cherries ripe and hard in here.'

Yasmin giggled. 'No, not cherries. More like – chocolate chips, if you like.'

He gently scooped her breasts out of the round neck of her dress and tucked the fabric beneath them. 'My God. You weren't joking. Lovely big chocolatey nipples. More like M&Ms than mere choc chips. I really cannot wait.'

His mouth fastened around one of her nipples and began to suck gently while his hand teased the other. Yasmin closed her eyes and concentrated on the growing pulsation of her sex muscles. This was going to be a treat. And as he said, she deserved it. Her just desserts.

Euan straightened up and stood to the side of her, one hand still toying with her breasts while the other traced the outline of her violet lips.

'Before you get too comfortable and that table gets too warm, I'd like to inspect the other side of you.'

'Now I feel like a carcass you're about to cut up into joints.'

'Gorgeous girl, what a sordid imagination.'

She brought one arm down to lean on and turned on to her side, facing him, and then over on to her front. The table had heated up slightly from her body, but the unyielding surface was still a shock to her bare breasts and nipples, warmed into fiery peaks by the attentions of his mouth and hands. However, her mons was more than grateful to slide up the solid surface and she could almost feel her clit tensing into a hard bud in anticipation of something to push against. As she moved her hands up to grab the edge of the table as before, Euan pushed her skirt up to her waist and circled both hands round her bare buttocks, so forcing her pubic mound down on to the cold metal. The muscles of her sex started to feel deliciously shivery and she was afraid she would come before he even had the chance to touch her there. But though she wasn't going to push it, she wasn't going to fight it either; she almost felt like she could come and come again tonight.

Before her body could take over, Euan turned her round again and pulled the thong off her legs, then pulled down his chef's trousers and pulled his cock out.

'Great turn on, these pants,' he observed ironically before she could. 'Now chefs are becoming sex symbols I'm sure there's an alternative design on the drawing board for occasions such as this, but I'm afraid at the moment there's nothing more I can do.' He grinned as he fished in his pocket and brought out a condom. 'At least there are handy pockets to carry essential equipment in.'

She watched as he dropped the foil on the floor and rolled the rubber quickly and efficiently over his cock, giving her little time to inspect it. Not that she cared what it looked like; it was big enough to fill her up satisfyingly, and she guessed his dextrous fingers would be as efficiently successful on her clit.

'Like pulling an icing bag over a nozzle,' he quipped as he finished.

'Better than a skin on a sausage.' She laughed.

'Oh, God, yes, after all this is –'

'Yeah, yeah, the dessert table,' she finished for him.

'Correct. Of course I should make sure that you're actually ready for dessert.'

She doubted that he could seriously think she wasn't, but as his fingers touched her for the first time not only did he exclaim at the copiousness of her wetness but she couldn't help a noise escape her own throat at his touch.

'Peachy,' he said, running his fingers slowly up to her clit from her entrance and back again. 'Like poached peaches, slippery with syrupy juice. In fact –'

Before he could finish a door banged somewhere behind them and voices came towards them. Obviously the sous chefs back from their break.

'Blimey, there's a sight for –'

'Fuck off. And I mean that,' said Euan, his voice dangerously low, without taking his eyes or his fingers off Yasmin's glistening slit.

The three men didn't fuck off straight away, but jostled each other, one whistling at the sight of Yasmin.

'Just for you, chef, or –'

'Just for me,' said Euan in the same tone of voice. 'And if you don't get out now, you're fired.'

He raised his eyes to hers. She'd blushed a bit at the thought of three strangers seeing her spread out on the kitchen table like a banquet, practically naked apart from the velvet around her middle like a wide belt, while Euan fingered her obviously wet pussy. But at the same time the admiring, envious tone of their voices and the mere fact of the public display was a turn-on. After all, she wasn't famous, they'd never find out who she was. She wondered what it would be like to star in an erotic film rather than write a scene for one, how it would feel to be fucked while people watched, instructed, commented, and whether they would get turned on by it themselves. As she imagined the sous chefs going to tell the others what was happening and the covert glances in her direction, Euan pushed his cock hard in to her.

'Put your legs round me, gorgeous girl,' he murmured as he thrust slowly in and out of her. 'Sorry about them.'

'I don't mind,' she whispered. 'It's a bit of a turn-on.'

'You mean you weren't turned on already? Jesus, woman, you must have dipped your hand into the peach juice when I wasn't looking and poured half a pint of it up yourself.'

Her laugh came out high and girlish; she was prepared to let him call the shots, as he was obviously expecting to.

'Move your arms down and hold on to the sides of the table,' he told her. 'You fuck me, Yasmin. You go at your speed.'

Obeying his direction she gripped the edges of the table as low as her hands would reach. Bracing herself on them she slid her body up the table gradually until his cock was inside her by no more than half an inch and then pushed back equally languidly. She did it twice more, distracted by his fingers still insistently stroking her clit, and then thrust down on him hard and fast, two, three, four times.

'I'll come in no time if you do that, woman,' he told her, though she could tell he had no objection to that, none at all.

A smile played round his lips. 'With those oafs coming in I lost my thread for a minute,' he said softly. 'I don't suppose the table feels cold any more, does it?'

She shook her head as she resumed her slow, tantalising movements, wondering whether to ask him to increase the pressure of his fingers on her swollen clit. It was amazing that such battle-scarred hands could be so gentle.

'Do you want to feel a little more coldness?'

He was reaching round and opening a fridge door.

'No. No funny tricks, Euan. I don't want ice cream shoved up me, if you don't mind. Someone tried that once and I wasn't impressed.'

He was laughing. 'God, he must have been a sadist. No, I was talking about peaches.'

In his hand he held a large, halved, juicy peach. 'Poached in vanilla syrup, and just fridge-cold, not frozen.'

Without waiting for her agreement he rubbed the fruit on her clit. He was right, it was only fridge-cold, but it was chillingly and thrillingly so compared to the heat of her body. And it was yielding but still slightly firm, and slitheringly covered with syrupy juices.

She moved faster down on to him and he pressed the peach faster and harder on to the swollen bud.

'You like it, gorgeous girl. You like it, don't you?'

'Yes,' she gasped. She wasn't far off coming and his lilting voice was bringing her even closer to the edge of her climax.

'Do you like me talking to you?' he demanded.

'Yes,' she said again, half aware that she couldn't say any more than that.

'And you like the guys looking over at us, don't you?'

'Yes,' she said again but it was for the last time because she wasn't capable of saying anything more as his fingers manipulated the velvety peach over her clit and his equally soft but insistent voice manipulated her mind. And really, he was Scottish and not Irish so it was hardly appropriate to do a Molly Bloom. Instead she concentrated on the very second when her climax took her over the edge, that blissful moment just before her muscles exploded around his cock, and she knew why they called it ecstasy, like a religious experience. Indeed, lying on the table, his voice murmuring low words she could barely hear, and the noise of other people and other things happening in the room made her think sacrilegiously of the devoutly religious spell she had gone through as a child, when the priest had said the prayers and the congregation took turns in communion at the altar and at the moment that she too drank the blood of Christ she had felt as though she was having a mystical revelation. Of course she had discovered sex shortly afterwards and that had been the end of her holy phase, but she suddenly wondered if it was coincidence that the majority of the churchgoers had been women . . .

'Hey, are you OK?'

She realised that Euan, who had obviously also found his own connection with the sublime, was talking to her.

'More than.' She sat up gingerly, her back and arms stiff from bracing against the unforgiving table. 'That was brilliant, but I feel like I've gone ten rounds with Prince Naseem.'

'Yeah, I reckon you got quite a workout there. Anyway, it was brilliant for me too.'

He was eating the peach; for some reason she felt absurdly touched, as though he wished he could literally eat her. But enough was enough. She pushed her breasts back inside her dress and pulled her skirt down.

'Now what would you like for dessert, Yasmin? I can offer you poached peaches, cranachan or sticky toffee pudding.'

She laughed. 'Oh, I really get dessert? What's the middle one?'

'Scottish speciality. Oats, cream, raspberries, whisky. Well, of course, that's what you want.'

He opened the fridge again and removed two large glasses full of a creamy mixture layered with raspberries, then picked up a bottle of whisky lying on the worktop and poured a slug into each glass. Handing one to her along with a spoon, he clinked his glass against it.

'Cheers, princess. Thank you for a most fantastic fuck.'

'And you.'

Yasmin realised that she was suddenly starving. They perched side by side on the edge of the table and ate the delicious mixture like two kids stealing from the fridge after lights out, and as they finished he put his glass down and linked his arm through hers.

'Now, after a suitable break I wouldn't mind an encore – how about it?'

She was taken aback. She'd not expected anything more and wondered whether she could assume U would stay the night with Amelia and she could take Euan home, or whether that was just tacky, or whether if she went home with him and U did get back after all he'd worry about her, and even whether she wasn't just quite happy with her little Highland fling.

On the other hand, she didn't want to go home alone and have U not return. At the moment she felt extremely pleased with herself, fairly forgiving towards U, and as though the world could be not quite as shitty as it had seemed an hour ago. And didn't Euan deserve a little more of her, if he wanted to?

After all, they'd talked about desserts all evening, and he hadn't even mentioned Turkish Delight. Sod U. She turned towards Euan.

'Your place?'

'Great.'

So, maybe the revenge fuck was childish and maybe she was imitating Lisanne, but the cloud that had hung over her earlier had lifted and life was sunny and simple and uncomplicated, just like when she was a child, and she didn't want that feeling to change. She left a quick message on the answerphone to say she was staying with a friend and had another delicious pudding while she waited for Euan to finish work.

2

From her seat in the front row of the balcony Amelia rose to her feet to applaud as the orchestra played the final flourish of *La Traviata* and the curtain closed on the expired body of Violetta. She loved the form and formality of opera, the stylised conventions and the total suspension of disbelief necessary to accept plot, dialogue and the inappropriately strapping figures of the singers. She clapped vigorously as the curtain parted to reveal the assembled cast and for several more minutes as the individual artistes took their bows and Violetta her bouquets, the orchestra was enthusiastically acknowledged and the curtain rose several more times on the whole cast.

Even as people began to disperse she stayed looking down from the vertiginous heights of the Coliseum balcony, trying in vain to see her friend Dickon pick up his violin and leave, though if he looked up with any gratitude or appreciation for her attempt to settle his first-night nerves she didn't notice it. Not that she wanted any; her own pre-show performance had been for her own benefit as well as his – not to mention the pleasure she would get in telling U about it. Hopefully he would be waiting for her.

The auditorium was practically empty by the time she finally moved, and she had the ladies' toilet to herself at first, though as she was flushing the loo she heard someone else enter and bolt the door of the adjacent cubicle. As she washed her hands she inspected herself in the mirror, just in case U was outside. Hair blonde, almost shoulder length, shaggy and teased so that it haloed her head. Face regular, nose slightly snub, cheeks slightly round, skin as peachy and fresh as only a nineteen-year-old's could be. Tits heavy and firm, totally visible behind the transparent white muslin top. Legs lithe, tanned and muscled and almost completely visible thanks to the tiniest of skirts. And thanks to the tingle she still felt at the encounter with Dickon and his friend, combined with the one that anticipation of seeing U provided, pussy decidedly moist. Like her tits, that too was free of underwear. Amelia believed in ease of access.

As she regarded herself in a self-satisfied, lazy, voluptuous way, the other woman flushed and came out of the cubicle.

'Great tits,' she said without preamble. 'Can I feel them?'

'Sure.'

Amelia sighed almost reflexively as the hands cupped a breast each, squeezing and coaxing her nipples to hardness. It didn't take long. She was sleazily pleased that the woman hadn't bothered to wash her hands – they had gone straight from wiping her piss off with a bit of hard tissue to stroking her tits. Smiling, she allowed the woman to kiss her. Strong face, not pretty but handsome, probably about thirty. Short dark hair, big glasses, black and tortoiseshell frames, obviously designer. Her hands felt slightly rough through the thin muslin but her fingers were expert. She herself had tiny tits over which she wore a black vest which disappeared into a pair of black shorts. Her legs were in fishnet and on top of her vest and shorts she wore a loose open jacket, the black relieved by silver chains round her neck. It was a good look. She buried her face in Amelia's breasts for a minute, then raised her head.

'Great. Thanks.'

'No problem.'

They left the ladies' together and started down the seemingly endless stone stairs that led directly to the street. There was hardly anyone else left on the balcony level; one old lady with a stick who was obviously going to take her time getting down, and an usher. Wordlessly they skittered noisily downwards, still meeting nobody. At one of the landings Amelia took the woman's hands and pushed her hard against the wall, then shoved her right hand down inside the woman's shorts and fishnet tights. She felt wetness and softness and brought her hand back until she caught the hardening bud of the woman's clit. As she rotated her finger on it smoothly, the woman's head sought her tits again, and her mouth closed around one of her nipples, nuzzling and sucking, then the other. Amelia scooped up more of the molten liquid seeping from the woman's sex and then continued teasing the clit, but suddenly they heard the unmistakable sound of the old woman on the stairs, as her stick tapped first on the next step followed by her heavy tread. They grinned at each other and ran down another two or three flights of stairs until Amelia judged she'd have time to finish the business. Her hand continued its exploration, her fingers pushing in and out of the woman's pussy then moving to her clit, alternately pushing and stroking, until she felt the unmistakable pulse that meant the woman was about to come, and as her hand moved faster she brought her mouth down on to the woman's and kissed her hard and fast, pushing her head back against the concrete wall almost savagely as she felt the contractions tighten and relax, tighten and relax, until all was still.

Amelia immediately turned and started down the stairs again.

'Hang on,' said the woman. 'Come home with me?'

'No thanks,' said Amelia. 'I don't do that stuff.'

'What, do you like guys? So do I ... I've got a friend ... we could both –'

'No, sorry, I mean I don't do more than quickies. That's it. I'll think about you tonight, I promise, but otherwise, that's it.'

She ran lightly down the stairs, without looking back, and as she guessed, U was waiting outside for her.

'There's a woman looking after you,' said U as the taxi pulled away. 'All in black, fishnet tights.'

'Yeah, yeah, I just gave her a hand job on the stairs.'

'Of course.' He stared at the wet patches on her top. 'While she sucked your nipples.'

She smiled at him, touching the tip of his nose with her finger. 'Don't worry, I'm going to tell you all about her. And Dickon and his friend.'

'Amelia. You just fucked two guys and gave a woman a hand job. But you won't fuck me.'

'No, dear U. I told you, it will spoil everything. Sex and love don't belong together. One fucks up the other. You know that's true.'

He was looking slightly exasperated, and she almost understood why. She was right, of course, but telling him in that tolerant, amused way was the way the old explained the obvious to the young, rather than the other way round, and he didn't like it. She amplified.

'If we were to have a full-on sex and love relationship, it would end in probably weeks, maybe even days. We would become irrationally emotional, we would depend on each other, we would crave each other's bodies as a substitute for each other's souls. If we keep everything in the right compartments, we can have a good relationship. Which may turn out to be love.'

'But I think I may be falling in love with you. And it's natural to want to express that love by making love to you.'

He was so beautiful, so talented, and yet, Amelia thought, so immature in his old-fashioned insistence on love and sex going hand in hand.

'U, that kind of love you're talking about *is* sex. It's just that our minds are still caught up in that repressed Victorian morality and the only way they can accept pure lust is to define it as love. I want *our* love to be the love of true friendship, something that will survive mere physical attraction.'

She felt incredibly wise as she explained to him what was, to her, so obvious.

'Look, I've been through all this love and romance and sex stuff too, you know. But when I got to New York and met Melinda Sue and took her philosophy on board, it seemed so kind of obvious – and so uncomplicated.

'Melinda Sue's mother is from Thailand and she brought her up with an awareness of Buddhism. Her dad's a real American and the neighbourhood school was Christian, of course, so Melinda Sue went through a few years of confusion before determining to sort out her own spiritual exploration. And the one thing she took on board was the instruction, "Commit Random Acts of Kindness".'

'Sure, everyone knows that.'

'Yes, but they don't actually do anything about it. So, Melinda Sue started doing that, once, twice a day, as she grew up. Then she discovered sex and, like me, went through the love and stuff, got really hung up on some guy and suffered quite a lot. Then she realised, the best way to approach sex is like a random act of kindness. Brighten someone's day with a totally unexpected fuck or a blow job, and you'll feel better about yourself, you may even enjoy it yourself, and if you don't you sure as hell will enjoy going over it in your mind later while you do pleasure yourself. We used to swap experiences every night. It was just amazing.'

'So you got off on each other? If you could do it with her, why not with me? What's the difference if you fuck me instead of her?'

'Shit, U, we didn't fuck. We masturbated, together, while we shared the stories of our experiences. We never laid a finger on each other, except as friends do. And we became true and loving friends. Like I want to be to you.'

She held his face between her hands, lightly, and looked deep into his eyes. 'You have your amazing intuition, U. Surely you know what I'm saying is right. It's the only way to leave adolescent fantasies about true love behind. Consign sex to its rightful place in our lives, an animal instinct and desire, and let your mind concentrate fully on love and friendship.'

'Right now the only thing my mind can concentrate on is the thought of you and Melinda Sue wanking together while you tell each other about your erotic adventures. Half Thai – don't tell me, incredibly long black silky hair, beautiful delicate features, great figure –'

'That's right. But don't forget her American side – she's also five feet eight tall and has got the most beautiful eyes you ever saw, a smoky purply-brown colour.'

'And was it her idea to get rid of your underwear along with your Victorian morals?'

'Oh no, that was me. I just like showing my tits – if you've got it flaunt it, right? On the contrary, she was so amazingly into underwear – she normally wore push-up bras, laced-up corsets, and always stockings and suspenders. Usually showing under a tiny skirt, or sometimes under a long transparent one.'

U smiled sardonically. 'You have to admit, Amelia, you must have looked like a pair of hookers stalking the streets of New York.'

She gazed at him thoughtfully. 'Of course one will always encounter outmoded attitudes like yours, U.'

His face registered a brief flicker of irritation, and Amelia felt quite sorry for him for a moment. After all, U was the style guru; to dismiss his ideas as outmoded was tantamount to heresy. But Amelia wasn't out to soothe his ego. She wanted him, badly, but she wanted him to understand her terms.

The taxi stopped outside Amelia's, or rather Pandora's, house in Holland Park. As U paid the driver, Amelia said, 'You know, tonight I think we should masturbate together, U. I won't just make you watch. I'll tell you about my evening.'

'Bloody hell!' exclaimed the taxi driver. 'You lucky bastard!'

'Yeah, yeah, that's fine,' said U, hurriedly tipping him a fiver. Amelia laughed, amused at seeing the normally ice-cool U looking embarrassed, and also quite taken with the frank exclamations of the driver. He was quite attractive, too, with dark curly hair and a just-back-from-Majorca tan, about U's age, a bit of a medallion man but quite nice in a husky, Tom Jones kind of way. If U hadn't been with her she would have suggested he parked up for a quickie but, then again, he was probably used to screwing a few of his lone female clients from time to time. And really, the after-shave was just too pungent.

There was no sign of Pandora as they entered the large, elegant house and went straight to Amelia's room. U sat in the sole armchair while Amelia poured them both a glass of wine and settled herself on the bed. U's eyes were on her as, on their previous dates, she adjusted her pillows behind her, pulled off her top and raised her skirt to reveal the delectably pink, always moist lips of her pussy and, thanks to her full Brazilian, the firm, already aroused bud of her clit.

'I think the woman was the best one of the night,' she decided. 'So if it's all right with you I'll start with Dickon and his friend.'

'Who's Dickon?'

'The reason I went to the opera tonight. He's a brilliant violinist; I know him from summer schools. It's his first job – I went to give him moral support. He was really tense beforehand so I suggested he might feel a bit more mellow after an orgasm. He was with another new guy who looked so kind of wistful I told him to come too. We went to the toilet, I had the friend sit down, and I bent over and blew him while Dickon entered me from behind – U, you're supposed to be wanking, too.'

U had been totally absorbed in watching Amelia's fingers; slicked with moisture they had slid from her pussy and drawn lazy circles round her clitoris, while her other hand ran idly around her sex lips and down towards her arse.

'The point is the story, not ogling me,' she admonished, quite severely, because she wanted him to know who was boss. 'Look, take your trousers off and lie down on the bed opposite me.'

It was the first time she had seen U's cock. It was gratifyingly erect; in fact it was really quite big, even though not the hugest she had ever seen, but a pleasing deep pink and, to her surprise, circumcised. He lay down as she had instructed, his legs straight and careful to avoid contact with Amelia's flesh. She drew her legs up and knees out to take up less room and watched him until he felt compelled to take his cock in his hand. He groaned and started pumping vigorously.

'U, the point is the story. And after this story there's the story about the woman. So, calm down, don't try to come in billiseconds, and just listen.'

He obeyed instantly and Amelia nodded with satisfaction as he spat on his hand and started to touch himself delicately. She dimmed the light to nothing more than a glimmer, then lay down and stared at the ceiling. She could see nothing, and all she could hear was the tick of her clock and U's breathing. Satisfied that he had nothing to concentrate on but her voice, she continued.

'As it happened, I've already masturbated in public today. Going back to the toilet – I really got into sucking Dickon's friend, he tasted really good and I wasn't rushing it, enjoying Dickon thrusting into me as well. Then Dickon said, "I want to change," and he turned me round and sat me on his friend's cock after giving him a condom. He pulled off his own condom and asked me to blow him. I never really enjoy it when it tastes of rubber, but it was OK. They were both dressed up in bow ties and white shirts – it was like screwing identical twins. It was hard to concentrate on moving my hips up and down on the friend's cock without losing the rhythm of my mouth round Dickon, and just to make it harder he said, "Play with yourself, I want to see you touch yourself". Christ, it was worse than juggling, and in all honesty I never really want to come when I'm committing a random act, but Dickon was so tense I guessed it would be really good for him to see me come, so I just let go, though I have to admit I completely lost the plot as far as his cock in my mouth was concerned. The friend had taken over by now, lifting me up and slamming me down on his cock, and he felt me coming and said, "Jesus, Dick, she's throbbing like a fucking train", and Dickon just shoved his cock into my mouth, just fucking well fucked my mouth, and he came almost straight away. The friend had already come, I guess, I didn't care.'

Her pussy pulsed again as she remembered, enjoying the savagery with which Dickon – normally such a sweet and gentle guy – had pushed his cock in and out of her mouth, and how contrite he had been afterwards. She didn't tell U that he had implored her to go home with him after the performance, nor how bewildered he had been by her explanation of her sole preference for casual sex. After all, U was having trouble taking it on board, and it wouldn't do to reinforce his own reluctance to accept her philosophy by admitting that nobody else seemed to accept it either.

'As for the woman,' she began, noting that U was breathing harder and faster, 'I didn't make any move on her at all. She was the one to begin it . . .'

'It's just not cutting it, Yasmin love,' said Milo flatly. 'The woman's found out her husband's having an affair, for Christ's sake, and you're making her sound as though she's just discovered that her vacuum cleaner's broken. You've got to get some real raw emotion in there. Try putting yourself in her place and imagine what you'd say. Frankly, darling, if I heard this on screen I'd think the scriptwriter was taking the piss. Postmodern irony's got its place, love, although personally I feel it's a tad passé these days, but for soaps we need real feeling and honest emotion. I want the viewer to have tears in her eyes for poor Lisanne. Feel it yourself, Yasmin. Have imaginary conversations with your own husband and imagine telling your friends about it.'

For the second time that week Yasmin felt as though she'd been battered around the head with an iron bar. She burned with fury at the realisation that she couldn't expose the irony of Milo's remarks, unless she wanted to share her sorry domestic plight with the producer, director, storyliners and other scriptwriters.

You should have eavesdropped on my conversation the other night, she wanted to say. You would have realised how cool I am and how so uncool it is to rant and rage just because your husband's getting a bit elsewhere – especially for someone cool enough to enjoy a little sexual experimentation herself. But she couldn't and didn't say it, instead just nodding and gritting her teeth and saying she'd work on it.

'Well look, love, we've decided the best thing would be for you and Josh to work together on the next couple of scripts, just to see how it goes. I know you both usually work alone, but just for me, let's try this little experiment. You know how well US comedy scripts work with a team of writers bouncing ideas off each other? Well, we thought a man and woman working together on this really emotional stuff could come off just as well. OK, both?'

'Sure,' said Yasmin, teeth still gritted, smiling as well as she could at Josh, who was nodding enthusiastically and saying why not, try something new, good experience, load of crap. She'd quite liked him up till then, but Jesus, she'd gone through the team-writing bit already and though it could and did work well with comedy she most definitely thought drama was better done by one person. Over the last couple of years she'd become used to working alone and at her own pace.

'Your place or mine?' she asked him with forced lightness.

'You can work here if you like,' put in Bernie, the director. 'There's a free office next to Sandy's.'

He looked slightly put out himself, and Yasmin guessed that Milo had overruled him on this one. So at least Bernie was somewhat on her side, though as for Milo – she wondered if she'd upset him in some way without realising it. She knew her script wasn't that bad. In fact she didn't think it was bad at all, and belatedly realised that if it hadn't been for the irony of her own situation mirroring that of the deceived Lisanne she would have defended herself better.

She'd never liked Milo anyway. He was a smooth shark, a real career type, going from theatre to the BBC to one of the main independent production companies in no time. Why he'd left his last company to move to this one was a mystery. She could only presume he thought *49 Madison Avenue* was going to be really, really big.

She realised Bernie was waiting for an answer. 'Why not,' she said listlessly. Why not have to come in to the production office instead of being comfortable at home? Why not get tied to an office routine instead of being able to take a break when she wanted to shop or, now she had promised Euan they could have a rematch, indulge in a little illicit sex?

'Well, that just about wraps it up, I think, unless you've got any more input, Bernie?' asked Milo briskly.

'Story's absolutely great, let's just get those scripts perfect. The sex scenes are terrific, by the way, Yasmin. It's just the emotion that's a little lacking.'

'Thanks,' she muttered drily. 'OK, Josh, you wanna get seriously emotional now?'

'Sure.' Josh smiled. 'I just want a quick word with Bernie first. See you in – our office?'

She nodded with a weak smile. Everyone was picking up their laptops and papers and scripts with obvious relief – Yasmin had been the one to be picked on, not them. She heard the sympathy in their voices as they said goodbye to her and, after responding unenthusiastically, she walked into the tiny office next to the secretary's and sat down despondently.

Her relationship had taken a nosedive and now the boss was criticising her work. Was she paranoid, or was someone seriously out to get her?

It was just a crappy coincidence, she knew that. It was just that once one dog's pissed up your front door all the other dogs in the road have the compulsion to follow suit. She might have been able to fight her corner better if she hadn't been feeling down about U's affair. In retrospect she realised she should have defended herself properly and strenuously resisted being relegated to a team player rather than a star solo artiste. But her reactions were out of kilter at the moment.

Ever since U's revelation on Saturday night her mood had been seesawing dangerously between total depression and reckless euphoria. Wandering aimlessly around the streets of Soho after he had first told her, her emotions had plunged as low as she could ever remember. Then, after her night with Euan, she was on a most definite high. But when she got home to face U and he had told her in some detail about Amelia's

philosophy, her stories, and the fact they had masturbated side by side, she had hit rock bottom again. She
had tried to counteract it by throwing at him Willie's
hypothesis that Pandora had set Amelia up to reel him
back in for herself, and been gleefully amused by his
indignation. His frigid rejoinder that he was going to
dedicate the next issue of *Slice* to the new sex made
her laugh out loud, but his resulting coolness had
plunged her back into the depths of despair. To cheer
herself up she had imagined another session with Euan
– after all, they'd done puddings, what about the main
course? – but that only led her to damn herself as a
shallow little tart whose only means of coping with an
adult situation was a childish tit for tat. And the really
depressing aspect of it all was that her situation was
mirroring bloody Lisanne's.

'Thought you'd like a coffee.' Josh came in with two
plastic cups. 'Not exactly palatial, is it?' He surveyed
the utilitarian cubicle that was hardly deserving of the
name 'office', apart from the fact that it contained a
plastic table – not even a desk – and two stacking
chairs. Sandy's voice came clearly through the prefab-
ricated partition and the phones were ringing non-
stop.

'I know you hate this and you'd rather be at home
writing alone, and to be honest what I heard of it I
didn't think your script sounded bad at all. Milo's
bloody good, though, we've got to accept that. If he's
not happy with it, we'll have to sort it.' Josh's look was
almost pleading, as though he suspected she would
take her irritation out on him.

'Good or not, Milo's a complete arsehole,' she
retorted. 'He's too smooth by half and all he cares
about is promoting his own self-interest. In any case, I
reckon he's got it wrong.' She sipped the disgusting

liquid that bore no relation to anything that came from a coffee bean. 'We're not talking *EastEnders* here, Josh. Lisanne's smart and beautiful and educated, and she's not going to mouth off like a stallholder getting pissed and shouting the odds in the Queen Vic when she finds out about Johnny. Sure, she's upset, but look at the storyline. She doesn't rush round to Imelda's apartment and give her a good slapping, does she? She takes her revenge.'

'Yeah, yeah. But maybe while she's taking her revenge, say in the scene where she's talking to Tom, we could put in a bit more pain. Give me your hard copy and you get it up on screen and we'll act it.'

Yasmin passed the printed script to him, and as their hands touched she felt a definite jolt of electricity communicating itself to her. Surprised, she looked up at his face. Josh was attractive in a quiet, understated way, with dark-blond hair and very deep-set grey eyes. He exuded an air of calm and self-possession, and she suddenly realised that she knew absolutely nothing about his private life.

'Do you have a partner, Josh?'

'Not any more. Look, let's read the scene in the gym. "You don't have to tell me anything, Lisanne, but I know something's going on. You can't keep anything a secret in this place. Mandy saw you coming out of Room 22 yesterday shortly followed by Simon. She swears she's not told anyone else, and I threatened her with all sorts if she did. I know it's none of my business either, but Christ, you and Johnny are the mainstays of this place. If you're falling apart, the whole thing could follow –" that's no good, two follows in there, we'll sort it in a minute "– and that's what makes it my business. Do what you like, but don't shit on your own doorstep. If Johnny should find out –"'

'"If Johnny should find out? Fuck it, Tom, Johnny's fucking around. With Imelda. With the most glamorous, coolest, hippest head receptionist anywhere in town. With someone who we daren't upset, otherwise half of London will be after her as a greeter. So there's nothing I can do. Except grab a bit of revenge. Savvy?"'

'I don't like "savvy",' said Josh, preoccupied. 'And to be honest, Yas, even though you did a good job of putting anguish in your voice, I don't really think that speech works. Don't you think she'd be a bit more hyper?'

Yasmin gritted her teeth and decided that there was one sure way to establish the integrity of her writing. 'OK, Josh, let me let you in on a little secret. My husband's fucking around too, as I found out on Saturday night. I haven't been exactly hyper either. Like Lisanne, I'm a sophisticated adult. And now you know why Milo's idea that I put myself in her place is a load of bollocks. Oh, and *never* call me Yas.'

She scrolled down the screen. 'That's all I want to say. Let's go back to the script.'

'Shit, I'm really sorry. I had no idea – oh, God, what a stupid thing to say, of course I had no idea.'

'Yeah, yeah. I said, let's go back to the script.' Yasmin felt his eyes on her, felt waves of sympathy emanating from him, and had a sudden urge to burst into tears and lay her head on his chest for consolation. But as she had just said, she was a sophisticated adult.

'Sure.' He carried on reading. '"Shit, Lisanne, I'm really sorry. I had no idea –" Christ, that's just what I said.'

They laughed, Yasmin with a touch of irony and Josh with some embarrassment.

'Hey, you certainly hit that reaction speech right on the head.' He put the script down and, taking Yasmin's hands in his, swivelled her chair round so they were facing each other. 'Let's improvise and see where we go. This might sound heartless to you, but it's a fantastic opportunity to really replicate a real-life situation.'

He let her hands go just to pull a tape recorder from his case. 'OK? We'll just take it from the top?'

Yasmin shrugged. 'If you like. What happened to your partner?'

A cynical look came into Josh's eyes. 'She decided she was gay and ran off to Lesbos with an older woman.'

'Wow. Recently?'

'No, two years ago. I've not bothered with women since, though maybe it's time I put it behind me and re-entered the world, as it were.'

His eyes were on hers, as though he wanted to enter her world. Yasmin felt the current flowing from him again. When their hands had touched earlier she had felt the force of the attraction she obviously had for him; maybe now she had confided her own situation to him, he felt she was inviting him into her world.

Just like Lisanne and Tom, she realised with dismay.

'I don't know if this is a good idea,' she said quickly, but Josh turned the tape on and grabbed her hands again.

'Trust me,' he said quietly. 'I'm not Josh, I'm Tom.' He released the pause button and turned his eyes to hers again.

'I had no idea. Well, nobody could have any idea that Johnny would be unfaithful to you, Lisanne. At the risk of sounding like Mr Spock, it's illogical. It just doesn't compute. I mean, Johnny's a nice guy, but you –'

'Oh yeah? What about me?' Yasmin put an amused note into her voice as well as a confrontational one.

'Lis – can I call you Lis?'

'*Never* call me Lis,' said Yasmin mockingly. 'I hope that was a joke.'

'Sorry, couldn't help it. I'm Tom again now. Lisanne, you are so not the sort of woman a man fucks with. Christ, if you were my wife, I'd cut my bloody cock off rather than be unfaithful to you.'

'You wouldn't be much use to me without a cock.' Yasmin put a gravelly note into her, or rather Lisanne's, voice.

'Yeah. That was pure metaphor, kid. Let's say I'd let you put a chastity belt round my cock any minute I was away from you, if there is such a thing, as long as I could come home to you and have you take it off.'

'Nice one, Tommy. I like the idea of unstrapping your cock and having it spring out, huge and distended, ready for action.'

'It would be for you, baby. Jesus, Johnny must be a complete idiot. I'm sorry I even mentioned you and Simon, I don't blame you for wanting revenge. Though . . . well . . . why Simon?'

'He was there; I was furious.'

'Aren't you still furious? I'm here.'

'Tom, don't say it unless you mean it. No, ignore me. I'm not furious now, either. Just a bit – a bit sort of miserable.'

To Yasmin's dismay a tear slid down her face. 'Fuck it, Josh, I can't do this.'

Almost before she knew it his arms were around her and he was cradling her head on his chest, just as she'd imagined earlier. Her misery disappeared almost as quickly as it had arrived and when Josh lifted her head and started to kiss down the track of her tear it most definitely vanished, only to be replaced with a powerful urge to put her lips on those tender ones that were on her face. And, like Lisanne, she liked the metaphor of a huge cock unfurling just for her.

She didn't have to do anything. Josh's mouth was purposefully heading for hers and before she knew it they were urgently kissing, his tongue penetrating deep into her mouth and her own responding just as desperately.

'Is it me or Lisanne you're tonguing so ardently?' she asked archly as they came up for air.

Josh's breathing was heavy and ragged. 'It's you, you sexy bitch. I've always had a thing for you. It was too much of an opportunity ... Christ, I wish I was Tom and you were Lisanne. I'd like to get you – where is it? – over the pec deck and fuck the arse off you.'

'Very elegant language for a writer,' mocked Yasmin, her hand moving to his crotch. 'Oh, there's nothing restraining that, is there?'

His cock was hard and huge inside his old cords and he moaned as she ran her hands over the outline.

'I like you calling me a sexy bitch,' she said softly. 'I guess I am a bitch, really. After all, I'm just like Lisanne. I've already had one revenge fuck, and now I'm grabbing you by the balls.'

Josh wasn't slow to pick up the hint. 'You're a beautiful bitch,' he whispered as she slowly undid his flies. 'A fucking, hopefully also ready for fucking, beautiful sexy slut. I want to get inside you. Let me get inside you.'

Yasmin liked being a slut as much as she liked being a bitch. Her breath, too, was coming faster as she felt the warm, throbbing flesh of his hard cock, easing it out until it was fully exposed. The phones were still ringing next door and, just as in the restaurant kitchen, she felt a thrilling sense of exposure.

'What did you call me, you fucking prick?' she murmured as she ran her hands up and down the shaft.

'Slut, bitch – you name it. Don't tell me you're not up for it, Yasmin. Look at you. Your tits are almost falling out of that top, your knickers are showing at the back and your jeans are only just covering up your pubes, aren't they?'

His hand slid down the front of her jeans. She knew only too well that he would find out he was right, because just that morning she'd tried leaving the top button of her new low-slung jeans undone but realised it would have meant exposing the first few stray black curls. Since her new diamanté-trimmed thong was peeking saucily above her jeans and her V-necked top was already leaving quite a lot of her breasts on display, as Josh had noted rather baldly, not to mention the fact that her waist and stomach were also bared to the world, Yasmin had decided that exhibiting her pubic hair was really going too far.

'I bet your pussy's wet, you dirty bitch. Let me feel it.'

Yasmin registered Sandy's voice, almost full volume behind the flimsy partition, telling a caller untruthfully that Bernie was in a script conference as Josh unbuttoned her jeans and pushed his hand down to find that she was indeed wet. She had pushed her arse forwards in the chair to allow him access, which meant that her head was leaning back and she could no longer touch him. But she had a better idea.

'You know the working title for this show was *69 Madison Avenue*, not *49*, don't you?' she murmured, taking a leaf out of the script by pretending she was in the gym and dipping her triceps on the chair seat and sliding to the floor. 'My feminine instincts could be completely wrong and despite the fact that you've not bothered with relationships for a couple of years you're carrying a packet of three round in your wallet but, if I'm right, well I haven't got anything either and so we'll have to skip the full monty.'

Josh pulled her jeans and the diamanté-encrusted scrap of satin Elle Macpherson called a thong down to her thighs and started teasing her clit with deliciously tantalising feather-like strokes.

'You're right,' he admitted. 'I have to say I thought I was in here for a quick meeting then home to get on with some work. But if you don't mind me rejecting your kind invitation, the old *soixante-neuf* has never been my thing. I like to concentrate on what I'm doing – OK if we take turns?'

Without waiting for her reply he peeled her jeans and knickers off completely, dislodging her flower-decorated mules as he did so, and pulled her hips upwards to meet his mouth as he leant forward, still in the chair. Fleetingly Yasmin thought that with her upper back and arms the only parts of her body still on the floor she looked like she was on another item of gym equipment, but as his tongue slithered smoothly over her swollen lips and then penetrated her she stopped caring what she might look like. Josh hoisted her legs over his shoulders and she braced herself against him as his tongue started seriously engaging her clit. The only disadvantage in having his mouth engaged was that he was unable to murmur obsceni-ties to her, but her muscles leapt in response to the voice of Milo from the adjoining room asking Sandy where the fuck Bernie was. What if he decided to come next door and ask them how it was going? 'Bloody marvellous,' she would have had to reply. But he didn't;

instead he just carried on giving Sandy instructions when not interrupted by the phone, and to the background of Milo's orders, Sandy's slightly resentful questioning of them and phones ringing all over the place she felt her muscles tense, ready to come. But just at that moment her mobile sang out its 'Ode to Joy' and, to her surprise, Josh, without even missing a lick, handed it to her.

'Yeah,' she said, distantly and slightly irritably.

'Hey, princess, you sound a bit miserable. Everything OK?'

She laughed jaggedly, smiling with half-closed eyes at Josh, whose tongue was purposefully heading away from her clit and towards her slit, where it did a fairly convincing imitation of a tiny penis.

'Everything's fine, though it would have been better if you'd called five minutes later. I've got the most wonderful tongue in my – Christ, no it's not, it's on my clit now – oh, Christ – sorry, Euan – and I was just about to come. But perhaps this is even better, because it'll last longer.'

'Oh, you gorgeous girl, I wish I was there. I presume it's not the old man?'

'No way. It's someone at work. We're in the office. And to think I was afraid that working here would curtail my sexual freedom. Anyway – oh, God – I'll have to phone you back.'

'No you won't. Tell me what he's doing now. Is it a he?'

'Yeah, though I bet you'd like it better if he was a woman. He's tonguing my clit like . . .'

She couldn't go on.

'Oh, my God, I'm hard for you, princess. Are you coming? God I wish I could see you, see your lovely lips swollen and glistening and throbbing and your clit hard and pearly and your fucking brown nipples poking through your dress. Are you coming?'

Not surprisingly she was, not just from Josh's skilful tongue but also from the double exposure of Euan on the end of the phone and the boss railing next door. Mindful of the thin walls she stifled her cries but knew that Euan would hear the faint sob she couldn't help escaping as she came. The need to contain herself contributed to the excitement and if orgasms could be rated on a noise scale it was a herd-of-elephants-on-the-rampage orgasm, not just a few-cats-mewling-on-a-dark-night orgasm.

'Yasmin? I'm glad it was great. Just tell me you'll come and see me soon. Not only do I most definitely want to fuck you again, but I've got some news for you. At least, my prep chef has.'

She just about managed to follow his conversation as her sex continued pulsing gently. She didn't want to miss one tiny scrap of sensation.

'How's that? I don't even know him.'

'Her,' corrected Euan. 'Come round after service tonight?'

'No, not tonight. Tomorrow – maybe. I'll call you.'

She disconnected and in turn disengaged her legs from Josh's shoulders.

'Sorry about that. But you didn't have to pass the phone over.'

'No problem. Thanks for the compliments. I was pretty sure that it was OK. If you don't mind me saying so.'

'Definitely not. False modesty's not very attractive,' she agreed, carefully rolling over and rising to her knees next to Josh's chair. 'I hope this'll be equally satisfactory.'

She held the root of his penis and licked gently around the head before opening her lips over it, sucking gently just on the tip at first and then taking his cock deeper into her mouth, deeper and firmer, wanting the soft flesh inside her mouth to feel like that other soft flesh to him.

'Oh, yeah, that's – that's definitely satisfactory,' groaned Josh. 'Christ, Milo doesn't half go on. I thought it might have put you off. I just wished we were fucking and I was talking to you rather than you having to listen to him, especially as he's hardly your flavour of the month at the moment. Oh, Christ, what is this, 49, 69 or Deep fucking Throat?'

She had taken him down as far as she dared, not wanting to gag – she'd never discussed it with a man but always felt it was rather an insult, despite the implication that the cock was particularly huge – but wanting him to have the best blow job ever. Cupping his balls with one hand, she moved the one that was holding the root of his shaft down to his arse and rubbed gently along the sensitive flesh between arsehole and balls.

'Oh, my Christ, delete that sexy bitch remark, you are *the* sexiest bitch I've ever had. In a manner of speaking. I'm gonna come in a minute and I'm gonna come even faster because I'm imagining you swallowing it all, then I'm imagining you taking your mouth off just as I'm coming and pumping me all over your tits, or I'm imagining you sucking me till the very last minute and rubbing it all over your face, oh, my Christ . . .'

He was finally lost for words as Yasmin managed to take down just another half a centimetre of his cock and, with her hands working as they knew only too well how to, he came, copiously. Being a practical sort of girl really, despite also recently taking on the dual role of deceived wife and pushover for any guy she met, Yasmin knew that swallowing was the only possible option out of Josh's three scenarios unless she wanted to walk past Sandy and Milo with come all over her face or her tits.

Their luck in being undisturbed wasn't going to hold out for ever, she realised, and quickly she pulled her jeans back on and adjusted her top. The slick of moisture from her own juices and Josh's mouth wasn't going to be absorbed by the satin, and she felt pleasantly sluttish as she imagined her jeans darkening with the wetness.

'I've had an idea,' she said, a little hesitantly, as Josh made himself respectable again. 'Don't worry if you don't want to do it, but I wondered if you'd like to do a little bit of spying for me.'

'Hey, sounds like fun,' said Josh idly, seemingly preoccupied with the sensations he'd just been experiencing rather than giving her 100 per cent.

'Tell me if I'm wrong, but you're a bit off women,' she said, her voice as neutral as possible. 'I know I encouraged you to call me a bitch and a slut and stuff, but I reckon your girlfriend going off has made you a tiny bit cross with us girls.'

Josh stirred uneasily in his chair. 'Hold the analysis, Yasmin. It was just sex, OK?'

'Yeah, yeah, I'm not interested in analysing you, sure it was just sex, bloody great sex. What I want is for you to fuck Amelia, U's – Jesus, I suppose I should call her his mistress. Apparently she fucks anything that moves out of some sort of charity, so I don't see it'd be that hard. And you might get some information about what she's doing with U.'

'Christ, that's a bit heavy.'

'Not really,' said Yasmin quickly. 'It's just a sort of favour, though I guess it means using her. That's what I meant about you being off women – I hoped you wouldn't mind doing that. Not that I think you're bitter.'

He threw his head back and laughed softly. 'Great. You fuck me for revenge and now you're encouraging me to take revenge on my ex by fucking your husband's bimbo. One minute you're complaining you're being influenced by the script of *49*, now you're trying to influence me.'

Yasmin dimpled at him in her very best, though not terribly effective, Felicity Kendal way. 'OK, try this as an option. Instead you could fuck Pandora, which might lead you to finding out even more. That's Amelia's aunt, who used to be my and U's boss. I've got a funny feeling she could be behind this little affair.'

'Good grief, perhaps I could have them both at a family tea party. How can you be offering me an aunt and a niece? How old are they? I've got a niece and she's only four, that's a thirty-two-year difference.'

'Mmm, well, that could be the stumbling block with Pandora. Amelia's only nineteen, and according to U is blonde with attitude not to mention being a prodigy on the violin, so I don't suppose you'd mind having her pluck your strings. Pandora looks about forty-five, but she's lifted and lipo'd and Botoxed – to be honest, she's got to be at least fifty-five.'

'Blimey. Even older than Mrs Robinson. Attractive?'

'In a magazine editor kind of way. And let's get this in perspective, you're a damn sight older than Benjamin Braddock as well. She's too thin, got what they call that lollipop look, you know, big head on a stick?'

Josh shook his head. 'Sorry, you're not a great saleswoman, Yasmin. I'll take the niece.'

Yasmin realised it was more than she'd really expected. 'OK. But think about Pandora. I mean, maybe if everything you did to her, you repeated with me – does that tempt you?'

'Sexy bitch,' he said by way of reply. 'I'm not saying yes. After all, I've given you enough for the first date. I don't want you to think I'm too easy.' He yawned. 'The trouble with sex is it makes me want to go to sleep, and I guess we better get something done today.'

'After lunch. On me. Wherever you like.'

Josh raised his eyebrows. 'Really? Wherever?'

'Sure. Damn the expense.'

He laughed. 'I'm quite cheap, actually. A pint of Young's and a steak pie at the Rose and Crown – that all right with you? Or are you a vegetarian alcohol-free zone?'

'Like hell. I like food and drink almost as much as sex.'

'Good girl. I almost wish the bugger would run off with his little violinist and leave you to me.'

'No, you don't. You don't want a full-on relationship at the moment, I reckon. Just a little playmate.'

He laughed and stood up, pulling on his disreputably creased jacket. Yasmin ruffled his hair affectionately. Really, to think she'd been cross at the prospect of working with him. Things really were looking up. A mate, a colleague, a good shag – well, from his performance with his mouth she guessed he would be – and a willing spy. What more could a girl ask for?

3

The violin lesson hadn't gone at all well. Benito, Amelia's old, fierce Italian teacher, accused her of not practising enough.

'I am, honestly,' she protested. 'It's just hard to concentrate at the moment.'

'Why? You're out partying, I suppose. Too much drink, too many men, not enough practising. It's simple. If you want to succeed you must practise. I don't care what else you do, as long as you make enough time for your violin.'

'I really am, Benito,' said Amelia, almost despairingly. 'It's just that my mind's focused on my relationship with U.'

'I beg your pardon?' The music teacher's head swivelled round sharply.

'Oh, sorry. Not you. U, that's the name of my lover. Well he's not my lover, he's the man I'm involved with.'

'Ah,' nodded Benito, like a wise owl. 'You're not such a silly girl as I thought you were. Going around with all your wares on display – I assumed you were having sex all over the place. But really you're not even sleeping with your lover.'

Amelia giggled. 'Oh, Benito, I couldn't really expect you to understand. You were right, I am having sex all over the place. But not with my lover.'

'*Dio!* Don't tell me any more, Amelia. I don't want to know about this ridiculous situation. Just go away, practise more, focus on your playing and on your instrument. I can't give you any more advice. You know how talented I think you are. If you want to throw it away by thinking about your relationships, sexual or otherwise, I can't stop you. But you have a rare – not unique, but rare – talent. If you don't make the most of that talent it will be a sin. More of a sin than your silly sex games. Practise and focus, and next week you will be better. Goodbye.'

Amelia wandered disconsolately out into the street from Benito's bedsit. Really, he was hardly a model for devoting life to the violin; though he had played in orchestras when he was younger he had been teaching for some years and all he owned was one scruffy room in Earls Court. It was true that his financial situation wasn't helped by the fact that he gave many lessons free or at least subsidised where he thought the violinist showed promise. She decided that, honourable as that was, she didn't want that sort of life. She wanted success, money, adulation – Yeah, yeah, she told herself. So go home and practise.

Her mind was on Benito rather than where she was going, and she bumped straight into a man walking down the road as she left the front door.

'Sorry,' they said simultaneously. Amelia was about to carry on when the man grabbed her arm – in a friendly fashion, thank God.

'I can't believe this. You'll hardly believe it yourself. But I have a real thing for violinists. And you are probably the most beautiful I've ever seen. I love Vanessa Mae and Anne-Sophie Mutter – but you are so sexy. Look at your clothes. You are fantastic.'

Amelia couldn't help but be amused by his praise. 'Well, thanks a lot. I'm just not as famous as the others.'

'I don't care about fame. I only mentioned them

because they're well known. Look, I'm not a nut, honestly, just a normal guy who has this – well, obsession, if you like.'

She looked him over carefully. He didn't look like a nut, that was true. His hair was a sort of dark blond with the odd grey hair, cut fairly short but in no way fashionably, with a strong face, quite a big nose, nice chiselled lips and deep-set grey eyes. He was dressed carelessly in a creased linen jacket, T-shirt and old cords, rather like an academic type whose mind is on higher things than his attire. It was a look that Amelia liked. She was tired of young guys all looking the same. This one was probably mid-thirties. He was OK.

'Would you play the violin for me?' he asked. 'A private audience? I can't think of anything more exquisite than having a girl play just for me. Especially one as beautiful as you. And especially dressed as you are.'

Amelia knew she had to accept that the way she dressed would always cause comment, although it was a warm summer day and she didn't think she looked anything out of the ordinary in her seersucker halter top and short, pleated gingham skirt, worn like a real fifties girl with short white socks and flat shoes. She guessed, however, he was seeing the outline of her heavy breasts behind the seersucker, and he was old enough to find youth even more alluring if wearing schoolgirl socks. But hey, she liked the look of him.

'OK. We could go to the park. Or to my place. My name's Amelia.'

'Nice to meet you, Amelia. You won't be surprised if I say I'd rather go to your place.'

His hooded grey eyes were looking at her with a calculated desire which pleased her. She believed him; he wanted to hear her play. But that wasn't all he wanted – which was just fine. She felt the first tingle of desire as their eyes locked. He was nice, but not too nice. It wasn't going to be a gasping, oh how wonderful, kind of screw. He was going to be in charge, and that was good. After her telling-off from Benito she felt submissive.

'We'll get a cab.' It was only yards to the busy main road and they started walking.

'So where have you been with your violin?' he asked.

'Lesson. Not a good one. Benito, that's my teacher, he says I've not been practising enough, which is totally unfair. It's just that I've got other things on my mind at the moment.'

'Oh, yeah? Like?'

'Oh, relationships and stuff.'

'This Benito, is he a strict teacher?'

'Oh, yeah, he's hard. But he's the best.' She raised her arm. 'Taxi!'

'If you don't mind me saying so, doesn't he get a little distracted by the way you dress?'

'No. Why?'

'Well –' they got in the taxi and Amelia gave the driver the address '– when you hailed that cab with your left arm, half your breast was hanging out of your top. Which I should imagine it does when you're holding your violin. And your top is not exactly opaque.'

'No, but that's nothing. Usually my tops are much less opaque. He doesn't notice.'

'I bet. How old is he?'

She shrugged. 'Sixty or so, I don't know. Old, anyway. He's not interested in that kind of thing. He's a little fat old guy with a beard, come *on*!'

His eyes were on her as the cab stopped outside the house. '*I'm* interested in that kind of thing. I thought I should tell you.'

She felt she was drowning in the deep grey waters of his eyes. 'I would be disappointed if you weren't,' she answered simply, then got out of the cab.

The thing was, she wondered, did he still want her to play?

Once in her room she indicated he should sit in the one chair, but he wandered around the room, picking up books and running his fingers over the cases of her other two violins.

'Three? Is that necessary?'

'Not really. The one on the left is my good violin, too good to lug around London and risk getting stolen, and the one on the right is extremely old and not really worth playing but I keep it for sentimental reasons. This one is OK, but not good enough for concerts.'

He nodded. 'Right.'

'I'm assuming you meant it when you said you wanted me to play for you,' she said, starting to open her violin case. Oddly, she felt she would almost be disappointed if he said no. Not that she thought it was anything but a casual pickup, but it would be nice if it was true that he really did have a thing for the violin.

'Of course,' he said, with some surprise, sitting down as if to emphasise his willingness to be her audience. 'Bach?'

'Mozart,' she countered, and before he could agree or disagree launched into the rondo from the 26th.

Josh sat watching her intently for a few minutes. Amelia was used to an audience but not an audience of one, apart from her teacher, and felt slightly nervous and made one or two mistakes.

'Too many notes,' he said softly. 'Someone said that about Mozart, and I agree. That's why I suggested Bach. It's more spare, more haunting. Still, at least it's not the *Four Seasons*.'

'You don't like Vivaldi?' Amelia continued playing.

'I did. It's too universal now. Don't you know any Bach, or is this your party piece?'

She lowered the violin. 'OK, you win. Bach it is.'

He looked satisfied as she started the B Minor Partita. She was pleased to see he actually seemed to know the music and a smile crept across his face as she played. More confident now, she played better.

However, it wasn't long before he stood and walked towards her, then positioned himself directly behind her.

'Don't stop,' he murmured in her ear. 'I'm just going to take your top off.'

Amelia almost missed the next phrase as his fingers gently pulled the ties at the back of her neck and her waist, pulling the halter neck off her and placing it carefully on the bed. She waited for his next move, but he just sat down in the chair again and surveyed her as she continued to play. It might have been her imagination but she thought she understood why he wanted the Bach rather than the Mozart; it felt shiveringly sexual to be playing bare breasted to the stark severity of the music, whereas the jolly sprightliness of the Mozart would be preposterous.

After another few minutes he once more moved to stand behind her. She knew, this time, what he was going to do. It took him a few seconds to find the buttons on the wraparound skirt but soon that too was discarded, again to be placed neatly on the bed.

It would have been easy to predict the look on his face, too, as he resumed his seat and gazed upon her naked pubis. Amelia was aware that the slightly-legs-apart stance required to play the violin was not necessarily erotic, but she knew that her hairless pussy would be the focus of his attention. Her excitement had increased with every note, every touch as he undressed her, and she guessed that her clit was standing out as hard and firm as a miniature cock. She guessed, too, that his own cock was standing out hard and firm as well.

She expected him to undress, at least take his trousers off, and tell her to ditch the violin and come over and fuck him, but for five minutes he just sat watching her intently. The lack of action was more exciting than any touch or word could be. She felt her sex muscles pulsing in expectation, and the longer the expectation went on the more urgent her desire became.

'Don't you want to screw?' she asked eventually, her voice hesitant and unsure.

He raised a shaggy eyebrow. 'Why, are you in a hurry? Do you have to go somewhere?'

'No. I – I just thought – '

Amelia was unable to explain. She felt embarrassed at what must have seemed like her crude desire to fuck in a brisk and mindless fashion, whereas he – what was his name? It didn't seem the right time to ask – was prepared to savour their encounter. Dismayed, she thought that maybe her deconstruction of sex into anonymous random acts had eliminated a sense of the erotic.

She kept playing. She didn't know what else to do. All she did know was that she was longing to feel him touch her again.

'You're too impatient.' He walked towards her and her eyes closed in relief as his hand reached out to her sex. 'Because you're ready for sex, you want to fuck – like an animal. Is that so?'

He had touched her just briefly, just gently parted her sex lips and felt the copious moisture that was welling up inside her. She couldn't deny his statement, although she felt she should be able to justify her sexual philosophy. But somehow she felt humiliated by his assertion, and kept quiet.

His hand moved to her breast and flicked over her hard nipple.

'You need discipline. You need to learn how to wait. Have you never waited, patiently and longingly, for sex?' he asked. 'Have you never been tied to a bed, not knowing whether the man will screw you, wank over you, fuck your mouth or your arse, let you come or not – and just been driven to crazy heights of longing because of it?'

She shook her head. This was weird shit. But she liked it.

'You need to learn about the darker side of sex. I want you to feel now as though you're tied up. As though you're rooted, chained to that spot, as though you can't stop playing. You're wearing a collar with a short chain attached to it and boots with chains. They're fixed to the wall behind you. Your arms too are on chains just long enough to allow you to play. Apart from playing, you can't move, you can't turn your head, you can't move your feet further than a couple of inches. Can you imagine that?'

She nodded, trembling, hoping that it wouldn't be too long before he did whatever it was he was going to do. But he just walked behind her, out of sight. Although she wanted to turn to see what he was doing, his instruction to her to pretend she was chained to the spot hit the mark.

He was opening something. A violin case. Maybe he too played? Maybe he was going to join her in playing, then they would fuck? Nothing happened for a long minute. Amelia closed her eyes and bit her lip. It was weird. But it was fucking brilliant.

Then she felt a stinging blow on her buttocks. It wasn't painful. She knew instinctively what it was. It was a bow.

'You do need some discipline,' he said, once again hitting her lightly with the bow. 'Maybe you need to learn real discipline, but I'm not the man to teach it to you. But you need to learn to wait, to savour, to appreciate.'

She almost stopped playing as, instead of applying the bow to her arse again, he ran it gently along her sex. Backwards and forwards. It was almost impossible to concentrate on her playing. Focus, Benito had told her – it was a good thing he couldn't hear her now.

'Is that what you usually want? Just bring a man home, get him to touch you till you come, then fuck him and dismiss him?'

'No.' She felt indignant. 'No, I don't. I fuck, sure, but I don't come, not usually.'

'Why? Can't you? Is that why you go round looking like you're gagging for it? Because you're looking for the man who'll teach you how to come?'

'God, no. I can come just fine. I just prefer to masturbate.'

Amelia felt as though she could come just fine any minute if he didn't stop running the bow slowly along her sex. If only it was a little faster, she would. But of course she didn't want to.

He moved the bow away and walked round to face her. 'Explain to me. If you'd picked up someone else apart from me, what would have been the scenario?'

She shrugged. 'Well, if he'd wanted me to play for him, I would, maybe he would have undressed me like you did, then he would have taken the violin out of my hand, undressed himself or just unzipped, fucked me, however he liked, I don't mind, and then gone.'

'And you wouldn't have wanted to come?'

'No. I – I like to come later. To masturbate. Thinking about the sex I've had that day. Sometimes with my lover.'

She said the last phrase a little defensively. As she could have predicted, his eyebrows raised sardonically.

'You masturbate with your lover? You don't have sex with him?'

'No. That way we have a pure relationship.'

He laughed sarcastically. 'Poor guy. You fuck complete strangers but you only wank him off because you prefer to have a pure relationship.'

'I don't wank him off,' said Amelia irritably. 'He masturbates too.'

'Well, at least *he* doesn't need to learn self-control,' he said in a tone of waspish admiration. 'You need me. I'll be back.'

'What do you mean?' Amelia lowered the violin in astonishment. 'You're going? You don't want to fuck?'

He shook his head. 'No, I don't want to be just another lay. Next time I will tie you up and make you wait.'

'Do it now!'

She felt almost embarrassed at the eagerness in her voice, especially when he laughed again.

'Don't you want me?' she added lamely.

He pressed her hand to his crotch and she felt the hardness and solidity of him. 'Obviously,' he said. 'But like you, I don't always have to come.'

'We could maybe both come,' she offered, feeling absurdly as though she were begging him to fuck her.

'Well, that's better than your other scenario,' he said

consideringly. 'But you're still chained to that wall and you're still playing.'

'Sure.' Hastily she lifted the violin to her chin once more as he again walked past her.

The next thing she felt was her old violin, obscenely parting her legs and rubbing its polished wood along her.

'No!' she cried out.

'Why not?' he enquired. He removed the instrument, but only to walk round and face her and then press the round base of her old, loved instrument past her clit and towards the source of her slippery moisture. The wax she treated the violin with made it move easily along her sex.

'It's like – like being raped by your best friend,' she moaned, half in despair and half in relief as she felt something solid for her aching pussy to grip on to.

'Don't sentimentalise objects,' he said, grinning slightly. She realised he really did want to discipline her, in his way. Whatever, she wasn't going to be able to turn him away now. For the first time in an age she had put herself in the position where she really was desperate to come. She was going to have to let him go ahead and fuck her with her violin while she played.

It was worse than that.

He stopped moving and let the violin rest immobile, pressing hard but not hard enough against her.

'You do it,' he said, with almost contemptuous amusement. 'I want to see you rub yourself off on it.'

'No way!' Amelia said fiercely, though she knew, almost with despair, that her refusal was only going to be temporary. She was going to do whatever he asked.

The bow descended on to her buttocks once more, harder this time.

'Do it. And don't stop playing.'

'I can't!' she wailed.

The bow stung her again.

'You will do as I say,' he told her. 'I'm not going to take my satisfaction until you've had yours. And you want to, don't you?'

It wasn't a case of wanting to, it was a case of having to. Amelia's fingers worked mechanically on her violin as, with a feeling of utter degradation, she rubbed herself against the blessedly hard wood. He held it in place rigidly, not helping her, but not humiliating her further by moving it away and making her seek out its hardness again. She felt her muscles start to swell inside her, ready to explode into her orgasm.

'Have you ever come while you're playing before?' he asked, as though making polite conversation, as though he wasn't really interested.

'No,' she said breathlessly, her eyes fluttering closed as she prepared for her orgasm. She was moving faster and had lowered herself further on to the violin, almost groaning as she imagined that she would look ridiculous to him, and ridiculously eager to achieve her satisfaction.

'Nearly there?' he enquired urbanely.

'Yes,' she breathed.

Suddenly the violin wasn't there any more.

'What the fuck –'

She stopped playing abruptly, opened her eyes and glared at him.

'I'm calling the shots here,' he told her. 'Play. And say please.'

Almost weeping with frustration, humiliation and rage Amelia started once more to play. She looked him in the eyes, her own look furious and scornful.

'Please,' she spat.

'Oh, no.' His look was stern. 'You must ask me meekly, not angrily. Learn to curb your impatience. Let it go. Now, look at me with a little pleading in your eyes and ask me again.'

Amelia closed her eyes for a few seconds and tried to relax and lose the anger.

'Please,' she said quietly, looking almost beggingly into his eyes.

The violin nudged at her again and with what she realised was undisguised relief she moved on it again, this time keeping her eyes on this stern stranger who was completely fucking up her sex life.

'Will you masturbate tonight?' he asked, almost in amusement. 'Or won't you need to? Will you tell your lover about this?'

'Will I, will I, will I, will I, will I . . .' Amelia couldn't say any more as her orgasm crashed through her like a sudden violent crescendo on the piano, a mighty blast of the organ or even the cannon shots in the 1812.

As she recovered, the front door slammed shut. He moved the violin and ran his hand along the now wet wood.

'You'll need to wipe this – flatmate?'

'It's my aunt. It's her house.'

He widened his eyes. 'In that case, you'd better get dressed.'

'Shit, no, I mean, she's like a flatmate. She doesn't interfere in my life.'

'She's your aunt? And she doesn't mind you bringing strange guys back for sex?'

'Of course not. Forget about her. I'm going to fuck you now.'

He looked at her consideringly. 'No, I don't think so. I'll go and introduce myself to your aunt.'

'Fuck you,' said Amelia, furious. 'You haven't even introduced yourself to me.'

Maddeningly, he laughed and extended his hand. 'Josh. I'll be seeing you, Amelia.'

'This is absurd,' she protested sulkily, putting her hand in his. 'Are you seriously going?'

'Why, don't you seriously want me to? You said you've got a lover and only pick up guys for casual sex. I don't really want that.'

'Well – what do you want? I think I'm in love with U.'

'Christ, that was quick.'

'U's my lover,' she said wearily, already starting to realise what an idiotic abbreviation it was. 'I mean, I don't want to have a love thing with you.'

'Just as well. There's no way I want a love thing with anyone at the moment,' Josh told her. 'But if you're prepared to learn a little discipline – I'll be in touch.'

She scribbled down her mobile number. 'You're a sadist,' she observed.

'Not really. Just a little mental discipline, that's all I meant. I won't whip you. Now do as I say and stay in here till I've met your aunt and gone. And when I say gone, if you dare to show your face till you hear that front door slam, you'll be sorry. OK?'

'OK. And thanks.'

Amelia threw herself down on the bed. Whatever the fuck was going on, she liked it. God knows what he was going to tell Pandora. Not that she cared. She just hoped he would call.

'Hi. Sorry, did I startle you?'

The woman had straightened up suddenly from moving a cushion on a sofa. It was Josh's turn to be startled. He'd expected an old woman, but the black-clad figure in front of him was slim and girlish.

'It's OK.' She put out her hand. 'Pandora Fairchild.'

'Josh Elliott.' They shook hands. He realised that she was indeed older than she had appeared from the doorway, but hardly what you'd call ancient. A perfect Mrs Robinson figure, in fact. True there was more make-up than complexion on display, but it was flawlessly applied. The eyes were compellingly dark and the lips a deep red. Her hair was an auburn that he'd never seen in nature and he guessed it probably covered up grey, but there was no sign of root growth. The haircut was obviously extremely expensive, a layered chin-length bob with a fringe which he presumed would hide some lines. The slender, yes, maybe too thin, body was clothed in an exquisitely cut black dress with long sleeves and a high neck at the front, though dipped to a deep V at the back. Her tits held up well, whether by nature or surgery it obviously wasn't possible to say. The dress ended at the knee in sheer black stockings, though in contrast to the elegant look her feet were encased in what he guessed was a very high-priced version of Doc Martins. She might look forty-odd but she was bloody gorgeous.

'I suppose you're one of Amelia's random fucks,' she observed, slightly scathingly, although her eyes lingered on him as though she wouldn't mind fucking him herself.

'No. She thought I was going to be, but to be blunt her ideas are rather way out for me. I declined to fuck her.'

'Really!' Pandora sank on to the sofa and patted the cushion next to her. 'I hope you haven't upset her. I'm not going out this evening and I don't want her sulking around the house.'

Josh laughed. 'No, she won't sulk. She's a very talented girl. She's been playing for me.'

'Oh, isn't she just? And what about you, Josh? In
what direction do your talents lie?'

He smiled into her eyes. She was game, and he
wasn't going to turn her down. What a family.

'I'm a writer. You know, the novel in the desk drawer
– though at the moment I'm engaged in some . . . some
undercover investigative reporting, as a sort of favour.'
He hoped she wouldn't ask the nature of the investi-
gation. 'Nothing to do with your line. Amelia tells me
you edit Black Box.'

So, he lied. But she might have done.

'Yes. Well, it's always good to meet a real writer.
But –' she eyed him with curiosity '– did you really
come back here just to hear Amelia play?'

'I love the violin,' he answered, simply but not
directly, guessing she wouldn't notice. 'I'd like to hear
her play again. She said that's OK.'

Pandora looked at him suspiciously. 'You know she
has a lover?'

'Of course, she told me. She's actually rather young
for me.'

Josh thought he was asking for trouble but couldn't
resist playing up to Pandora – after all, that's what
Yasmin had asked him to do. And whatever he might
have told Amelia, he was just dying to fuck. Anyone
would do, he realised. It seemed brutal, but then he
hadn't felt his cock inside a woman for so long and,
though Yasmin's mouth had been a fantastic substitute, he wanted to feel a warm, yielding pussy around
his cock. Equally, he guessed that Pandora just fancied
a quick shag and he just happened to be there. They
could both use each other.

He wondered if she was wearing stockings or tights and decided he had nothing to lose.

'Can I ask – are they stockings or tights?'

Her laugh was sexy and she took his hand and slid it up her skirt. He felt the end of the silky softness, the suspender and the warm thigh above. Already halfway there, he moved his hand questingly further up and encountered warmth and lace.

'I don't think Amelia should come out and find you doing this,' she whispered.

'She won't,' he assured her, hoping rather than knowing the power of his command for her to stay put. 'Anyway, it doesn't need to take long – does it?'

He had pulled the knickers down and encountered the second moist pussy he'd felt in the last hour, while Pandora made no bones about unzipping him and pulling his cock out. He rubbered up and, pushing her elegant dress up to her waist, sat her astride him on the sofa. She was wet and he pushed into her, not exactly roughly but with cool and purposeful efficiency. Despite her age she was tight and it felt better than he even remembered.

She didn't seem concerned with elegance as she bounced up and down on top of him; on the contrary she seemed to be totally absorbed in grinding herself against his bone. He grabbed her firm tits but not for her sake; obviously all she was interested in was her orgasm. She didn't even waste time with words and, realising she was old enough and experienced enough to look after her own needs, Josh just let himself go, and along with the physical rush of bliss experienced a moment of pure joy at the total lack of complication involved.

He realised Pandora was making a little noise deep

in her throat as she came, too. For a couple of moments she continued to move against him more slowly as her breathing returned to normal, then she smiled at him and slid off both his deflating prick and the sofa.

'Great, just what I needed after a hard day at the office,' she said impersonally, putting her knickers back on. 'Would you like a drink?'

'No thanks,' said Josh, following her example and rearranging his clothing. 'I'll have to be going now. But thanks a lot. That was just what I needed, too.'

'Especially after being teased by my niece, I expect,' observed Pandora. 'I guess you must think casual sex runs in the family – well, obviously it does. But it'd be nice to see you again.'

Josh had his hand on the doorknob and thought he could chance his arm.

'Yeah, well, as I said, I told Amelia I'd like to hear her play again, so I'm sure I'll be running into you.'

The change in Pandora was instantaneous; one moment all sweetness and light, the next the Wicked Witch of the West.

'I think I told you Amelia's already got a lover.' Her voice was smooth but with a dangerous undertone.

'Indeed. Though from what she told me they aren't technically lovers. So she's more or less free, I guess.'

'You'd guess wrong,' said Pandora sharply. 'She's deeply involved with him. And I have to say it's a relationship I approve of wholeheartedly. In fact, I introduced them.'

'Really?' said Josh, trying to sound as incredulous as he could. 'But I thought she said he was in his forties – far too old for her.' He crossed his fingers on the door handle as he told yet another lie. If Pandora were to question Amelia on how much she had told him, she'd find out that he had insider knowledge. But it was unlikely, and anyway it was worth a try.

'What difference does age make?' She shrugged. 'I'm older than you. Does it matter?'

'Well, we're not *deeply involved*, as you say they are, for one thing,' said Josh. 'I was just curious as to why you would introduce your niece to someone twice her age and then approve of their involvement. Most people would try to turn her against him.'

Pandora narrowed her eyes. 'Actually, it's none of your business. You know nothing about us, do you? So if you don't mind, leave her alone.'

Josh realised that if he was going to be able to find out any more he had to get back in Pandora's good books.

'Hey, I'm sorry. You're right, it's none of my business. And it was a great fuck. I'd like to take your number. If that's OK.'

Mollified, Pandora reached into her handbag and gave him a card. 'Sure. Call me.'

'Count on it.'

He was gone. Josh 'Bond' Elliott was going back to report to Mother, or whatever he was supposed to call Yasmin. He couldn't suppress a smile as he walked down the affluent street. What an afternoon. Amelia had been fun, though perhaps he had been rather cruel. And Pandora – well, a shag was a shag. If Yasmin wanted, he'd have another go.

As the front door slammed, Amelia pulled a wrap on and went into the sitting room. Pandora was making a gin and tonic.

'Drink, darling?' she asked without turning round.

'No thanks. You had a long chat with Josh.'

Pandora swung round, drink in hand. 'And? What makes you think it was just a chat?'

Amelia stared at her. 'So what was it?'

Her aunt's smile was tinged with triumph. 'Nothing, darling. Anyway, you're not interested, are you? These random guys are just so you can tell U and ... do what you do together.'

Although she knew Pandora thought her sex life was weird, Amelia hadn't realised before that she obviously thought it was really a little distasteful.

'Masturbate,' she supplied. 'Or wank, if you prefer. In fact there are all sorts of names for it, but I doubt you'd approve of those either. That's what we do. I didn't realise you had a problem with that.'

Pandora sighed. 'I don't have a problem, darling. As long as U's happy with it. Don't forget he and I used to be an item − I know a little about his sex drive.' Her mouth twisted into a secret smile of reminiscence.

'An occasional item,' corrected Amelia. 'That still doesn't give you any right to criticise our relationship.'

'Oh, darling, I know!' Pandora put her drink down and hugged her niece. 'I'm sorry. I really don't want to interfere. It's just that ... well, you and U make such a fantastic couple. I'd hate you to spoil it by insisting on your ... your philosophy, as you call it. But I won't say another word about it.' She sat down and looked at Amelia sideways. 'Though I was a bit surprised that − what was his name? Josh? said he was going to see you again. That doesn't sound like playing the game. I'm sure you don't want to risk jeopardising your relationship with U for him.'

Amelia sighed. 'You know, I do have to face the fact that U's a married man. He's never pretended for a moment that he's going to leave his wife.'

'Maybe not. But I thought you said he was falling in love with you.'

'Yes. Isn't it wonderful?'

It was amazing what a swift reaction the words 'falling in love' could provoke. Amelia was immediately transported back to a young girl with the perfect lover. Josh was forgotten.

Pandora patted her knee. 'It is wonderful, darling. U is so special. He's worth fighting over. Not that I'm saying it'll come to that, but – well, don't give up without a fight. And if that means thinking further about going on with your odd sex life, then think about it. But don't throw it all away on someone like this Josh.'

Amelia thought Pandora was probably right. But on the other hand, Josh's words about the dark side of sex had excited her. If she did see him again, she'd just have to do it when Pandora was out or at work. However, what had Pandora done with him?

'You're right.' She pretended to play along. 'I won't. So tell me, were you just chatting?'

Pandora crossed her elegant legs and smiled. 'Well, if you're sure you don't mind – we had sex, right here, on the sofa. And very nice it was too.'

'He wouldn't screw me,' said Amelia slowly. 'He said he didn't want to be one of my random fucks.'

'Darling, you really can't blame him.'

'So how come he was happy to fuck you – at random?'

Pandora shrugged. 'Maybe he prefers older women. Anyway, if you're not going to see him again, it's not important, is it?'

Amelia shook her head. She was confused. For years she'd admired Pandora – indeed, she'd aspired to be like her. Having a relationship with U, following in her aunt's footsteps, still almost seemed like a dream. But now Pandora had screwed Josh – Christ, she couldn't work it out. She was jealous! But it was U she wanted – wasn't it?

'I think I will have a drink after all,' she said weakly. She wasn't expecting U that evening, and she'd done enough practising for one day, even though it was during sex, or rather yet another twist to masturbation. All she wanted to do was veg out in front of the TV with a takeaway. Shame Pandora wasn't into food.

She sighed at the thought of her aunt's disapproving gaze on her as she pigged out on pizza, and made her vodka a large one. Hopefully Pandora would spend much of the evening on the phone to New York as usual, and she could slum it. Just for once. And maybe she would indulge herself in imagining Josh tying her to the bed and making her wait for him. What had he said? Not knowing if he was going to come back and screw her, or maybe wank all over her. Maybe letting her come, maybe not.

Random sex was a brilliant idea, she thought, but possibly it could be refined. Like, her love for U could still be untainted by the inevitable complications of a sexual relationship, but instead of limiting her sexual activity to one-hour stands she could have a purely sexual relationship with someone else – well, with Josh of course – untainted by the complications of love or friendship.

As the vodka kicked in she let her imagination go into overdrive. She saw herself dressed by Josh in a tight black leather corset, her tits pushed out supplicatingly, her legs in high-heeled boots, her arms in long black gloves and a wide collar around her neck. Like he had told her to visualise, she was chained, though not to the wall, just to the floor. She was playing the violin as he ordered, and she was blindfolded. He might make her play for hours, without her knowing what he was doing, whether he was completely ignoring her, maybe wanking at the sight of her, or maybe not even in the room. Then suddenly he would take the violin from her, force her to her knees and push his cock into her mouth, still without saying a word. She would suck him as well as she knew how, and he would pull out and come all over her face. Then she would be raised to her feet again and the violin put back into her hands and again she would start to play, feeling his spunk trickling off the blindfold on to her cheeks, running into her mouth. Maybe, after a while, he would take the violin away again, unchain her from the floor and lead her to a bed, where he might condescend to penetrate her, and might even let her come too.

If this was the darker side of sex he wanted to teach her, it was more than all right by her, though she couldn't suppress a fleeting vision of Josh fucking Pandora on the sofa. Could she have lied? She pushed the picture out of her mind and checked her watch: six thirty. Plenty of time to phone Melinda Sue before ordering a takeaway, to discuss the possibility of replacing random acts with a highly sophisticated relationship consisting entirely of sex games. She went back into her bedroom and dialled up New York, letting her wrap fall open. Her fantasy of Josh making her wait in chains for sex had already aroused her again, and telling Melinda Sue about the events of the afternoon was only going to increase her desire. Masturbating with Melinda Sue – it would be just like old times, only an ocean apart.

4

'So there I am playing fucking Svengali, and there she is playing the bloody violin with nothing on, not even a pubic hair, bloody well oozing for me to fuck her, and instead I make her rub herself off with her violin and then order her to stay in the bedroom while I go out and fuck the aunt.'

Although she wasn't a prude, Yasmin looked round uneasily. She suspected most of the customers enjoying their mid-morning latte didn't really expect to hear something quite that graphic, especially as Josh seemed to be taking on the character of Danny, the chirpy cockney head porter in 49.

'Yeah, yeah, well maybe hold the four-letter words, Josh,' she said, feeling slightly guilty all round. 'I know I said you could play out your vengeance against women on Amelia, but – you don't think you went too far?'

He grinned and shook his head. 'She loved it. She wants to see me again. And thanks for the tip: it did get rid of a lot of anger. Anyway, what you want to know is, Pandora the Wicked Witch of the West was the one to introduce them and they have her blessing. It all sounded a bit odd to me. When I said I wanted to see Amelia again, she more or less told me to fuck off, or rather, that I could have her and not the niece, and I shouldn't poke my nose in their business, which incidentally I knew nothing about. Bizarre, eh?'

Yasmin stared at him. 'More than bizarre. I mean, I

know Pandora was really put out when U and I got together because she liked to shag him every so often. It was U's idea that we have our sexual freedom but not talk about it, which at first I thought meant he wanted to carry on seeing her occasionally, and I was a bit pissed off but thought I should be adult about it. Anyway, it was only a few months later that I saw her and she was very cutting about me tying U to the apron strings, and I realised whatever or whoever he was doing with his sexual freedom it certainly wasn't her. So, I could understand her trying to get him back for herself, but introducing him to her niece? I would have thought that would have made the old bat even more jealous. And talking of whom, what was she like?'

Josh grinned. 'Fucking A. She can't be that old. Her tits are firm and her pussy is as gripping as any I've ever had, I reckon.'

Yasmin was laughing.

'All right, I guess the tits are fake – they're a bit too firm. But as for the rest of her, I don't see she's any older than forty-five. Which is only about ten years older than me.'

'You're a sweet innocent, Josh.' Yasmin still couldn't stop the smile on her face. 'Haven't you ever heard of vaginoplasty?'

'Do what?'

'You have your vagina tightened. Bloody painful, apparently, and extremely expensive. But good for two things, like, feeling – I mean to a man – a lot younger than you are, and also, great orgasms. Which I presume she had one of.'

'Fuck me.' Josh shook his head. 'I know you said she'd been facelifted and all the rest, but I didn't know anyone would go that far. Like blokes can have a penis extension, apparently, but I didn't think I'd ever meet a real person who had anything like that done. Jesus.'

'Pandora's not a real person, dear,' said Yasmin briskly. 'She's an institution. And she's been around long enough to be one.'

Josh looked at her suspiciously. 'I seem to remember you saying in all honesty she was fifty-five. Which I have to say when I met her I didn't believe. So were you being honest?'

She squirmed a little in her chair. 'I don't lie, Josh. And what I said was, and I chose my words carefully, that to be honest she was at least fifty-five.'

He looked just a little cross, she thought, as he raised his eyebrow to encourage her to go on.

'I knew if I told you there was no way you'd do it, even once you met her. But she's actually getting the old-age pension.'

'Oh, Christ. I've fucked a pensioner. Screwed a senior citizen.' He gulped down his coffee. 'Jesus, I would have thought there was some law against that, like taking advantage of the elderly – isn't there?'

Yasmin couldn't stop laughing. 'Only if you use force. Come on, you loved it. Don't be ageist.'

'Ageist, now you call me ageist for unwittingly conning me into having sex with someone old enough to be a grandmother!'

'Actually she could be a great-grandmother, if you think about it,' went on Yasmin remorselessly. 'Say she had had a child when she was eighteen, then that child had a child when *she* was eighteen, and that child had –'

'Enough already!' groaned Josh. 'Oh fuck it, it is ageist, isn't it? Let's face it, nobody thinks it's that strange for a sixty-year-old bloke to fuck a thirty-something woman, so what the hell. She's still gorgeous and, however she's done it, she's got a brilliant fanny.'

'Let's get out of here,' said Yasmin quickly, aware that a man at the next table had looked up in astonishment. 'We'd better get back to work anyway. That last episode needs a bit of sharpening up before mighty Milo gets it.'

As they walked down the busy streets of Soho Yasmin took his arm. 'So tell me, which was best, being the gentle sadist with Amelia, or having a quickie with Pandora?'

There was just a faint trace of bitterness in Josh's laugh. 'Amazing, isn't it? One moment I'm playing the severe and slightly sinister dominator for a nineteen-year-old, the next thing I'm a human dildo for the OAP.'

'So? What did you like best?'

He grinned, and Yasmin could see how easy it would be to fall for him. Not that she could bear to make her life even more complicated than it was.

'I'm a man, darling. The best sex is the one where you get to fuck and get to come. The rest is – well, preparation.'

'Not for women, though,' said Yasmin slowly. 'You were right on the button with what you said to Amelia, about the excitement of waiting. That's the erotic side. That's what women like.'

'Well, I know. I didn't just open my mouth and spew out a load of rubbish.'

She looked at him curiously. 'How do you know? Did you have that sort of relationship with someone?'

He sighed. 'You might as well know my sad story – yes, Veronica and I were well into games. I've never had such fantastic sex with anyone. Our sex life was dominated by fantasy, bondage, anticipation – you name it. Sometimes we'd not have sex for three days, we'd just come home and she'd dress up, you know, really sexy underwear and stuff, and we'd kiss and caress but never let our hands touch each other's genitals, but we'd be so aware of the tension, every night for three days, and then at midnight on the third we fucked – that was fucking A. Then we did the tying up and waiting thing, and the slightly S&M thing – only slightly, neither of us were really into pain. But we just kept the sexual tension going. You can't imagine how good it was.'

'No. Especially as you said she ran off to Lesbos with a woman. How the hell did that happen, if sex with you was so bloody good?'

'Not Lesbos, Naxos. Or was it Paxos? She doesn't write,' he said, though without bitterness. 'It was my fault, Yas.'

'Never –'

'Yeah, yeah, sorry. Well, as you can imagine we talked about fantasies a lot, and one of hers was to have sex with another woman, and as I'm sure you know most men wouldn't be averse to a bit of lesbo action. So anyway, we'd talked about various girlie fantasies, and dickhead here decided to give her a special present on her thirtieth birthday. A big crowd of us were going out to dinner, and I found a bisexual girl to join us. I said she was a budding scriptwriter I'd been assigned to mentor. When everyone started saying goodnight, she just hung on with us, then as prearranged went into the loo when everyone had gone and wrapped a big red ribbon round herself, so I could give Veronica her real present.'

'Wow! You *found* a bi girl? What, hanging around on the street with a sign round her neck? Or was she a friend?'

Josh looked uncomfortable. 'No, I didn't actually know anyone who fitted the bill – anyway, I wanted a stranger. I planned it for ages, and advertised in the Girl Seeking Girl columns. Not that I lied; I told the truth. After a couple of non-starters, I met Fen, who was perfect.'

Yasmin looked at him incredulously. 'You're not telling me that Veronica left you for her, are you? After you set it up?'

'No way! But – well, to get back to that night, it was brilliant, the best present I could have got her, she said. I suppose when Fen was going down on her and Veronica was saying she'd never had it like that from a man, I should have taken the hint, but you can imagine, I was pretty well turned on myself, not to mention more than a little high. Fen had already agreed she'd like to fuck us both, so we more or less had a bloody orgy. When Fen left, Veronica took her number, and I was imagining we'd all do it again sometime, and what a smart bloke I was. But then Veronica said she was going clubbing with Fen and it was women only, and then she started to go off our sex games, and then before I knew it she was hardly home and talking non-stop about Christine. The rest is history.'

'Bloody hell.'

'Yes. So, if you've got a very, very hot fantasy you're unsure about acting out, maybe give it a miss. It could change your life.'

'Sorry, mate. So no chance of you trying a threesome with Amelia and Pandora?'

He burst out laughing. 'You're impossible! They're aunt and niece, for God's sake. The fantasy sort of depends on the two women together. You're not seriously suggesting –'

'I'd put nothing past Pandora,' said Yasmin grimly. 'But no, not for the time being anyway. But you'll see them again, separately?'

He groaned. 'Yes, if you like. As long as granny – sorry, auntie – doesn't find out about me seeing Amelia again, otherwise she'd screw my nuts off, I'm telling you. But since you ask, I don't mind the thought of a few games with Amelia.' He glanced at her quickly. 'I mean, don't think I'd see her in preference to you, given the choice, I mean –'

'Get out of here. I know you're doing it to help me. I'm just glad you're going to enjoy it. And if you want my point of view, you don't have to go too easy on the discipline.'

'Ouch, you vicious bitch.'

'She's fucking my husband. Give it to her good.'

'Yasmin! Maybe just a little light spanking?'

'Yeah. Not too light. What did you call me?'

'Bitch. Vicious bitch. Vindictive slut. Sexy, sadistic vixen. You want to fuck?'

They had just reached the office.

'No. I'm seeing Euan later, who I hope will be another little spy for me. Not that I'm using him. He's a great lay, too.'

'I'm jealous.'

'No, you're not. Let's go and read episode five. You know when Tom and Lisanne are pulling each other's clothes off in the gym . . .'

Josh gave a little smile. 'You horny bitch.'

That was right. Imagining Josh smacking the naked Amelia with her own violin bow, making her stand playing while he did nothing, not to mention the picture of Josh and his ex and the other woman – she was horny, all right.

'Don't forget you bribed me into fucking Pandora

with the promise that I could repeat everything I did with her with you,' he said in her ear as they walked through reception. 'That means you owe me a quickie.'

Yasmin wasn't one to back out of a bargain. And though she was indeed seeing Euan later, he'd mentioned some other chef being there, so maybe they wouldn't get to screw. Too many erotic images crowded in her head to let her risk not getting any today, and reading the part where Tom and Lisanne got down and dirty in the gym was going to prove too much. Anyway, she knew Josh had bought a packet of three the previous afternoon, and he'd only used one. There was no need to hold back this time.

It was absurd, but Yasmin felt guilty as she let herself into the flat that evening. She hadn't wanted to go home at all, but obviously Euan would be working until late and she didn't want to sit around Over the Border all evening waiting for him like a culinary groupie. Josh had suggested they went to dinner or even just for a drink, but having – of course – fucked him that afternoon she realised she couldn't go straight from seeing him to Euan. She tried telling herself she could just have an aperitif and a starter with Josh and then let Euan provide the main course, but it just seemed a bit tacky.

Besides which, she wanted to go home. She was used to working at home after all and, although thanks to Josh working in the office was now even more delicious than her previous solitude, she liked her flat and it was absolutely idiotic to avoid it just because she wanted to avoid U. Almost as idiotic as feeling guilty for a little light adultery, when he was the one who started it and what was more was the one who was serious about it.

She hoped he would still be at work, or maybe out on one of his endless walks where he picked up on the next big thing, but no such luck. Although the flat was quiet, as she picked up a wine bottle in one hand and the coffee pot in the other and tried to make the sensible choice, he came down the stairs from the meditation room.

'Hi,' she said laconically.

'Hello. You're never home these days. I miss you.'

She laughed. 'Sorry, U. Difficult to know how to cope with this. Seems easier just not to be here. Though I can assure you it really was not my idea to write in the office. That was a fait accompli engineered by Milo. I would much rather work from home.'

'Sure, I believe you. It's just that – never mind. You have remembered that we made a date for our anniversary tomorrow?'

Yes, she had remembered. They had booked The Ivy ages ago – before Amelia had come between them. Or rather, Yasmin thought with dismay, before U had told her that Amelia had come between them. It was hard to imagine celebrating their marriage in the circumstances, but tomorrow was another day.

'Of course. I'm looking forward to it.' A white lie seemed unimportant in the face of U's deception.

'Good, so am I. What about tonight? Are you in for dinner?'

Shrugging, she decided, almost regretfully, that she needed the wine rather than coffee, and poured herself a glass and handed the bottle to U.

'Yeah, but I'm going out about ten, and I don't want anything too heavy. There are some mushrooms and salad – I could make a risotto.'

U nodded eagerly at what he probably thought was

a peace offering. He should have known better, she thought. While she didn't mind cooking, time-consuming dishes like risotto were not her favourite thing at all. She had only suggested it because it demanded full attention for about half an hour, which meant any attempt at conversation would have to be postponed. She was irritated to find that her contrivance had made her feel guilty again.

'You're not seeing Amelia tonight?' *Again*, she wanted to add, slightly nastily. She turned her attention to chopping shallots and garlic so she didn't have to face him.

'No. Well, actually I was going to go round earlier but she phoned and put me off – apparently she needs to practise.'

Yasmin nodded as she melted butter in a saucepan and tipped in the vegetables, then turned her sharp knife to the mushrooms. She had plenty of practice yesterday, she wanted to say. Before an audience, what's more. And her relationship with her violin is frankly more intimate than the one she has with you.

However, she kept quiet, smiling to herself at the thought that U would probably soon find out about the violin's part in Amelia's last orgasm.

'We're not talking at the moment, Yasmin,' U began as she put the kettle on for vegetable stock and weighed out the rice. 'I almost wish I hadn't told you about this. It's come between us – I didn't mean that to happen.'

'Oh, fuck off,' said Yasmin exasperatedly. 'Don't be so bloody naïve. There's no way I can carry on as normal knowing you're not-fucking a nineteen-year-old relation of your ex-mistress. You should have thought that one through before you told me. You're supposed to be the one who picks up on things – I would have thought you would have been just a bit more sensitive to my feelings.'

She threw the rice and mushrooms into the pan and, switching the extractor fan on to full to make conversation even more impossible, glared at him. 'And this is why we're not talking, and why I'm not home much. Because we can't help but talk about your little affair, and it makes me mad. So why don't you just go back to meditating for half an hour and then we'll eat and try to have a conversation about something else – OK?'

Turning her back to him and her full attention to stirring the rice, she waited for him to leave the kitchen. He stayed for about half a minute and then left, closing the door softly. Yasmin immediately turned the extractor down and carried on stirring furiously, though she couldn't help a few tears going into the rice as well as the stock. They would eat, try to talk about other things like work, then she would have a long bath and get ready for Euan. U didn't know it, but she was going out to enlist another recruit to help her fight for him.

He should be flattered, she thought cynically. Two gorgeous women fighting over him. It was just a shame her pose of fearless female warrior was interrupted every so often by the appearance of weeping deceived wife.

Over the Border was quiet when Yasmin arrived just before ten thirty, and to her delight Willie was sitting alone on the wrong side of the bar.

'Yasmin, pet! What a nice surprise.'

He pulled up a stool and signalled to the barman, yet another clone in a kilt.

'Whisky or beer, petal?'

'Neither, Willie. I don't want to get too pissed nor do I want to spend half the night pissing. Any chance of wine in this establishment?'

'Any chance of it? We've got a wine list as long as the Forth Bridge, darling girl. Red?'

'Great.'

At Willie's command the barman brought a bottle and two glasses and removed Willie's beer.

'Whisky and beer do have their disadvantages, right enough,' he said, clinking glasses with her. 'And if you're planning a wee session with my head chef, you don't really need to be pissed, nor wanting to run to the ladies every ten minutes.'

'Oh, really? And why should you think I'd be planning a "wee session" –' she managed a passable attempt at a Scottish accent '– with anyone?'

Willie laughed. 'Och, silly me. Just because you screwed on the kitchen table in full view of the rest of the staff last time you were here, and just because the regularity of your visits has gone up from once a year to twice in a week – how dare I jump to such a preposterous conclusion?'

'All right, Taggart, or whoever the latest Scottish detective is, you're right.'

'Taggart died, actually, so if you don't mind I'll pass on that nickname. Look, petal, there was one reason only I took you out back last time, and I bet you know that only too well. You and Euan are made for each other. Anyway, he certainly seems to think so. And as I said, you're back here within the week, so I guess you think so too.'

Yasmin gave him a troubled look. 'Willie, I think U and I were made for each other. Oh, fuck, not you and I –'

'I know, pet. To be perfectly honest I don't know

how anyone can seriously live with a man called U. But joking aside, when I say you're made for each other I mean as lovers. What they call fuck buddies in the States, apparently. You wouldn't want to have a proper relationship with a chef. The hours are terrible and they always stink of onions and raw meat and –'

'Christ, Willie, that's enough. You're putting me off anything except getting a cab back home. Anyway, Euan reckons he wouldn't mind helping me with my little detective work – which incidentally is going quite well.'

She filled him in on Josh's role as secret agent and Pandora's confession to being instrumental in introducing U and Amelia.

'I told you the old cow had something to do with it,' said Willie, glowering. 'God almighty, she's a nasty piece of work. What's in it for her? I bet I was right: she just wants him back.'

Yasmin sighed. 'Who knows, Willie. But that's not all. First I fucked Euan, in revenge I suppose, even though I said that's just what I didn't want to do. The next thing is this guy Josh at work, and you know it's just like the bloody script I'm writing. Lisanne fucks Simon when she hears about her husband having an affair, then despite feeling guilty about going for the cheap revenge trick she fucks a guy at work and asks him to help her. I don't know if I'm being influenced by the plot or whether it's just a coincidence.'

'Bollocks,' declared Willie roundly. 'Of course it's just a coincidence.'

'Well, U reckons coincidences always mean something.'

Willie poured them both another glass of wine. 'See, I was right. U talks a load of bollocks.'

'Willie! I'm surprised at you!'

'Oh, come on, pet. Surely you don't really believe all this business about fashion trends floating around in the ether, do you? Nice work if you can get it, especially if you can do what U does and make thousands of gullible people hang on to your every word, but for God's sake! I mean, go on, tell me, what's the next big thing?'

Yasmin burst out laughing. 'Well, sex. Like Amelia's philosophy of it. The casualisation of sex. The relegation of the erotic to the mundane, and the elevation of relationships beyond the taint of sex. Oh, and the rise of modern classical music.'

Willie chortled. 'Christ almighty! So I was right, it's complete codswallop. Anyway, getting back to this plot business, what's happening next?'

'Well, I don't know. That's what I didn't tell you about. The plot of 49 isn't planned out months in advance like normal soap operas. We're only told the next part of the plot a week at a time.'

Willie looked mystified. 'And what's the point of that?'

'So that we make the characters act as though they're in a real life situation, rather than our forward knowledge influencing what we make them say. It's a good idea – if a bit frustrating.'

'Good idea, my arse. You'll be doing yourself out of a job at this rate, pet. The characters might as well improvise if they're only reacting to the current situation.'

'That was one idea,' admitted Yasmin. 'The original one was that at the end of every episode they'd give the viewers a chance to vote on three possible outcomes for the next episode, but they realised that wouldn't work. It would mean too much in the way of resources tied up in taking calls, plus either having to write three scripts – more manpower – or have the writers sitting there furiously scribbling away after the votes were cast. Apparently Milo was really pissed off when it was rejected.'

'Christ, you didn't tell me Milo was involved. You poor wee girl. You've got cow bitch Pandora messing with your marriage and mouthy Milo at work. Good thing you've got us. Let's have another bottle.'

Yasmin looked at her watch. 'Well, I did sort of expect to see Euan this evening, not that I'm not enjoying our chat. But he's got something to tell me, or rather some other chef has. As you're so quiet, Willie, do you think –'

'Get away with you! I almost forgot you came here to screw my staff, rather than talk to me.' Willie waved her off in the direction of the kitchen, grinning. 'You know the way, I believe?'

Yasmin felt suddenly shy about going through to the kitchen on her own.

'Actually, last time we went through the side door from the back room.'

Willie heaved himself off the bar stool and put his arm round her. 'God, you're such a wee girlie. Let me take you through.'

He pushed open the swing door to the kitchen. Euan was in deep conversation with a woman, also in chef's whites, at the main table.

'Eh! Your guest has been waiting for you, chef!'

Yasmin was pleased and relieved to see Euan's face light up with its incredibly joyful smile.

'Yasmin! Why didn't you come straight in? I was afraid you weren't coming.'

He bounded up to her and gave her a big hug. 'Willie, you've been hogging her, you bastard.'

'No, we've been having a good old chinwag. Anyway, don't let me stand between you, and I shan't let you stand between me and another drink. Cody, do you fancy joining me?'

'In a minute, Willie,' said Euan quickly. 'Cody's got some information for Yasmin about her ... little marital problem.'

Willie raised his eyebrows. 'Right enough. I just thought you two might like to be left alone – or fairly alone.' He looked round at the almost deserted kitchen. 'Anyway, if you fancy a drink, I'm out front.'

He saluted them and left the kitchen, leaving Euan to hug Yasmin again.

'So what's this information?' she asked suspiciously, eyeing the other chef. She had a strong face with big features, brought into prominence by the white cap covering her hair, and stylish black and amber glasses.

'Cody,' said the woman, holding out her hand. 'Nice to meet you, Yasmin. Curiously enough the night you were here last I met your husband's girlfriend.'

'Hello?' said Yasmin faintly. 'How?'

Cody smiled at the puzzlement on Yasmin's face. 'I had last week off, so as you can imagine filled every night with the sort of things I never get to do working here. Last Saturday I went to the opera.'

'Yeah, yeah, don't tell me, *La Traviata* at the Coliseum.'

'Right. Well, it's not only cultural activities you don't get much time for in this job, but sex as well. So when I saw this babe with very large tits showing under a transparent blouse I figured she might be up for something, so I followed her into the toilets at the end.'

'Yeah. I heard. Well, mostly. U told me she gave a woman a hand job on the stairs.'

'That's right. I was a bit pissed off, actually – when I approached her I was kind of expecting a bit more than that, like maybe a bite to eat and a night of it. I was actually going to ask her to come back here and pick up Euan, but she wasn't interested.'

Euan held his hands out expressively. 'Can you imagine that? Here I am with you on the table and Cody brings your husband's girlfriend back for a bit of a threesome – even I might have been a bit fazed by three women at once.'

Yasmin laughed. 'It would have been a touch ironic, wouldn't it? I haven't seen her for a few years, so I don't suppose I would have recognised her. Though of course if U hadn't been going off to meet her, I wouldn't have been here at all.'

She suddenly realised that it was unlikely that Amelia had told her that she was having an affair with a guy whose wife had worked on a Scottish soap opera. 'How did you know who she was, anyway?' she asked Cody suspiciously.

'Because I'm a magazine junkie, and I've seen your husband's photo in *Slice* often enough,' she explained. 'Whatshername – she didn't tell me what it was – skipped off into a taxi with some handsome bloke in white. As he turned round to pull the door shut I recognised him. To be honest I was just kicking myself that she didn't invite me to go with her.'

'Well, don't take it personally. You were just a random act of sexual kindness, a quick fuck she could talk about to U later while they both jerked off.'

'Wow. Sounds totally sad.'

Yasmin shrugged. 'Too totally fucking sad to talk about, that's for sure.' She yawned. 'Anyway – thanks for the info.'

'I wondered if Cody could maybe do a bit of spying for you – get in touch with her and ask her out, or something,' suggested Euan.

'I don't know – I thought you would be better. After all, she's had Cody. She's like lightning, she doesn't like to strike in the same place twice.'

'Apart from with your husband,' Cody observed.

'No, that doesn't count. They don't actually have sex – their relationship is on a higher plane,' said Yasmin bitterly. 'Which leaves me not knowing what my relationship with him is. Are we supposed to have sex? We used to, but does that mean our relationship wasn't precious enough? Or now he's taken her ideas on board, does that mean we don't any more because our relationship *is* special?'

'So have you? Since he told you?'

'No,' admitted Yasmin. 'But then again I've had both you and Josh since then, so I'm actually having more sex than I'm used to. Not that I'm complaining.'

Euan laughed wickedly. 'Thank God for that. I'm not used to complaints, whether it's about food or sex. In fact, I don't like them at all. I'm liable to get all Gordon Ramsay if someone dares to criticise my food.'

Yasmin raised her eyebrows. 'And how do you get if someone criticises your fucking?'

'Never happened, gorgeous girl,' he assured her with a wicked glint in his eye. 'Anyway, that's enough talk for one night. You know Cody is my prep chef.'

'You said,' acknowledged Yasmin.

'So. If you don't mind, I'll just let her prepare you for me.'

Yasmin's pulse notched up a few more beats to the minute. She looked at the woman, who had a faint smile on her face. Obviously she was bi – so what did Euan have in mind?

'What does that mean? Prepare me how?'

'Well, if you'll just come over to the prep table,' said Cody, taking Yasmin's hands and leading her to her second encounter with a stainless steel table, 'I'll give you some idea. Preparation in the kitchen sense can involve many things, depending on the size of the brigade. As we're quite small here, it includes peeling and chopping, cleaning and washing, tying into the right shape, and generally getting the raw ingredients into the right state for the chef to finish them off.'

Yasmin faced her as she sat her on the edge of the table. She felt that Cody's large, expressive grey eyes were looking her over as if she were nothing but a piece of meat for the table, but knew that was her own imagination. Studying the big-boned face she felt no desire for the other woman, although she had had her share of girl-on-girl encounters, but the anticipation of what she was about to do sent a frisson through her. She guessed that she didn't need to be turned on by Cody; she literally was going to get her ready for Euan's attentions.

'So, peeling. Actually, this is normally done in the prep sink round the back there, but for convenience we'll keep all the operations in one place.'

Cody matched her actions to her words as she peeled Yasmin's dress from her body. Yasmin had dressed appropriately for the evening's planned activities in a short, sleeveless chiffon dress with a dropped waistline reminiscent of the 1920s, expecting it to be raised to waist level as on her previous visit. However, Cody reached behind and undid the zip and then pulled it to the floor, leaving Yasmin sitting on the table in her new strapless bra and knickers, white cotton trimmed with red broderie anglais.

'Very pretty,' observed Cody, running her hand over the bra and, of course, Yasmin's breast. 'In fact, very pretty indeed.'

Her other hand stroked the other breast and then,

working gently together, they reached into the bra cups and scooped her breasts out to sit over the top of the underwiring.

'You weren't joking, Euan. Fantastic nipples. I've never seen any this dark.'

Whether it was part of her preparation role or not, she lowered her mouth to suck gently on one of Yasmin's nipples, which were quickly becoming erect, while still toying with the other. Yasmin closed her eyes and concentrated on enjoying the sensation, not just for its own sake but also for the fact that Euan was watching. The boy at the washing-up sink may have been watching too, she didn't know. Or care. It registered somewhere in her mind that if Euan had told Cody about the colour of her nipples, he had probably described the sex they had last time. She felt sleazily pleased that she had been the topic of conversation between the two chefs, and that she was now the centre of their attention.

'Mmm,' said Cody. 'As you may have gathered from my meeting with your rival, I adore breasts. Not just big ones, but all breasts.' Her hands were still gently scuffing Yasmin's nipples, now wet with saliva. Yasmin opened her eyes and looked into Cody's. They were now narrowed with desire, and Yasmin's sex muscles gave a corresponding leap.

Alarm went through her next, however, as Cody produced a large black-handled knife.

'Chopping – well, maybe that's not appropriate to this scenario,' the chef mused. 'Slicing, rather. Keep still, because it's very sharp. But don't be afraid: I assure you I'm very experienced with a knife.'

Yasmin was pushed back on to the table, her breath coming quickly. She assumed Euan hadn't let a mad woman loose on her, but couldn't help but be a little worried as to what was going to be sliced. She soon found out as the blunt side of the knife was pushed up under her bra between her breasts, and the blade cut through the virgin white cotton. The point of the knife was inches from her throat and, while she knew, deep down, that Cody was only planning to slice her underwear off her, she allowed herself a little tremor of fear. The knife moved then, the blunt side pushing each cup of the bra away, grazing over her nipples as it did so. Cody then pushed the point of the knife in one side of the bra and pulled it out from under Yasmin and tossed it on the floor.

It was obvious what was going to happen next. Prostrate on the table Yasmin could only wait, unable to see Cody now she had moved back to stand in front of her. The chef had obviously decided that, as Yasmin had just confirmed to Josh, anticipation and imagination were what turned a woman on, and left her untouched for a full minute. Lying on her back, the fluorescent lights overhead, she was reminded as on her previous visit of being in a hospital operating room, waiting for some incision to be made, wanting to cry out that she hadn't had the anaesthetic but unable to speak.

She felt the knife, but not where she had expected. Following on from her performance with the bra, she guessed that Cody would push the knife up each side of her knickers and cut the fabric and take them off. But instead she felt the slightest pressure on her clit. It wasn't hard to obey the order to stay very still.

Relief flooded her when she felt Cody's other hand lift the knickers up, away from her body – presumably she wasn't about to go in for a clitoridectomy. Instead the knife cut sharply through the cotton, making a tearing sound, as she moved it down the front of the knickers, from just below the waistband right down to Yasmin's arse. The knife had finished its work and Cody's hands pushed the cotton apart, exposing her from clit to arsehole.

'They were too pretty to take off,' she said by way of explanation. 'I wanted to see Euan's cock going in and out of you surrounded by that red cotton lace.'

'So when does my cock get to go in and out?' Euan's voice was husky. He had obviously been as turned on by Cody's knifework as Yasmin.

'Not yet,' tutted Cody. 'First there's a little matter of trimming. She's all over the place.'

Pulling Yasmin's arms back behind her neck, she produced a ball of string and wound it round her wrists. It wasn't too tight but as Yasmin pulled against it experimentally she knew she couldn't move far.

'And cleaning,' added Cody. Before Yasmin could wonder what on earth she meant, the chef pushed her thighs apart and, kneeling in front of the table, licked softly at her clit, as though not knowing if she would find it to her liking. With her hands still on the soft inner flesh of Yasmin's thighs, Cody started moving her tongue more deliberately across the now hard bud of flesh. The sensation was almost too much for Yasmin; she started moving her hips towards the woman's mouth, willing her to finish her off, regardless of the fact that Euan was waiting to satisfy her – or, at least, himself.

As if she wanted to make Yasmin wait for satisfaction, Cody's tongue slipped down to part the swollen sex lips and then her lips were kissing those softer, more fleshy ones, kissing them and driving her tongue into the moist opening as though she were kissing

Yasmin's mouth rather than her pussy. As if by reflex Yasmin's mouth pouted in return, wishing she could join in the caresses.

Although her eyes were narrowed and clouded with lust, she couldn't help noticing the expression on Euan's face as he watched Cody kissing Yasmin's sex almost passionately. His fleshy features were distended, almost ugly, with desire, but it was an ugliness that was pure animal.

'When we spoke on the phone you said you had a tongue on your clit. How does Cody's compare?'

'Just as good. Better? I don't know,' muttered Yasmin, her voice throaty and breaking slightly. 'I don't want it to end.'

'Not even for me to fuck you?' asked Euan.

'Yes, of course I want you to fuck me. God, I want everything.'

I was an almost-faithful married woman until a few days ago, and now I want everything, Yasmin thought. I don't want this woman's face to move from my clit, but I want Euan's prick inside me. A shiver went through her as, unbidden, the picture came into her mind of the little guy who was washing the dishes coming over and pulling his cock out and pushing it into her mouth. Although she'd never before fantasised about an orgy, she suddenly wished he would come and take her mouth while Euan fucked her and Cody continued her caresses. She even imagined the other kitchen staff coming back in and pulling their cocks out and wanking over her, all while she was lying helpless on the table, pinioned by bodies with her arms tied above her head, a willing vessel for anyone who wanted to use her for their own satisfaction.

'Move over, Cody,' said Euan roughly, pulling his

cock out of his checked trousers. The woman obliged, standing and watching Yasmin.

'Thanks,' said Yasmin, rather absurdly.

Cody smiled rather ironically and then, as Euan pushed his beautiful and welcome cock into her, Yasmin's mouth finally found employment as the other woman kissed her as passionately as she had just laboured on her other lips. Yasmin's tongue responded with furious energy and was rewarded when Cody's slightly rough hands started mashing her breasts. Although Euan had barely fucked her with two or three firm strokes she felt like she could orgasm almost straight away.

Cody had other ideas, though. She stood abruptly, leaving Yasmin's mouth and breasts feeling abandoned. Although she felt disappointed, Yasmin concentrated on Euan's rhythmic strokes and his big hands clutching hard at her hips. She imagined bruises forming and felt a masochistic delight at the thought of seeing them come out the next day, purple marks against her honey-coloured skin.

Then, cold steel once more touched her flesh, as Cody lowered the kitchen knife to press on Yasmin's mons. The blade was laid flat on her fleshy mound, just above her clit, and the woman pressed the blunt edge of the knife down, centimetres above the swollen bud and Euan's cock. Yasmin let out a moan.

'Come on, gorgeous,' urged Euan, his voice thick. 'Come all round my dick, you beautiful wee girl. Cody, you're an awesome fucking bitch, press down on her, Christ, I can feel you, my God, I can feel you coming, Jesus, I can feel your come running out of you, it's dripping down my cock, Jesus Christ, oh God, help me.'

Yasmin half heard Euan's profanities, though the

orgasm that swept through her overpowered her senses completely. She couldn't even manage words herself, though as the waves subsided she realised she was making a little noise at the back of her throat.

'That's a hell of a big appeal to the good Lord for an Episcopalian,' Cody was saying to Euan with an amused voice. 'Anyway, as you're committing adultery, I doubt he'd have any time for you.'

'Fuck off, Cody,' said Euan happily, a beatific smile on his face. 'Yasmin, you have the nicest pussy I've ever had the privilege to put my cock inside.'

'Charmed,' sniffed Cody.

'Och, apart from yours,' he added hastily. 'Christ, I suppose you want some attention as well.'

'Don't worry, Raymond's outside,' said Cody, her voice resigned but amused. 'I guessed you were going to waste yourself in one fell swoop.'

'Who's Raymond?' asked the ignored Yasmin.

'Oh, just one of the kitchen hands. He's always up for it.'

Yasmin sat up with some difficulty, not having her hands free to help herself with. 'I thought that was a load of rubbish, chefs casually screwing each other at work. I read a couple of books about restaurant kitchens in preparation for *49 Madison Avenue*, but the storyliners reckoned it was just boasting.'

Cody laughed. 'Everything you read is true, especially the bits about harassing the female staff. That's why we women have to be *strong*.'

She emphasised the last word as she walked purposefully towards the back door, opened it and called out.

'Raymond! Get your arse in here!'

Almost immediately a figure appeared to stand in

front of her. He was one of the kitchen staff who had watched Euan screwing Yasmin a few days earlier, a big black guy who had asked if there was any chance of Yasmin being passed around.

'You really want my *arse*?' he drawled affectedly. His eyes flickered down the room. 'Hey, lady, you back! Don't say I missed the floorshow.'

'Shut up, get in that prep room and do what you do best,' ordered Cody, her hands pushing his buttocks into the alcove next to the back door. 'See you later, guys.'

'Hey, gorgeous,' said Euan as he untied Yasmin's wrists and handed her dress to her. 'You coming back with me again tonight?'

She shook her head regretfully. 'No, it's too confrontational. Especially as tomorrow's our anniversary and we've got to go out to dinner and act like a loving couple.'

He whistled, then grinned. 'Why don't you come here?' he suggested teasingly. 'I'll cook you a special meal, then afterwards you can come through to the kitchen and he can have Cody first hand rather than by repute, and I can think of something else for you.'

Yasmin giggled. 'Oh, great. While we're at it we can dress his little girl up in a mini kilt and get her out front serenading us with her violin before she joins in the fun afterwards.'

'Just trying to help. So where are you going?'

'The Ivy. I'm going to spend all tomorrow getting ready. I've got a new outfit, gypsy style, so I've made an appointment to have my hair unbraided – I thought it'd look better with curls.'

Euan was shaking his head wistfully. 'I wish I could be the one taking you out tomorrow. I vaguely remember you with curls – I think I liked it better than the plaits. I'd like to see your gypsy outfit, too. Especially as it comes off.'

'Well, you'll be working. And you'll be working most nights, Euan, so don't pretend you wish you could be a full-time lover.'

His face dimpled. 'I'm not good at that,' he confided. 'Not enough time. That's why it's so tempting for chefs to fool around when there's a break in service. It's the only chance you get for a sex life.'

'That's cool. Anyway, as Willie said, you chefs stink of cooking all the time.'

'Did he? Drunken lowland bastard, I'll get him for that. Better than stinking of whisky. Anyway, what about this spying?'

Yasmin shrugged. 'I don't know. Josh is doing a pretty good job at the moment. Maybe you don't have to get involved, especially as you're working all the time.'

'Well, I know Cody wouldn't mind seeing her again – she might help. Give me a call if you change your mind.'

'There's one thing I'd like to ask you.' Yasmin felt a little shy about it. 'She's got a Brazilian – do you think I should do mine?'

'Och, do I hell,' said Euan, putting his arm round her. 'Don't copy the silly little bitch. Your pussy's just fantastic with hair and all. Is that all?'

'Yeah. Well, she doesn't wear undies – what do you think?'

'After that trick with the knife, I think wearing undies is the best thing ever,' said Euan gravely. 'In fact, I think your husband will probably realise that underwear is the new black pretty soon. I bet they were expensive – I hope you thought it was worth it.'

Yasmin smiled. 'Absolutely. We're not exactly hard up. And I'm going to keep those knickers for coming to see you in. Even if you're busy you can bend me over that prep sink and fuck the arse off me without me having to expose myself to the rest of your staff.'

'Is that a promise?'

She nodded, feeling tremendous affection for him. 'I'd better go, Euan. Thanks for a great time. And the offer of help. Thank Cody for me, too.'

'Thank me yourself.'

Cody strolled towards them, smiling and relaxed. 'Sorry, didn't mean not to say goodbye. I knew I wouldn't take long. Thank you, too.'

Yasmin nodded. 'Maybe next time I could be a bit more active with you.'

The other woman winked. 'Any time. Really.' She cupped Yasmin's breast in her hand. 'Want me to sew up the bra? I've had a lot of experience with kitchen string and a darning needle.'

Yasmin laughed. 'Thanks, but no. Keep it as a souvenir. I think I'm moving on to sexier underwear, on Euan's recommendation.'

She kissed both of them on the cheek and went back into the bar, where she couldn't help soliciting Willie's advice on pubic hair, bras and crotchless knickers. Not that she wanted his views, but she knew it would amuse him and, despite having been fucked and sucked in public, she still felt a bit flirty. What am I like, she thought, as she had one more glass of wine for the road and then allowed Willie to escort her to a taxi.

5

'This is what's coming. Sex – is the new –'

'Gardening?' suggested one of the journalists flippantly as U hesitated. 'After all, it wasn't that long ago that they were saying – correction, even we were saying – that gardening was the new sex. So what is sex but the new –'

'Can it, Kip.' U frowned. 'I mean, sex is on a new plane. Sex and relationships are getting divorced. Sex is fun, pure and simple. Relationships are mellowing into friendships and spiritual communion, unsullied by sex. But we all need sex – so we take it randomly.'

'Gays have been doing that for *ever*,' sniffed Kip, tossing back his black quiff. 'I don't see what's so smart about this. Tons of people fuck randomly. Indiscriminately, I'd call it, but I suppose randomly sounds better. Like the lottery.'

Stevenson, the photographer and Kip's special friend, stifled a snort. 'Actually, that's not a bad idea, U,' he said languidly. 'The lottery of love, the fuck that turns on the throw of a dice.'

'I don't think I could turn on the throw of a dice,' put in Terri, a plump Californian who needed quite a considerable space to turn in. 'U, this sounds like those tacky holiday programmes where young people go to shag as many other people as possible. What's the difference?'

U was struggling to maintain his usual imperturbability as the others round the table laughed and nodded agreement.

'Believe me, this is where we're heading,' he said earnestly. 'I see what you're saying, Terri, but it's a difference of perspective. Our readers just aren't the sort of people who go on these holidays to Cyprus and so on. They're stylish and sophisticated and their sex lives are nothing like shagging by numbers. Look, we know that thirty per cent of our readers have partners. What proportion of them do you reckon still fantasises about screwing other people? And what proportion finds sex with the partner a little dull?'

'In my experience, most people find shagging their partner dull,' said Yvonne, who at fifty-plus with at least three marriages and several other live-in lovers under her belt was the most qualified to talk about sex within a relationship. 'I like this idea, U. So I tell Vincent that he and I move our relationship on to a more spiritual plane and go out fucking younger men every night, is that it?'

'That's where your problem lies,' interrupted Kip. 'Yvonne, dear heart, do you think it's going to be easy to go out finding younger men to screw every night? Frankly, random fucking only works for young and attractive women and for gay men.' He looked round the conference table maliciously. 'I bet if we all go out tonight on the pull, only Lucy will score. Apart from me, of course.'

'Yes, well, if you count pulling as opening your mouth to any passing dick –'

'That's enough!' U stopped Yvonne with a thump of his hand on the table. 'People, I'm not arguing. This is what the next issue is about. Random, uncomplicated, fulfilling sex. Putting sex in its rightful place, rather than as a bargaining tool in a relationship, or a bone of contention.'

'Bone of –'

'Kip, you always go too far, but today you're really overplaying the bitchy queen.'

'I'm bi, actually,' retorted Kip. 'It's just that someone has to put a bit of fun into these conferences.'

'Enough. Stevenson, I want some good raunchy pictures. I thought about illustrating classic sex tracks. You know, like "Walk on the Wild Side" – do you know any transvestites?'

'Thanks to my little friend here, of course,' said the photographer, patting Kip's hand. 'Sounds interesting. Leave us to come up with a few ideas.'

'"Relax". "YMCA" –'

'Don't take this as homophobia, Kip, but the majority of our readers are heterosexual.' U's tone was weary.

'Ignore him,' said Stevenson with a faint smile. 'Coincidentally a friend of mine – female, you'll be pleased to know – is coming up this afternoon to stay for a couple of days. She'll be into posing for me. That's what we want, a real person seriously into sex, not a soft-core model. I'm sure we can come up with something a little more acceptable.'

'Good. Yvonne, I want something from you on relationships – how eliminating sex can be liberating, find a few people who don't have sex but have a great relationship. Transatlantic viewpoint, Terri: bring in the new celibacy, the difference between postmodern Europe and post-apocalyptic New York. Lucy, speak to a few Club Med types, I'm thinking they're playing around before they find a partner, contrast with couples who play around in an adult way.'

'Well, OK, U,' said Lucy hesitantly. 'It's just that I don't think I know any couples who play around in an adult way. Unless you mean swingers –'

'No,' said U, almost crossly. 'Most emphatically not. That is so seventies. Look, I'll give you a number, a girl

I know who can explain it to you. And Anneliese, I don't really need to brief you on sexy fashions, I expect. We'll be seeing lots of transparent shirts with nothing underneath, the death of underwear, the thrill of knowing the woman walking down the street in front of you could just lift her skirt for access.'

Anneliese looked worried. 'It's not my department, U, but I don't think advertising will be too pleased by the death of underwear. We must get at least ten per cent of revenue from lingerie houses.'

'I like that idea of the girl lifting her skirt for you. It reminds me of that guy who was walking down the street in front of us the other day. He dropped his trousers and mooned, didn't he?' said Kip maliciously. 'Though I don't think that had anything to do with ease of access. More likely it was about having six pints of snakebite or something.'

'Kip, you're knocking on redundancy's door,' said U testily. 'And you can leave advertising to me, Anneliese. That's it, people. Let's see what you can come up with.'

He gathered his papers together and left the room for the peace of his office feeling extremely irritable. It was the first time his intuitions had been treated with complete ridicule. One or two of his ideas had drawn a blank over the years, but he had always triumphed when his predictions had been proved right. However, he wasn't used to being laughed at. What was more, he was even more annoyed that it was Amelia's philosophy that they were laughing at.

He hoped she wouldn't mind if he gave her number to Lucy. She would be far and away the best person to describe her take on sex in a convincing way, though he realised he should have interviewed Amelia himself. Never mind, he would rewrite Lucy's article.

Opening his office fridge he pulled out the freshly squeezed juice he had had sent in for lunch: his favourite, organic pear and watercress laced with wheatgrass and spirulina. Sipping the biliously green concoction, he sat back and relaxed in his ergonomically designed office chair.

Although he'd silenced Kip, he was aware that he wasn't – to be blunt – getting any either. Indeed, when he had gone out once or twice deliberately resolved to find some random action, it had totally eluded him. Even when he found a woman he liked the look of, he just didn't have what it took to suggest sex.

Taxis, for example. Amelia spoke enthusiastically of taxi drivers as sure-fire participants in random sex, but on the one occasion he'd had a woman taxi driver she was large and butch and he was afraid he'd get a kick in the balls if he'd offered her a quickie on the back seat. He felt that if he were a woman he'd almost scream rape if a stranger suggested sex, or even if he wasn't afraid he'd feel too vulnerable to accept.

The ironic thing was that he wasn't getting any from Yasmin either. Since he told her about Amelia she'd almost completely avoided him altogether until bedtime, and he had just known that she would have been outraged if he'd tried to come on to her in bed. They had always scorned the idea of the married couple having a quick, unthinking screw between turning the TV off and going to sleep, preferring to make love on the sofa or in the meditation room, fucking with concentration and energy.

Still, it was their wedding anniversary and they were going out for dinner. Maybe if they had a few drinks, a good meal, became friends again, they could finish off the evening the way they always used to, with a joint and maybe another drink up in the meditation room. He hoped so.

A thought came into his mind, one that had tried to get a foot in there before but which he had managed to shut out before it did so. This time it arrived without warning. What if Pandora had never introduced him to Amelia? What if Yasmin hadn't been away for that break at the spa two months ago? And what if he had just done the sensible thing, had a pleasant evening, been delighted to reacquaint himself with a now-grown-up Amelia and come home and looked forward to Yasmin's return?

What if Pandora hadn't had an urgent meeting come up unexpectedly the next day, and suggest U accompany Amelia to that concert at the Wigmore Hall? And what if Amelia hadn't come back from a prolonged visit to the ladies during the interval and told him that she had just given head to the distinguished-looking man in the front row while his wife guarded the toilet door?

So many what ifs, and he knew the answer. If those things hadn't happened, he would be looking forward to the evening's celebrations. He would probably have picked up on some other cutting edge trend than the new sex, and he would have just left an editorial conference elevated by the admiration of his colleagues rather than deflated by their ridicule and distrust. He would certainly have been having regular sex with his wife, rather than masturbating with Amelia.

After all, wasn't he just a little too old to have a girlfriend who was saving herself and denying him – even if she were saving herself for complete strangers?

But while his mind was open to such negative thoughts, it was also open to the picture of Amelia that came into it. Her beauty, her attitude, her confidence, her naked pubis, her full breasts displayed almost arrogantly under her transparent tops ... he was getting a hard-on.

Synchronistically, his mobile vibrated in his pocket. Amelia.

'Hello, sweet one. How are you? I was just thinking about you.'

'Really? I'm not interrupting your work?'

'No. I've just left a meeting, and I was at my desk picturing you.'

He decided to leave out the fact that he'd also been picturing his previous life, the one into which Amelia hadn't intruded.

'Oh, U. That is so nice. I'm sorry to call you at work. I'm not feeling too good.'

He sat bolt upright in his chair. 'Why? Are you ill?'

'No, nothing like that. It's just – oh, I wish I'd seen you last night. I'm really missing you.'

'But why did you cancel? I would have loved to come over and hear you practise.'

'I know. Can you come over now?'

'Now?' U looked at his watch. 'Amelia, I have just an hour and a half till my next meeting, and that's with two of the top guys at the management company. It's serious, too. We need to increase circulation – advertising's down, what with fears of a recession.'

'U, an hour and a half will do. I just want to talk – and to hold you.'

He could hardly believe it. She wanted to hold him. Not to tell him of a previous conquest, not to have a mutual masturbation session, but to hold him, affectionately.

But – an hour and a half.

'Amelia, you know what the traffic's like at this time

of day. I could only just get there and back in that time, let alone spend any time with you.'

A kind of bravado seized him. 'Look, why don't you come to the office? Right now?'

There was a few seconds' silence.

'U – is this a good idea? After all, won't everyone there know Yasmin? What will they think?'

He felt slightly bewildered. Amelia was supposed to be the bold one, the one who set no store by public opinion.

'Well, does it matter what they think? Look, I've told them about your philosophy. The next issue is going to feature it in a big way. I even said I'd give your number to one of the reporters, so you can explain it properly. Come on!'

'I can't. Sorry, U, but – well, I'm having so much self-doubt, I don't even know what I think of my philosophy any more.'

His heart sunk. 'Amelia – oh, hell, why don't you just get on the tube and get over here?'

He felt slightly guilty as he made the suggestion. He would never set foot on the tube himself, but he had to acknowledge that it could be quicker than taxis, especially in the middle of the day when nobody was throwing themselves in front of the rush-hour trains.

She was sobbing. 'I'm so sorry! I'm so sorry! I really don't know what's the matter with me! I really need to see you!'

'Shh, shh,' he soothed. He set his jaw grimly. OK, so neither he nor Yasmin was looking forward to the so-called celebration dinner. What the hell if he was a bit late.

'Amelia, I'll come round as soon as I can, as soon as the next meeting's finished. I can't cancel that, but I'll take a rain check on the next appointment.'

'When will your meeting finish?'

'I don't know. Around five thirty, maybe. I'll see you before half past six, I hope. OK?'

She sniffed, but had stopped crying, thank God.

'That's fine. Thank you for understanding. I'll just practise for a few hours. Hurry, U!'

'Of course. You take care, little one.'

He sighed as he put the phone down. Yasmin was supposed to be coming to the office at seven, which was the time he had expected to wrap up for the day, and they were going to have a couple of drinks before going on to the restaurant. Well, he could be back, especially if the meeting with the management company could be hurried along, or he could just call her and get her to meet him at the bar or restaurant if need be. Although she had lied that she was looking forward to dinner, he guessed that she thought it was a sham to celebrate their marriage at the moment.

The night before he had been sure that he would be able to convince her that they were still solid together, but Amelia's call had made him wonder if their relationship was as firm as he thought it was. Amelia wanted to hold him, and that was enough to make him cancel a meeting and risk being late for his anniversary dinner. How much of a good husband was he?

New hair, new clothes, a massage and facial did absolute wonders for a woman's self-confidence, thought Yasmin as she entered the *Slice* building and took the lift to the third floor where the magazine's offices were. Or maybe it was having two sexy men and one sexy woman paying her every sexual attention a girl could ask for, not to mention wanting to be her best friend and spy. She was totally invincible in her new guise and just knew that this evening was going to be the last round of the fight. She was getting U back this evening and no mistake.

Instead of the normal quiet hum of a well-run office she came out of the lift to a row at the reception desk.

'Julie, we've set everything up for you coming tonight. We were going to do a sexy photo session – Kip's even been out to buy the sex toys.'

Stevenson, the rather attractive photographer who had set the female pulses in the office racing when he first arrived but had disappointed them by taking up with the even newer journalist Kip a few months later, was obviously angry. His well-modulated voice was almost steely and his face was set in severe lines as he waited for the reply from the person on the other end of the phone. With his hair tied back into a ponytail and his usual black garb, his uncompromising features made him look more like an influential Californian guru than a photographer, albeit one acknowledged to be the best.

'Julie, I thought you were interested in a job here. I've even told U that you'd be around tomorrow, not to mention the fact that you were going to be my model tonight. Don't you think he'll remember your non-appearance should you deign to favour us with your presence at an interview in the future, for example?'

'Mrs U! You are looking extremely attractive. Not that you don't always, but you really are done up like a dog's dinner tonight.'

Yasmin was, as usual, amused by Kip, whose motor mouth often got him in trouble. He just couldn't help being outrageous.

'Cheers, Kip. Hopefully someone's idea of a pretty good meal, though hopefully not a dog.' She turned to Briony, the receptionist. 'Is U ready?'

The worried look on Briony's face gave her a twinge of uneasiness.

'Hi, Yasmin, U's been on the phone twice – he hasn't been able to reach you. Is your mobile turned off?'

Oh, shit. Not wanting to be disturbed at the hairdresser's or the spa, she had turned it off and then completely forgotten about it.

'Don't tell me, he's still in his meeting.'

'No – well, yes, a different one. Something urgent came up and he had to cancel his last meeting ... he's gone ... well, I don't know where he is.'

Yasmin looked at her watch. Quarter past seven. 'So when he was on the phone, what did he say about when he'd be back?'

Briony squirmed. 'Well, he took longer to get to wherever it was he was going than he thought, so he said maybe he'd meet you in the restaurant at eight thirty. Then he phoned just a minute ago and said for you to call him as maybe it would be better to put the reservation back till nine.'

For the first time in ages Yasmin felt a slight tic at the side of her left eye. Where the fuck was he?

'You don't know where he is?'

'No. He just took a cab after the management meeting finished about a quarter of an hour ago.'

'Briony, did you book the cab?'

'Yes.'

'So where was it going?'

The receptionist looked unhappy. 'Holland Park. But – I don't know if I'm supposed to tell you that or not.'

'Christ.'

Yasmin became aware that Kip and Stevenson were looking from her to Briony, half with fascination and half with alarm. She remembered she was invincible, despite the fact that U had obviously gone to see his juvenile mistress just before taking her out for their special dinner. And by the sound of it, he wasn't coming back.

She was invincible. And she wasn't going to get trodden on.

'What's this sexy photo session about?' she asked Stevenson, looking as sophisticated and nonchalant as she knew how.

He shook his head. 'Honestly, this is U's marvellous idea for a new sex edition. We're not exactly in favour, but he's usually right – anyway, I'm doing a few pix on sexy song tracks, and we were going to get my friend Julie to pose for us. Now she's stuck down at the seaside while her policeman lover sorts out a riot or something.'

'Sounds like she would be getting into a riot up here too,' said Yasmin, amused despite the fact that she really wanted to burst into tears of anger. 'What sexy song track was she going to pose for?'

Kip giggled. 'A Frank Zappa tune called "G-Spot Tornado" – heard it?'

Yasmin laughed. 'How on earth was she going to pose for that?'

'Ta-da!' Kip brandished a sex-shop bag. 'It's apparently the best vibrator for getting to your G-spot. Don't tell me you've never tried it.'

'No. Still, if you're not going to be using it, you might as well let me borrow it for the evening.' After all, I've got nothing else to do, she thought bitterly, despite being done up as a dog's dinner.

'It's a shame you're married to the boss,' said Stevenson quietly. 'Otherwise I'd suggest you come back to pose for us. You really do look exceptionally beautiful this evening. Your hair is marvellous – I remember when I first came here you had it like that.'

'That's just its natural style.' Yasmin acknowledged his compliments with a faint smile. He was looking at her intently, his rather cold blue eyes seeming to size her up for his lens. She wondered for the first time if he and Kip really were gay, or just a bi couple who happened to get on well together. She also wondered if there might be a possibility of salvaging the evening after all.

'So what does it matter if I'm the editor's wife?' she asked challengingly. 'If *Slice* is coming out in favour of sex – don't tell me, random sex outside relationships is where it's at – why the hell shouldn't I pose for you?'

Briony's eyes were like saucers as she listened to their exchange.

'Brilliant. Fucking brilliant. Sex doesn't belong inside relationships but outside them, so U reckons, which means that you and him don't have it – is that right? – so why not share your charms with our readers?' said Kip, slightly maliciously.

'Yeah, why not. Looks like he's blown me out this evening anyway. Where's this shoot taking place? Here?'

'God, no,' said Stevenson. 'Back at ours, accompanied by a few drinks and of course the appropriate soundtrack.'

'So? Will I do?'

'Most definitely,' said Stevenson, his thin lips curving into a smile that Yasmin could think almost spiteful. 'As long as you're happy with the situation. I don't know whether U will be.'

'Tough.'

'Yasmin, what shall I tell U if he calls?' asked Briony anxiously.

Linking arms with Kip and Stevenson, Yasmin turned to her with raised eyebrows.

'Well, how about telling him something urgent's come up and I've had to rush off too? And I also might be late for dinner, so it's up to him what he does with the reservation?'

'Oh, shit. He won't be happy.' Briony looked as though she was about to burst into tears, much to Yasmin's exasperation – after all, who was being stood up on her wedding anniversary? Well, stuff Briony and stuff U. She'd always fancied a spot of modelling.

The enormous windows of the warehouse apartment were open to reveal the Thames running below, a slight smell of seaweed wafting into the flat.

'Great flat. Must have cost a fortune,' commented Yasmin.

'Not to us,' Stevenson replied. 'We're not property-owning types. A friend of mine bought it then got an assignment abroad, so he's let me have it for next to nothing for a year. Which is how Kip comes to be living here too – it's cheap.'

Yasmin raised her eyebrows. 'You mean you're not a couple?'

'Very nosy,' chided Kip. 'Well, no. Yes and no. From time to time. We have a somewhat complicated sexual relationship, don't we, Steve?'

The photographer winced. 'In case you get any ideas, Yasmin, nobody calls me Steve. Except mighty mouth.'

'You certainly seem like the perfect couple to me!' laughed Yasmin. 'So tell me about your complicated sexual relationship.'

'Only if you tell us about yours,' challenged Kip. 'Or do I mean your husband's sexual relationship?'

'Why, what has he said?' faltered Yasmin.

'Nothing, nothing. But all of a sudden he intuits a new sexual philosophy taking us by storm, where random fucking replaces marriage, or rather marriage still exists on a friendship level – did he get that by walking round Clapham Common?'

She had to laugh at Kip's dismissive attitude. It was the second time in twenty-four hours, and only the second time ever, she had heard U's fabled skills laughed at.

'OK. He's got a lover. It's her idea, not his.'

'Stupid bastard,' sniffed Kip. 'Well, isn't he, Steve?'

'Absolutely,' agreed the photographer, looking Yasmin up and down again. 'Quite frankly, although I don't go in for full sex personally, I could happily spend a great deal of time with someone who looks like you. And I'm sure Kip agrees.'

'God, look at you,' agreed the other. 'I mean, *look* at you.'

Taking Yasmin by the hand he led her to stand in front of a full-length mirror.

'Look at this marvellous hair,' he continued, touching her abundant curls which cascaded halfway down her back. 'Why on earth you had it braided I can't imagine. Now look at this face. OK, not conventionally beautiful, but look at the arrogance of that nose, the cruelty of those eyes!'

'Excuse me,' muttered Yasmin, unsure as to whether arrogance and cruelty could be considered compliments.

'Trust me,' urged Kip. 'Now your figure. So you haven't got massive knockers, but then again I'm not so keen on those anyway. Small waist, childbearing hips. And what an outfit.'

It was indeed a marvellous outfit. A black lace top tied down the front allowed the black lace push-up bra to show through. Yasmin had taken Euan's advice on underwear and gone for downright sexy. The skirt was black and red with flamenco frills, slit up one side though not high enough to show the lace briefs that matched the bra.

'Drink,' said Stevenson firmly. 'We're rather into absinthe at the moment – that OK with you?'

'Sure. Not that I've tried it, but I quite like the historical significance – Verlaine and Rimbaud, all that decadence.'

'That's us, darling. Verlaine and Rimbaud, eh Steve? God, you're gonna make me lonesome when you go.'

'Christopher, you're becoming just a touch boring, so please shut up for five minutes and get the drinks. Yasmin, I think we should be told about your husband's girlfriend, if only for the sake of our careers. If he's really going ahead with this tacky sex issue, I predict – even without the benefit of U's foresight – *Slice* becoming a bit of a laughing stock in the industry. Which could mean our reputations ditto.'

She was surprised that he looked quite serious.

'I mean it,' he told her earnestly. 'I'm quite happy to take erotic pictures, God knows I've done it before, but in the right context. If *Slice* is heading towards becoming a tits-and-bums lads' magazine, I am most definitely brushing up my CV. So do tell, Yasmin.'

Yasmin was perversely pleased to feel dismay creep over her, dismay at the thought that U was on the wrong track and that his magazine would be compromised. If she was meaner, she would have relished the *schadenfreude*, but she realised that she must actually be quite a nice person to worry about her wrongheaded husband.

Which didn't stop her from a brutally frank summary of his situation.

'The totty in question is nineteen, big tits, shaved pussy, practically bares her all and I could say she drops her knickers for anyone except she doesn't wear any. Her mission is to have frequent and random sex, and then go home and tell U all about it while they wank together.'

Stevenson whistled slowly while Kip burst out laughing, making him drop ice into one of the glasses with such force that the forest-green absinthe splashed over the edge and on to the table.

'He's fucking lost it, hasn't he? You're right, Steve, let's start the schmoozing. I fancy *Black Box* – how about you?'

'That's something I forgot to mention,' added Yasmin. 'Amelia – the totty – is Pandora Fairchild's niece. Who is living with her.' She picked up the drink that Kip had poured and sat down on the sofa almost triumphantly. 'Cheers.'

Even Kip was silenced by her news.

'Well, well,' mused Stevenson. 'Like aunt, like niece, eh?'

Yasmin gave him an astonished look. 'How do you know? Don't tell me you and Pandora – no, *don't* tell me.'

'Surely U told you about the casting couch?' asked Kip, surprised. 'I thought everybody in the business knew.'

'As it happens I used to work at *Black Box* myself a few years ago,' said Yasmin tartly. 'And I can assure you I didn't get the job by screwing Pandora, or anyone else for that matter.'

'That's because she was screwing U at the time,' explained Stevenson. 'Or so legend has it. After she'd lost her reliable supply of German salami, if you'll excuse the racist slur, she started exercising her *droit de seigneur*, or *madame* or whatever, over the staff. A job interview took a whole afternoon.'

'And did you ever apply to *Black Box*?' Yasmin asked slyly. 'Because if you did, you obviously failed the entrance exam.'

'I did and I did,' said Stevenson tranquilly. 'I told you earlier, I don't go in for full sex, so I didn't get the job. That was six months before the job at *Slice* came up, so it was just as well. Or,' he added gloomily, 'I thought it was until U started sabotaging his own magazine.'

'God, we're stupid,' broke in Kip excitedly. 'Look, I've had one of those Eureka moments. He's only sabotaging it because he's under the influence of Pandora's niece, ergo, if you don't mind me mixing Greek and Latin, *Pandora*'s the one who's sabotaging it, because it's overtaken her circulation. She's probably in deep shit with the owners and this is how she's getting her own back.'

'I reckon you're right,' said Yasmin slowly. 'My friend Josh found out that it was Pandora who introduced Amelia and U, and she's very keen on them staying together. It's got to be so she can wreck *Slice*, and I bet she's quite happy if it wrecks U – and the rest of you – in the process.'

There was a long silence, only broken by Kip picking up the bottle and pouring another round.

'Well, we've identified the problem and we've established its cause, but I don't see how we're going to come up with a resolution. So we might as well just get totally off our faces.'

'We're taking pictures,' Stevenson reminded him. 'Seeing as we've got both Yasmin and the super G-spot-finding vibrator here, we might as well get the pix out of the way before we get wrecked.'

'I feel pretty out of it already,' admitted Yasmin. 'Wish I'd tried absinthe before – it seems so decadent. I feel like I'm in one of those Anaïs Nin erotic stories.'

'Do tell,' said Stevenson, a glint in his cold blue eyes. 'I love erotic stories.'

Yasmin registered his interest and her own body responded.

'Well, they're mostly set in Paris. There's one about an artist and his model girlfriend who have the artist's friends round, other artists I think, and they're drinking absinthe, or maybe that's just my imagination, and he starts fondling her right in front of the others, and she can't help getting wet, and the others know.'

'Excellent.' Stevenson's eyes hadn't left hers while she told him the story and, like the girl she'd just described, Yasmin realised she too was getting wet.

'That would make a great picture. Kip, go see if Patrick and Yamani are in and tell them to come over.' He raised an eyebrow eloquently. 'That's if you don't mind, Yasmin? After all, it'll be slightly less revealing than a vibrator attempting to find your G-spot.'

Kip had bounced out on to the balcony and was calling across to the adjacent flat as the photographer moved to sit on the sofa next to Yasmin.

'Patrick and Yamani can sit over there and Kip's next to you,' he explained. 'He'll start by fondling your breasts.'

His actions followed his words and Yasmin's breathing quickened as he undid the ties of her lace top and pushed them aside, almost as though he were framing the picture he was going to take, though not completely dispassionately. Her nipples had already hardened and his hand brushed over them more than once as he adjusted the top.

'Then his hand will move down your body, over your belly and slide just over your sex to your thighs, and then he'll start slowly pushing his hand up and pushing your skirt up.' His hand seemed to be following his instructions on autopilot, while his pale-blue eyes bored into Yasmin's. As his hand made its way up her thigh her legs fell slightly apart almost automatically and she couldn't suppress a moan.

'Et cetera,' Stevenson finished briskly, withdrawing his hand abruptly and standing as Kip came back in from the balcony with two men who presumably had leapt across from their own flat. 'Hi, guys. Hope you don't mind just a few pix, watching Kip feel up Yasmin.'

'Pleasure,' said one, a thin pale thirty-something with black-rimmed glasses. In contrast the other man was bulkily muscular and dark complexioned. Yasmin had registered his name as Arabic and was quite pleased to register his looks as being those of a young Omar Sharif. He merely nodded, and Yasmin wondered if he realised she had some Arabic blood and what he thought about the situation. He probably disapproved of a girl called Yasmin being photographed in a sexually explicit way, and almost certainly pigeonholed her as a completely immoral slut.

Which, she felt, she was. And she was totally enjoying it.

'OK, Kip on the sofa, you guys over here – right, there's drinks all round. You're talking and drinking then Kip starts playing with her tits, undoes the top, then brings the hand down the body, starts up the leg, all the way, into the knickers, brings the hand out wet, few chuckles all round. Yasmin, you just look embarrassed and ashamed, after he starts up your leg close your eyes, then as he gets into your pants turn your head away, sort of hanging it in shame. Just go on as though you're in a porn film.'

'Oh yes, which we're all so experienced in,' said Kip caustically. 'Bit of mood music, if you don't mind.'

Stevenson nodded and went off to comply while Kip hooked his arms round Yasmin and pulled her back against him. 'OK, Yas?' he whispered confidentially. She decided there was no point in telling him to ditch the abbreviation and merely nodded, settling back against him and waiting for lights, camera and action. As the sound of Edith Piaf regretting *rien* filled the room Yasmin suppressed her own misgivings and decided to enjoy it.

Taking Stevenson at his word, the men carried on talking, incongruously about *The Simpsons*, while the photographer took a few shots. Kip handed Yasmin her glass and she took a gulp after he looked into her eyes, his slightly wolfish smile teasing her, and clinked glasses. Then he set down his glass and started to toy with her breasts through the double layer of lace while still talking cartoons. The other two answered him but Yasmin could see their eyes were on her as Kip followed Stevenson's earlier example and slowly and deliberately undid the ties of her top to reveal the minuscule lace bra, through which her nipples were obviously standing to attention. Kip gently twirled one then another in his fingers and the watching men laughed; she guessed he had winked or made some lewd expression. Her eyes closed as his hand moved firmly down her body, lingering over the slight swell of her belly and lingering even longer over the plump mound of her sex, before settling on her bare knee.

'Talk!' ordered Stevenson, still clicking away. Kip had fallen silent after running his hand over her body.

'Sorry, it's almost impossible to carry on a normal conversation,' complained Kip as his hand snaked tantalisingly up Yasmin's leg. 'So who are Wolverhampton Wanderers playing this Saturday, Patrick?'

'Bolton Wanderers,' corrected Patrick absently. 'Great legs. Do we all get a turn?'

'No, she's mine,' said Kip almost smugly as his hand found the warm, wet and welcoming place it had been aiming at. 'She's the boss's wife, so we can't let just anybody have a go at her.'

Yasmin's blush deepened as she turned her head away from the strangers; Stevenson's instructions had been forgotten, rather it was instinct that made her hide her face. Shame mingled with and enhanced her desire as Kip's fingers stroked rhythmically over the wet lace of her knickers. She wondered with some dismay whether she was getting just too used to having sex with an audience; even with Josh her excitement had been augmented by the fact that others were going about their everyday business behind a flimsy office wall.

She imagined the photographs: his white bony hands on the black lace, obviously damp, surrounded by her caramel-coloured skin.

'Course, if you want a bit of action, Pat, then you can tie me up and have a bit of a go after we've got rid of her, if you like,' said Kip in his most camp voice, as in an extremely uncamp way he pushed under Yasmin's briefs and pushed two fingers into her, once, twice, and then withdrew them to hold up the evidence of her wetness.

'Fuck off. If this really was a porn film we'd all be having a go at her now,' said Yamani roughly. 'I've had enough, sorry. I'm off.'

Stevenson carried on shooting as Yamani left the way he came. Yasmin thought they must be finished and was therefore shocked when Kip's other hand roughly pushed her head round towards the camera and brought up the other to smear her lips with her own juices.

'Like to bring you off, Mrs U, but we better save ourselves for the G-spot,' he said nonchalantly, then suddenly let her go and stood, stretching and yawning. 'I've got a stiffie, Stevie. Who's going to look after it?'

'Well, not me,' growled Patrick, also rising. 'Usual remuneration, I suppose?'

'Absolutely. See you down there later,' answered Stevenson, saluting him as he followed his friend out to the balcony. 'OK, both?'

'I guess,' said Yasmin, frankly unsure. 'What are you going to do with these pictures?'

Stevenson's thin lips curved into a smile. 'Not sure yet, but don't worry, nothing too sleazy. I won't sell them to *Readers' Wives* or anything. These aren't for *Slice*, if that's what you're worried about.'

Yasmin wasn't sure whether she was indeed worried or not. It would serve U right to see the pictures, and it might jolt him into realising that, although he might think Amelia a supreme turn-on, other men might prefer her charms.

'Now, let's get ready for the G-spot,' said Stevenson briskly, lighting a spill from a match and holding it to a series of large white church candles that adorned the room. 'The bed, I think, for this.' After lighting the candles he tossed the pillows from the king-sized bed and covered it in a black satin sheet.

'Much more appropriate. Now, the music.' He removed Edith Piaf from the stereo and rummaged for another CD. 'Kip, get the vibrator. Now, you point this against the front wall of your vagina, apparently, and you'll get a G-spot orgasm, or so the girl in the sex shop reckons.'

'Christ,' said Yasmin faintly, sitting down on the black satin and inspecting the pink apparition Kip was unwrapping. 'Can't we go back to Kip's hand?'

'Definitely not. Oh, except, take her kit off, Kip. Leave the bra. You see the thing about Kip is that he's basically just like a child – well, that's obvious. What I mean is that he only really likes playing when he gets a reward,' continued the photographer as Kip unzipped and removed her skirt and then pulled off her knickers in an almost businesslike fashion. 'He wants pain, Yasmin. Now, if you don't mind inflicting a few bites and bruises, he just might find your G-spot for himself. What do you think?'

It wasn't an easy call. Yasmin tried to weigh up the pros and cons of taking a swing at Kip while his cock probed her G-spot, compared with probing herself with the vibrator.

'OK, give me the toy,' she said, settling herself in the centre of the bed with her legs apart and turning the vibrator on. Music started again – a giddy electronic jangle. This was obviously the 'G-Spot Tornado'.

'Slowly,' urged Stevenson, moving towards her, his camera zooming in on her sex. 'Let me see it going in – oh, nice. Don't think this'll get past the censors, though. What's it feel like?'

'Just a vibrator,' said Yasmin, disappointed.

'OK, well get on your hands and knees, look back at me over your shoulder with it in your hand – lovely. Now, Kip, you take the thing and aim it at her from behind.' He moved round to Yasmin's face, which she realised had suddenly taken on a look of astonishment. 'Oh, it's working, is it?'

She nodded wordlessly. She'd always liked being fucked from behind but didn't know why it felt different. So this was the famous G-spot. It was even better with the vibrator that also caressed her clit. She found herself pushing back on the toy just as she would push back on a man fucking her from the rear.

'Give it a bit more, Kip, but I don't want her to come. Do you think you might be close?'

'Not yet,' breathed Yasmin at the camera. Nothing seemed real; the explosive music, the fact that this photographer she thought of as being mainly interested in food and fashion seemed an expert at soft-core porn, and the fact that she was being shafted with a battery-operated toy by a man she had assumed was gay, who was now hoping she would hurt him.

'Good. Kip, get undressed and rubbered up. Lie down and lift her up – can you get your dick inside her with that thing?'

Kip's slight frame belied his obvious strength, as he lifted Yasmin from her all-fours position to sit her up on her knees with her back to him, poised above his prick with the vibrator still buzzing inside and outside her. She had grabbed the vibrator herself as he had put his hands on her waist to move her, and now waited unmoving as he carefully nudged his prick between her open sex and the plastic buzzing phallus.

'Maybe,' he breathed. 'Hold on to me, Yas. Hard.'

She knew what he meant. The vibrator was now wedged inside her by Kip's cock so she let go and, reaching her arms out behind her, grabbed either side of his ribs and dug her nails in hard.

'Yeah, yeah, yeah,' said Kip, sliding her further down on to his cock. She felt distended, as though two enormous pricks were inside her. The vibrator was still thrumming more and more insistently on the soft flesh of the front of her vagina, while almost opposite on the outside it was massaging her clit equally rhythmically. And the two enormous pricks were pushing in and out of her more firmly now.

'Open your eyes, Yasmin,' interrupted Stevenson.

She realised she had forgotten about him and guiltily obeyed, at the same time moving her hands from Kip's sides down to his arse to grab the flesh there. His buttocks were small and muscular and once again she used her newly manicured nails to gouge his soft skin.

'Nice, Mrs U,' he whispered. 'Steve, it's pretty good fucking alongside this thing. Think you could get up my arse next to it?'

'If you like,' replied the photographer uninterestedly. 'Put your hands on her tits, Kip.'

There was no other erogenous zone left to be stimulated, Yasmin thought, as Kip's bony hands closed firmly over her breasts and rolled her nipples between his fingers and thumbs; though with so much going on in and around her sex the sensation on her nipples was of negligible importance. What did flash through her mind, though, was the feeling of Cody's mouth fastening on hers as she was being fucked by Euan; a kiss from a woman would make it only too perfect.

'What?' asked Stevenson sharply. 'What are you thinking about, Yasmin?'

'How do you –'

'Sudden smile on your face. What?'

'I was – I was just remembering a woman kissing me last time I was being fucked and how good it was.'

'Oh, yeah,' breathed Kip. 'Tell my arse, Yas.'

She interpreted it as an instruction to scrape even harder over his buttocks, this time going what she thought was dangerously close to his arsehole. Kip, however, obviously thought she wasn't close enough.

'Go on,' he urged, 'nail me, bitch. I'll tell you when to stop.'

'What was she like?' asked Stevenson, bringing her mind back to Cody.

'Strong, hard, sexy,' breathed Yasmin, as her index finger pushed up inside Kip's arsehole. She was sure he was more used to men moving inside him there rather than half an inch of pearlised Flamenco Red, but she was equally sure that he wanted whatever she could give him, the more painful the better.

'She held a knife against my mound and pressed down hard while I was being fucked.'

Yasmin stared straight at Stevenson, or rather straight at the camera, as she told him.

'Lovely,' he said, shooting away. 'Didn't realise you went both ways too. Shame Julie didn't turn up, though then you wouldn't be here – love to have you together.'

'You want to pass me a knife?' asked Kip of Stevenson, moving his hands from Yasmin's breasts to press hard just in the place Cody had pushed with the knife. The effect was instantaneous. Yasmin felt that the flesh, the tiny point of sensation between his hands and the vibrator, was growing and bursting into a huge, engulfing climax.

'Fuck no, G-spot moment, I think,' observed Stevenson with a small smile. 'Hands will do, Kip, she's having the time of her life. Yasmin, just dig your nails in harder and let the poor boy come with you.'

Her hands did as he said of their own volition; she was barely conscious of obeying him. She was barely conscious of anything except the fact that she knew for certain that the biggest, most explosive, most incredible orgasm of her life was just about to wipe her out like a hundred megaton bomb. Vaguely she realised that her expression, which she could do nothing about regardless of the fact that she was being photographed, was one of total bewilderment at the sensation that had taken her over, as Kip's hands pressed even more firmly against her, almost as if they were connected to the vibrator inside her, while also closing over the part of it that was massaging her clit. The incredible full-ness she felt inside her played no small part in it but she wasn't analysing it, she just gave way to the amazing, almost obscene wave of pleasure that washed over her, not just in an instant but for what seemed like minutes.

She was aware that Stevenson had left his camera and realised he was standing next to the bed behind Kip, taking his cock out and yanking the black quiff back viciously.

'Choke on this, Chris,' he said almost contemptu-ously as he pushed his cock into Kip's mouth. Yasmin guessed that Kip needed more to come, more pain, more humiliation, and while still luxuriating in her still-pulsating pussy she pushed yet another sharp-pointed finger inside his arse. Between them they were rewarded by Kip's groans, coming deep from his chest as Stevenson's cock filled his mouth and throat, and his final manic thrusts as he came inside her.

'Fuck, fuck, fuck. Brilliant, Mrs U.'

Kip had pulled out of her and pushed her off him and collapsed on to the bed. Yasmin felt rather ridicu-lous as the vibrator still buzzed inside her, and removed it and lay down next to him.

'I was "bitch" a moment ago,' she reminded him.

'Shit, calling the boss's wife a bitch is probably not the best career move I've ever made,' said Kip.

'It probably doesn't beat double fucking her while she sticks her fingers up your arse,' said Stevenson, who had zipped up again and was sitting on the edge of the bed, an amused look on his face.

'You didn't come?' asked Yasmin, surprised.

'God, no. I prefer not to,' he replied, as though it was the most normal thing in the world.

'It seems to me that U's new take on sex is slightly

less radical than the way you two go about it,' she observed archly.

'True,' admitted Stevenson gravely. 'But we know that we are – I almost said unique, which is obvious rubbish. Neither of us is like the common herd, Yasmin, nor would we want or expect the common herd to be like us. U's mistake is to try to preach, or rather predict, a massive shift in the sex life of the majority. He's heading for total disaster.'

'So, bitch, if we can do anything at all to help you fight this little tart to get him back with you and more importantly back to normal, let us know,' added Kip, giving Yasmin a kiss on the cheek. 'I like calling you bitch. Is that OK?'

'I like it, too,' she said, laughing. 'Frankly, anything's better than Yas.'

'I rather wish you would call *me* bitch rather than Steve,' said the photographer languidly.

'No, you can fuck off,' said Kip tartly. 'I heard you call me Chris. That is definitely out of bounds.'

'Just because it's your real name?' jeered Stevenson. 'It just slipped out along with my dick. God, Yasmin, sorry. We're getting into our nasty little queenly quarrels which can wait till you've gone.'

Oh, yes – when was she going? Yasmin suddenly remembered her – cancelled, postponed or still current? dinner date. She checked the time: quarter to ten.

'So, should I try to phone U to see if he's waiting for me at The Ivy?' she asked, almost rhetorically. 'Or should I just assume he's at home and go back there and see if we can make it up?'

'I think you should stay here and eat with us,' said Kip. 'Bitch here –' he turned to Stevenson, laughing '– got in food for his pal Julie, so there's enough for three. Not to mention special wine.'

Stevenson raised his eyes to heaven. 'Sorry, Yasmin, Kip is the very antithesis of a wine snob. It is actually rather a nice Riesling from New Zealand, though there's plenty of red if you prefer. Or more absinthe, of course.'

'What's for dinner?' asked Yasmin practically.

'Scrambled eggs with smoked salmon and asparagus and Poilâne bread, followed by *tarte tatin*.'

'Not the famous ten-pound loaf?' Yasmin's mind had fixed on the bread.

'The same.'

'Great, I'll stay.'

Kip yawned. 'That's brilliant. And when we've had loads to eat and drink, we can all go to sleep like friends in this lovely big bed. Friends who've just had a pretty good sex scene, that is. Which is a million times better than U's new philosophy.'

Too right, thought Yasmin. Euan, Josh and now Kip and Stevenson – her new, and frankly accidental, sex life had brought her new friends. It was indeed a million times better than U's, or rather Amelia's, philosophy.

She just wished for an almost tearful moment that she was sharing it with U, but pushed the thought aside. At least she had more allies in her fight for him, and at least she was going to have a nice dinner and bed down with two new mates. Things weren't so bad after all.

6

Innocence is bliss. Switching off her mobile had more than one effect on Yasmin's day. U wasn't the only one trying to get hold of her that afternoon. Back in the office Josh had tried to get her several times. First, when Milo had gone to see him for a heart to heart, as he called it, and, second, when Sandy had let him have the storyline for the next three episodes.

Josh couldn't work out what was going on. Milo definitely had it in for Yasmin and talked about paying her off. But why, when the project was still in the early stages? Josh couldn't believe that Milo hadn't had a hand in selecting the writers for the drama, so why suddenly had he taken against Yasmin?

Even more creepy was the fact that Milo hinted that he knew Yasmin's personal life wasn't going well. How on earth did he know that, Josh wondered? He was totally certain that Yasmin wouldn't have told him, and equally convinced that he was the only one at On the Edge productions who knew about U's little affair. It was most curious.

But even more curious was the storyline for the next episodes. It was certainly odd that Yasmin had ended up screwing both him and Euan after finding out about U, just as Lisanne had screwed first one then another of her friends and colleagues once she found out that her husband was having an affair. Yasmin would obviously have denied that she was following the plot of the soap in her own life, but it could have been argued that she was subconsciously copying the character. But how weird was it that Lisanne was to find out in the next episode that the 'mistress' was in fact not allowing her husband to have full sex either? Could that be just coincidence?

Josh knew that Yasmin and U were going off to their anniversary dinner that evening. What Yasmin didn't know was that Lisanne and Johnny were to have a reconciliatory meal in the next episode, but that Johnny cancelled to see his girlie, leaving Lisanne to visit her gay friends – only to discover that one of them wasn't so gay after all.

In his heart of hearts Josh knew that it was ridiculous to worry about Yasmin. Just because the reconciliation dinner was cancelled in 49, it didn't mean that U was going to cancel the anniversary celebration. And it would be preposterous to assume that Yasmin would take consolation with a gay friend.

Wouldn't it?

He tried again but again got the voicemail. She had obviously switched off because she was in the restaurant at that moment making it up with U. After all, Yasmin might have been influenced by the fictional Lisanne's behaviour, but she certainly couldn't be influenced by something she knew nothing about. It would be too ridiculous, almost like U latching on to ideas floating around in the ether. Unless U's work wasn't so ridiculous after all.

He couldn't help worrying, so he turned his mind to more practical matters. Whatever was happening, he could maybe help a little. He found the card in his pocket and connected with Amelia – only to find his fears seemed to have some foundation.

* * *

'I want to see you tonight. Meet me in Zanzibar at seven. I want you to wear black, including stockings and suspender belt. I'm presuming your lack of other underwear the other day was standard?'

Amelia's heart skipped a beat. Josh!

'Yes,' she said faintly in answer to his last question, while not knowing what to say to the rest of his – not invitation, but rather command.

'Yes to everything?'

'No,' she countered hastily. 'Yes to the lack of underwear. I don't have any, and that includes stockings and suspenders.'

'You'll have to borrow them from Pandora. I know she wears them.'

'Why did you do that?' she burst out. 'Why did you leave me and then have her on the sofa?'

'It's not your place to ask questions,' he said with a slight laugh. 'You're answering mine, and there's only one left. Do you know Zanzibar?'

'Yes,' she admitted reluctantly. 'But eight ... I've got someone coming round in a minute ... well, I hope so. He's late. I don't know how long he'll be staying.'

'Not a random screw,' he said in a weary tone. 'How boring. I was hoping you might have managed to avoid it for a day.'

'No, it's not, actually,' she retorted. 'And if you really want to know, I've actually avoided it for a couple of days.'

More than that, she thought silently, realising that the day she had seen Josh hadn't involved a screw at all.

'Excellent! So you'll be looking forward to seeing me. We'll make it eight thirty, if it's more convenient. See you then.'

Amelia was left holding the phone in astonishment. He'd rung off, assuming her complicity just because he'd changed the time by half an hour. His arrogance was astounding.

Not, she realised, as astounding as the way her body had reacted to the sound of his voice and to the very imperiousness of his orders. Which was worrying on several counts, not least because U was on the way, having rescheduled his afternoon thanks to her.

She picked up her violin again but put it down abruptly. Goddamn his insolence. She just wouldn't go. He could wait all night as long as she cared.

But then, what if she didn't see him again?

Stuff it, if he hadn't come on the scene and awakened all sorts of questions in her, life would be much less complicated. She would still be happy about random acts of sexual kindness, still happy to keep U in his previous place, and not at all wondering how long Josh planned to keep her waiting in a bar surrounded by strangers, knowing she would be wearing nothing but stockings and suspenders, a skirt and a see-through blouse.

At the last thought she shivered. That's just what he'd said, keeping her waiting. God, she was right first time. Let him wait. Maybe she could persuade U to stay longer than she'd hoped – and maybe it was time their relationship entered a new phase.

Just in case that last scenario wasn't going to happen, she seized the chance to pop into Pandora's room and borrow stockings and suspender belt. She felt guilty as she hid them in her wardrobe, while also making sure she had a black skirt and top ready. She almost certainly wasn't going to use them – but it did no harm to be prepared.

* * *

'Amelia, little one. Are you feeling any better?'

The straight lines of U's tanned face were etched with concern. As Amelia registered his anxiety about her she was swamped with guilt at the fact that she'd spent the last ten minutes fantasising about Josh. There was only one way to cope with such conflicting emotions: she burst into tears.

Immediately U's arms were around her. 'Oh, Amelia. Poor thing, poor thing. Don't worry any more. It'll be OK.'

Her misery was compounded by the fact that it was the first time they had embraced, and here he was cuddling her for comfort like a little girl rather than a lover holding her. When she told him on the phone that she wanted him to hold her, she had almost heard his sharp intake of breath, and she too had longed to feel his arms around her – and now it was actually happening, it just wasn't working on the romantic level. She cried even harder. Apart from her genuine upset and confusion, it was easier than talking.

Still, she couldn't go on for ever. Eventually her sobs subsided and U led her to sit down on the bed.

'Now, what is it? What's making you so unhappy?'

She tossed a mental coin. The truth, the whole truth, and nothing but the truth? Or a glib tissue of lies?

Wasn't it all about honesty?

Amelia dried her eyes and told him everything. It took a long time, because there were feelings she found it hard to put into words. U watched her, his piercing blue eyes on her with grave concern, making her feel like bursting into tears again for any pain she might be causing him. Though she had to admit that the cold fire from those eyes still turned her on. She hadn't stopped wanting him, just because she wanted Josh as well.

'So, I still want you,' she concluded, her voice strained and quiet. 'I still want you very much, though I'm totally confused as to whether I want to carry on as before or whether I want you to be my lover properly. Maybe ... maybe we should move on a stage ... and maybe instead of random acts of sex I could have this other guy as well. I know my relationship with him would never be anything but sexual, whereas I know my relationship with you is on a deeper level.'

She closed her eyes as U reached out and stroked her hair. She so wanted him to crush her in his arms and make love to her properly and exorcise the appeal of Josh. She so wanted that to happen that she almost felt she was propelling towards doing it by her own will – after all, wasn't that what he was so good at, instinctively understanding what people felt?

But it wasn't working with her. As much as she willed him to take her with overwhelming passion, he just stroked her hair as though she were a little girl. It reminded her of her first boyfriend, who had kissed her long and hard, leaving her breathlessly awaiting his next move – only to realise that he wasn't going to make one.

'Oh, my dear. I don't know what to say to you.' U's tone was grave. 'I believed so much in your philosophy. It just seemed as though it was the right thing, the next big thing, that I'm having a hard time taking in what you're saying now.'

He stood up and paced the room. 'You say that Pandora suggested you drop the philosophy and become my lover properly?'

Amelia nodded mutely.

'Don't you think, sweet one, that you're overly influenced by her? After all, she is your aunt, she is also *in loco parentis* and, let's not be coy about it, she is my ex lover. All these things must be in the forefront of your mind.'

He didn't give her a chance to reply before continuing.

'I think she's wrong. I don't think you really want to abandon your philosophy. She's just suggesting this because – why do you think she's suggesting this?'

'Because she thinks you'll get fed up with it,' said Amelia. 'That's what I'm trying to say. She's not trying to keep us apart, but bring us closer together.'

'That's not the way to go about it,' said U crisply. 'I believe wholeheartedly in your philosophy, little one. I'm even basing the whole of the next issue of *Slice* upon it, which goes to show how much I believe in you – in it. So why can't we stay as we were?'

'I guess because ... because Josh made me feel so ... so cheap,' said Amelia in a small voice. 'Like an animal just screwing because it was on heat. And I guess because I want to see him again.'

U exhaled wearily. 'Do you want us to finish because of him?'

'God, no!' she cried. 'I told you, I'm just so confused. If only he hadn't screwed Pandora – I'm afraid that I only want him because she had him. Which makes me afraid that I only want you because she had you.

'She's always been such a role model to me,' she continued. 'I was just afraid that I was wanting everything she had.'

'But if you don't actually have sex with me, you're not following in her footsteps,' said U, taking her hand. 'Let's leave things as they are, Amelia. You can see this other guy, I don't mind – well, what right do I have to mind? And we'll go on as we were.'

Amelia noticed him looking at his watch.

'What time is it?'

'Seven ten.'

She was aware that they both had appointments, and aware that, as he had refused her suggestion to commit to a sexual relationship, she was going to make her appointment after all.

'U, if you have to go, I understand.'

His eyes narrowed slightly. 'You mean you have to go, Amelia. I appreciate your earlier honesty, but I think we should be frank about this. You know that I postponed meeting Yasmin because of you?'

'U, I so do not remember you telling me about your dinner with Yasmin, I swear! I thought you were just rearranging a business meeting. If you'd told me when I called that you had dinner planned with her, I would have said not to worry.'

She felt self righteously sure that that was the case. Yet, at the back of her mind, something niggled. Had he told her about the anniversary dinner? And if so, had she really forgotten, or just blocked it from her mind, not wanting the thought of U and Yasmin sitting down to dinner as a happy celebratory couple?

'Sure.' U was trying someone on the phone – she presumed it was Yasmin, and from his snort presumed he hadn't got through.

'Look, if you have to go . . .' She was feeling something like remorse.

'It's OK. Yasmin's phone's still off, but I left a message at the office when I got here to say I might be late.'

Amelia was aware of her own timetable. The cab would take up to half an hour, and she would have to book one: when she was looking for random sex, waiting on the street in a see-through blouse was a plus, but as she was on the way to meet Josh it would only be an embarrassment. And she had to get ready. Her eyes most definitely needed redoing after her sobbing session, and of course she had to get into the black. However, she could hardly chase U out of the house.

She was saved, not by the bell, but by the door slamming. Obviously Pandora home from the office. U raised his eyebrows at her.

'You've got a date, so get yourself ready, little one. I want to have a serious talk with Pandora, if you don't mind.'

In her muddled state of mind she wasn't sure whether she cared or not. Perhaps she should be involved in the serious talk?

'I don't know – do you want me to be there?'

He shook his head. 'I want to talk about you, not to you.' There was a glimmer of humour in his voice. 'Go on, I know you want to get ready. I'll just leave another message for Yasmin and have a cosy heart to heart with your auntie.'

Amelia giggled at the word as U phoned the office with a message for his wife, though she knew her giggle was more nervous than anything else. He kissed her on the forehead and made for the door; she caught up with him and put her arms around him, hugging him tightly.

'It's a mess, isn't it, U?' she said sadly. 'I hope it all works out in the end.'

'Me too,' he said softly. 'Don't worry. Everything's going to be all right. You have a nice evening, and I'll have a drink with Pandora before I go to meet Yasmin.'

She felt lost and lonely again, a little girl playing in the grown-ups' world, a world where people had histories and relationships that went back years before, before she had intruded upon them and upset them. She almost wished she'd stayed in New York.

Then again, U's eyes ... but he was gone.

Even if she was a little girl, she was a little girl with

an appointment to keep with a man who might become a lover, or who might just be toying with her for his own amusement. Just the thought of that was enough to excite her. To meet him in a tiny cocktail bar dressed as he'd commanded, only to have him not deign to put even a finger on her – that was pretty cool.

She ordered a cab and had a quick shower before doing her make-up carefully and dressing exactly as he'd ordered, slipping out quietly so that U and Pandora, deep in conversation at the dining table, didn't see how she was dressed. It was all crazy, but that was how she liked it.

'Why are you trying to overturn her sexual philosophy? What business is it of yours?'

Pandora raised her immaculately plucked eyebrows at U's accusation and poured him a glass of Chablis. U picked up the bottle and scanned the label before drinking. He only ever drank the best. It passed muster.

'U, darling, I'm not trying to overturn anything. Honestly! I know how much she means to you, and you mean to her. I just suggested to her that it would be a terrible shame for you to lose interest just because of her absurd little ideas.'

'Pandora, I wonder how we worked so well together. We are just not on the same wavelength, at all,' said U moodily. 'I really buy into this idea of sexuality. In fact, I'm going to base my next issue on it. I wanted Amelia to give us an interview, under an alias, of course, and now it seems as though you're trying to sabotage the whole thing.'

He gave her one of his piercing looks. 'Did you know that? Pandora, do you have a mole in my office?'

She laughed uproariously. 'Oh, U, that's priceless.

What do you think this is, Watergate? *Slicegate?* Don't be ridiculous. Of course I don't have a mole in your office, you silly boy. And if you want my completely honest opinion, the only person sabotaging your magazine is you with this sex business.'

'I believe it's a fine philosophy,' said U doggedly.

'Well, think what you like. I think it's a teenage fad that she's already growing out of. Don't tell me your staff were enthusiastic about a sex issue, because I won't believe you.'

U was silent. He wasn't going to admit that Pandora was right.

'Look, U, let's not argue about this. I think it's complete rubbish, but it's your magazine and your relationship, even though she is my niece. But frankly, darling, if you're not screwing her, and I bet you're not screwing Yasmin at the moment, not now she knows you've got Amelia, then what the hell are you doing? Committing the odd random act yourself?'

U managed a grudging smile. 'That's where it does all fall down somewhat,' he admitted. 'I can see how easy it is for someone like Amelia to find men falling over each other to have sex with her, random or otherwise. But when you're a man in your forties – well, you know.'

'Of course,' sympathised Pandora. 'You know where I am, of course.'

'Thanks,' he said briefly. 'However, I have a date with Yasmin. Do you mind if I phone the office with a message? Her phone's not working.'

'Be my guest.'

Pandora looked disappointed at the thought that he was shortly going to leave her, but it turned out to be only a thought. Briony confirmed that Yasmin had arrived, had been given his messages and had gone off after giving him the virtual finger. He guessed she could have told him more about where she had gone, but he didn't pursue it. After all, what was he going to do? Chase after her and drag her to their dismal attempt at celebration?

'Well, this evening's a total disaster,' he said as he threw the phone on the table. 'Yasmin's blown me out. Not that I blame her, as I've put dinner back twice.'

'Well, that's no big deal, is it?' asked Pandora. 'It's a shame I've got an appointment, otherwise I'd let you take me out to dinner.'

'A small big deal, if you like. It's our wedding anniversary.'

'Oh dear. While I'm glad you postponed your anniversary dinner to rush over to see Amelia, I do think that in the circumstances it's an awful pity that you turned down her offer of sex and let her go off to see a friend. You seem to have come out of this rather badly, U.'

'Don't I. Especially as the guy she's gone out with is what she's proposing to replace random sex with.'

Pandora eyed him curiously. 'Which guy?'

'The one you had on the sofa after he turned her down.'

'Oh, for Christ's sake!'

U was surprised to hear Pandora react with such vehemence.

'Have I said something wrong? You didn't know she was going to see him again?'

'I told him to leave us alone,' said Pandora furiously. 'Little shit. I told him he could see me but not her.'

U smiled wryly. 'Obviously he preferred the younger model. Sorry, Pan. This is all too ridiculous.'

'Christ, I don't give a shit about him preferring her. That's just too bloody obvious for words. I just didn't want him to come between you and Amelia, that's all.'

U felt he was out of his depth. What did it have to do with her?

'Why not? Why exactly are you so keen on me and Amelia getting it together?'

He could have sworn that a shifty look came into Pandora's eyes, but maybe it was just that her expressions were limited thanks to the Botox.

She shrugged. 'I don't care either way,' she answered tonelessly, leading U to think that she most definitely did care one way or another. 'I'm just fond of both of you. You make a good couple.'

'You told me I'm only two years younger than her father,' reminded U.

'Yes, well, a lot of good he ever did for her, or anybody else,' said Pandora waspishly. 'God knows he had a good enough start in life, but then managed to go through his inheritance like water. My poor little sister – well, never mind that.' She shook herself as though to bring herself back to matters in hand. 'Reservation where?'

'The Ivy.'

'God, what a shame I have a meeting. I'd have happily substituted for Yasmin.'

U looked down into his glass of wine.

'No, you wouldn't. It wouldn't be right – I don't know why. I'd better go, Pan. I think I should be at home waiting when Yasmin gets back.'

Pandora's laugh could have shattered one of the crystal glasses. 'Now that is ridiculous. You've postponed your anniversary dinner twice, she's uncontactable and you say she didn't come home the other night – what's the point of going home? For God's sake, U, as a woman I can tell you that she'll pay you back by not coming home. Even if it means sleeping on a friend's sofa.'

She poured the last of the Chablis into the glasses. 'Now, going back to Amelia's philosophy, let me tell you something about sexual philosophy which I really think you should take on board. You say that as a man in his forties you don't seem to have much chance of getting much of this random action. Let me tell you about a little scene I was involved in once.'

She lit a cigarette, much to U's disgust. He couldn't stand the smell, and she knew it only too well, but he decided it was pointless to say anything.

'Quite a long time ago, before I knew you, I was involved with a man who was always looking for the next sexual thrill. There wasn't much we didn't go into together, but it was never enough. Something darker, more transgressive always beckoned to him. He always tried to get me to go to swinging clubs but one experience was enough – talk about random sex, it was just a big orgy and I didn't want to be just an orifice for complete strangers, some of whom were truly undesirable.

'I don't know how, but he met up with a group of guys who felt the same way. We were all in our early thirties and rather glamorous and successful and like me the others also considered themselves too good, too exclusive, for a full-on orgy. Straightforward swapping was also ruled out as being more than a touch suburban.

'One of the guys came up with a better idea. They all had a fantasy which they wrote down and then decided how it could most practically be enacted. They then assigned roles to the women, wrote them on cards and shuffled them for each of us to pick out. We called it a sex lottery – amusing to think that these days the majority of the population "does the lottery" every week, isn't it?

'The women drew the cards and read them silently – that was part of the deal. We showed them to our partners, who took us separately to the bedrooms in the host's house to prepare us.

'The first time my card said I was to be dressed in accordance with the desires of my partner but in a way to leave my sex accessible to anyone who wanted to penetrate it in any way. I was then to accept any sexual overture or demand that anyone should make upon me. He took me upstairs and dressed me in a black velvet basque with stockings and suspenders and a thick black velvet choker. He told me he was going to blindfold me so that I wouldn't be able to tell who was taking me at any time, but that he would only do so once I had seen what else was happening in the room.

'We went downstairs again and I found out what the men wanted. One of the women was dressed in schoolgirl clothes and bent over a table. She was there to be spanked, and if anyone wanted to – someone did, or the words wouldn't have appeared on the card – buggered. By the time we got there music was playing and another was starting a slow strip, which would continue on to what we would now call a lap dance. Two of the others were beginning to pet each other; they had to have sex with each other continuously unless one of the men decided he wanted to fuck one or the other. There were two others, and their role was the same as mine, except they were dressed differently, one in sluttish scarlet and black satin and fake fur and the other in nothing but a short, white cotton vest.

'I was blindfolded and sat on a sofa – there were two, with the other two girls on the other. Nothing much happened to me at first; I heard the music, imagined the striptease and the two women with each other. The guys were fairly subdued, but gradually they got more confident. They were talking about the stripper – who was a successful psychoanalyst, by the way – and the two women screwing, and then there were a few slaps on the other one's arse.

'I was suddenly pulled off the sofa and on to the floor on my knees and fucked, slowly and silently. I realised the other men were watching and I was the first one. Gradually they lost their inhibitions and it went on from there.

'There were seven couples involved and over the course of the evening I'm sure I was fucked by all seven men. Also by a vibrator, many times. One of the men was an American, a rival magazine editor but much more successful than I. He decided he'd keep me coming for as long as possible. I almost lost the desire for orgasm after that.'

U was silent. 'But, was it a bad experience? You were willing – why are you telling me?'

Pandora laughed softly. 'No, it wasn't a bad experience. It seems gauche and juvenile now, but then it was exciting and almost daring. Don't forget we're talking about the early seventies here. Here's the reason I'm telling you. We did this a couple more times, different roles and fantasies every time, and each time I was a willing participant. Then the women decided they should have a turn at assigning roles to the men.'

She knocked back the last of the wine. 'You can guess what happened. The men who were assigned to have sex with each other were outraged and refused point blank. One was supposed to be a slave, running around after the women with drinks and cigarettes, and he just got bored after the first ten minutes. Those who were supposed to be permanent fuck machines couldn't cope, of course. They needed too long to recover between orgasm and hard-on.

'And that,' she concluded, leaning towards him, 'is the problem with any sexual philosophy like Amelia's. First, men are happy to screw any woman who points her fanny at them, but they only want to do what they want to do, which means you will never have equality in this silly philosophy. Second, most women are like me – choosy about who they have sex with. Which is why your average older man will not find it easy to get an attractive woman to have random sex with him. And third, men are completely useless at the long haul.'

She stubbed out her cigarette. 'And if you want the punchline, none of those relationships, which were all based on sex, lasted. The only relationships I've ever known to stand the test of time are those where the couples are lovers and friends. Not one or the other. Which I think, my dear, puts the kibosh on Amelia's rather sweet but senseless ideas.'

U was smiling broadly. 'I wouldn't have minded being your partner then,' he said mischievously. 'Good tale, Pan. Every man's fantasy, I guess. All his equally attractive and successful friends' wives or girlfriends available without censure.'

'Did it turn you on?' she challenged, her eyes sparkling. 'It did, didn't it?'

U couldn't deny it. 'Of course. But –'

Pandora had stood up with her hands at the back of her neck. 'Let me show you something.'

U watched as she unzipped her black dress, pulled it to her waist, wriggled out of the sleeves and let it drop to the floor. Underneath she was wearing a black velvet basque with stockings and suspenders. Nothing else, apart from the black choker around her neck.

'Of course, this wasn't the outfit I was dressed in that night, though it was similar,' she told him, her voice husky. 'I couldn't resist bringing it into the story. What do you think, U? Can you resist me?'

His voice came out just as gutturally as hers. He knew that he was going to do the wrong thing before he even answered her, and he knew that he was helping to sabotage his marriage even more than he had already. But something in him just stood back and watched as he helped himself further along the road to self-destruction.

'No. I can't, even though I know this is stupid. But Yasmin's fucking someone else somewhere and Amelia's out with the other guy and, for heaven's sake, Pan, your story turned me on and with you standing there dressed like that it seems too much like old times –'

He didn't finish his sentence as he buried his head in her breasts and breathed in the sweet, familiar Diorissimo of her while unjustifiable self-pity washed over him. Amelia hadn't let him have sex with her until it was too late, and Yasmin had also cold-shouldered him. As Pandora helped him out of his clothes, he closed his eyes and blotted recent events out of his mind and regressed to memories the scent evoked and, for a few brief, sweet moments, to the uncomplicated life he had before.

'You're late.'
'Only five minutes.'
Josh looked her up and down, then stood and twirled her round in front of him. She seemed to have obeyed his instructions, but he decided to be absolutely sure.

He sat down again then lifted her skirt up at the front and looked appraisingly at the stocking tops and suspenders, the latter framing her naked pubis, which presented itself to him almost at eye level. She moaned softly, and though the lighting was subdued he saw a blush rise in her cheeks at his steady regard. He was seated against the wall and there was nobody at the tables either side, though he was aware that it could be obvious to anyone watching what he was doing, even though they couldn't see what he could see. He was equally aware that Amelia had registered that fact also.

'Nice,' he conceded. 'Do sit down.'

As she pulled out a chair and sat opposite him he reached a hand out to tweak first one then the other nipple.

'Very obedient,' he said mockingly. 'Although I was a bit disappointed that you wouldn't drop everything to get here earlier.'

'I couldn't,' she protested. 'I'd just asked someone to come round to see me – I could hardly tear out of the house straight away, especially dressed like this.'

'Hmm. From that I presume it was either your aunt or your lover. Drink?'

'Just white wine, please.'

Josh beckoned a waitress over. He was already three-quarters of the way through his Budvar and ordered another along with Amelia's wine.

'So? Who was it you had to see before me?'

'U. I mean, my lover.'

He had guessed as much, but couldn't help a shiver going down his spine. Johnny had cancelled dinner with Lisanne because his girlfriend had called on him – life was imitating art, and it wasn't funny.

'This is the man you call a lover but don't make love with.'

'I told you all that,' she said sulkily. 'Now because I'm here he's having a drink with Pandora.'

Josh laughed. 'Oh, great. So you're afraid that he'll end up screwing Pandora like I did.'

'No, I'm not!' she said fiercely. 'And since you mention that – why did you do it?'

'Well, I'm too well bred to use the expression "gagging for it", at least when describing a member of your own family, but if I weren't I'd say she was,' he said casually. 'And you had excited me, as you know. Seeing as you believed in random sexual acts, I thought I'd see what I thought about it.'

'And what did you think?' Her voice was little more than a whisper.

He leaned towards her. 'She's rather old, isn't she?' he said conspiratorially.

Amelia laughed. 'Sixty-two. But don't tell her I told you.'

Josh winced slightly. Although he had had no reason not to believe Yasmin, he had still rather hoped she had exaggerated Pandora's age.

'She's looking good on it,' he observed.

'Thanks to science and surgery,' said Amelia bitchily. 'God, I shouldn't say that. It's just that sometimes I'm not sure I believe her when she says she's got my best interests at heart.'

Josh swigged back his beer as the next round arrived. 'She certainly told me she had, when she told me to leave you alone.'

Amelia stared at him. 'She said that?'

'Yup. She said she entirely approved of your relationship with your lover, that you were deeply involved with him and that she didn't want me getting in the way. Though she wouldn't mind seeing me for an occasional screw herself.'

'God, that's too much,' said Amelia despairingly. 'She told me not to see you either. She said I shouldn't jeopardise my relationship with U by seeing you again.'

'Maybe you'll jeopardise your relationship with me by seeing me again,' quipped Josh.

'Yeah, yeah. It's such a stupid name. I'm really starting to worry about where Pandora's coming from. You know she used to have a relationship with U herself.'

Josh managed to look surprised. 'Really? And you say you left them having a drink together?'

Amelia nodded gloomily. 'Let's not go there.'

He realised that despite extracting a little information from her, he was hardly playing his role as Svengali.

'No. You wouldn't want to spoil your evening with me by imagining them making out on the sofa, would you?'

'Like you did,' she retorted.

'It seems like everyone's getting it but you,' he observed nastily. 'Still, I said you needed to learn patience – it's good for you.'

'So what . . . what have you got planned for tonight?' Amelia asked breathily.

Josh raised an eyebrow at her, realising he had in fact planned nothing apart from having her exhibit herself in public, obey his command to meet him and try to get her away from U. Having succeeded in that regard he wasn't quite sure what to do with her next, though the fact that U was left having a drink with Pandora rather than rushing off to his anniversary dinner with Yasmin was unwelcome news.

He leant his head towards hers and improvised. Really, it was just like work.

'I thought I'd take you up to King's Cross to see how you like prostitution,' he murmured, reaching out to take her hands as though they were lovers murmuring sweet nothings. 'I'll drop you off on an appropriate corner and watch to make sure you get into a car and do it. I'll want to see the money, just to prove you went through with it.'

He saw her shiver slightly. He also saw her nipples hardening and darkening under the transparent blouse.

'Drink up – you'll probably need it,' he said maliciously. 'After all, you don't know who you'll get.'

'Are you serious?' she said in a small voice.

'Doesn't matter,' he replied carelessly. 'If that's what I feel like when we leave here, that's what we'll do. Won't we?' He put menace into the last question, and then felt wretchedly guilty when she nodded meekly.

'On the other hand I thought I might take you to a hotel – it'll have to be a cheap one, with you dressed like that,' he said candidly. 'I rather fancy tying you up and gagging you and then see what I feel like doing to you. OK?'

She nodded again. He could see her excitement increasing.

'Or I might even take you home with me. Can you cook?'

'Not much,' she admitted. 'I'm pretty good at pasta, and can do a Thai stir-fry – apart from that it's jacket potatoes and scrambled eggs.'

He smiled in what he hoped was a satanic manner. 'Thai stir-fry sounds good. I like the image of you naked, except for your stockings and suspenders and shoes, cooking for me. What do you think?'

'I think I'll have to stand well back from the frying pan,' she said with a giggle.

Josh felt happier at her laughter. After all, he didn't really want to humiliate her, at least not badly. And he was seriously hungry – as usual.

'OK, it's a deal. I'll give you marks out of ten for your cooking, and reward or punish you accordingly.'

'Right, like S&M *Masterchef*? Too hot and I get ten smacks with a wooden spoon, too mild and I have to suck your toes?'

He shuddered. 'Nothing that inelegant. I can think of at least one part of my anatomy that would appreciate a sucking more than my toes. Though I'd have to admit that that would be a reward rather than a punishment.'

'You would!' she laughed. 'So what other punishments can you think of?'

'Don't worry, I can think of plenty,' he assured her. 'For example, I'd like to watch you touch yourself.'

'Punishment?' she queried.

'Only after you've cut up the chillis,' he explained. 'That should warm you up nicely.'

'Ouch. You won't be wanting me to touch you, then.'

'No, after that I'd have to tie your hands together out of the way,' he said gravely, picking up the bill and putting a note on the table. 'I don't need your hands. I've got two of my own, and you have a very nice mouth. And I'm sure that's not the only wet and luscious orifice you have.'

He took her hand over the table. 'I'm not a complete arsehole, Amelia. I'm aware that you don't screw your – your lover, as you call him. So I do feel a little guilty about what I'm proposing to do. After all, this was a date, we met before, I'm not one of your random guys.'

She shrugged. 'You feel guilty? Imagine how I feel.

For one thing, I asked him to come and see me tonight, when really he should have been having an anniversary dinner with his wife.'

'Christ.' Josh had an uneasy moment when he realised he'd forgotten whether or not Amelia had told him that U was married. Spying's not really my game, he thought. It wasn't hard to improvise, however.

'So you deliberately asked him to come and see you to wreck his anniversary dinner?'

'No! Honestly, I didn't. But when he mentioned it I realised that he had told me about it, but I'd forgotten. If I did ask him on purpose tonight, it was unconscious.'

Josh felt that the unconscious was featuring a little too much in his life at present.

'I believe you. Did he?'

'I think so. But apart from feeling guilty about it, I suggested that we forget the platonic thing and go for it, in so many words, but he more or less turned me down and said he believed in my philosophy.'

Josh couldn't hide his amusement. 'Oh dear. So I turned you down the other day and shagged your aunt, and now he's turned you down and – didn't you say you left him having a drink with the Wick– with Pandora?'

'Yes. But he won't –'

Josh read in her eyes the realisation that maybe, in fact, he would.

'No, he won't,' she said firmly. 'After all, he's on his way to his anniversary dinner. He'll have a quick drink and go off to meet her.'

'I hope so,' said Josh, thinking of the storyline for 49 and hoping that U did indeed go to meet Yasmin rather than let her fall into the clutches of her gay friends. But really, the storyline was too absurd. He would bet that it would be changed at the script conference. It was just so not probable that Lisanne, Yasmin or anyone else would inspire their gay friends to turn straight, whether in the unreal world of soaps or the real one.

Amelia's eyes were questioning, and he realised that he had spoken carelessly.

'Why do you hope so?' she asked curiously. 'Are you really hoping to see Pandora again? Does the thought of her screwing him make you jealous?'

'No way,' asserted Josh, wishing he could explain why he was hoping U wouldn't let Yasmin down. 'I mean for your sake, not mine. Now, if you're really up for it, let's go and get cooking.'

As he rose from the table he suddenly noticed a couple on the other side of the bar walking from the entrance at the foot of the stairs to a table where a lone man sat. He knew straight away who they were, but not why they were together. The man was Milo. And the woman was Pandora.

But why were they together? And who was the other man, now standing up and shaking hands with the new arrivals?

He thought quickly. As much as he wished he could try to find out what they were up to together, there was no way he could face them with Amelia in tow. Pandora would most definitely blank him in the circumstances and he'd blow it with her for good. There was no doubt that she would make Amelia suffer as well, which would probably mean that she wouldn't see him again either.

The only possible way he could barge in on them would be to dump Amelia, put her in a cab back home and return to the bar alone. But he couldn't be that cruel.

He just had to accept that he couldn't confront them

in any way, so he just had to let them get on with it, get Amelia out without Pandora seeing her and just be grateful that, after all, Pandora wasn't at home in bed with U.

In an unaccustomed gesture of chivalry he rose and pulled Amelia's chair back for her to stand. He was feeling guilty, worried about the connection between Pandora and Milo and uneasy about the clairvoyant nature of the script, but he was a practical man. Amelia was a sweet girl, despite having sort of seduced his friend's husband, and he was looking forward to her satisfying first one of his appetites and then the other.

7

'Why the hell weren't you answering your phone yesterday? All sorts of things have happened.'

Yasmin put her bag and laptop down on the desk and smiled sweetly at Josh as she took the lid off her latte.

'Good morning, Yasmin. How the hell are you? Did you have a nice anniversary dinner? And, I must say, how lovely your hair looks back in its natural curls!'

Josh just stood with arms folded, shaking his head wearily. 'You don't have a clue, do you? Things are very odd, Yasmin. I don't know what the hell's going on, but it's definitely not all for the best in the best of all possible worlds.'

She stretched and yawned and ran her hands through her curls. God, it was good to have them back.

'Sorry, dear. I had a most enjoyable evening, thank you. Though not attending my anniversary dinner, which U decided to cancel. Or, I should say, postpone twice, so when a better offer presented itself I decided that I wouldn't wait for U to finally cancel, and I took that instead. It turned into an all-nighter, which means that he was very grumpy this morning when I went home to change.'

'Well, you might feel a bit grumpy yourself when I tell you something,' said Josh tersely. 'For one thing, I know he postponed. That's because Amelia desperately needed to see him.'

'How do *you* know?' Yasmin sat bolt upright in the plastic chair.

'I'll tell you in a minute. The other thing I know is that he had a talk with Pandora after he saw Amelia.'

Yasmin eyed him suspiciously. 'I hope it was just a talk. He was cross this morning because I'd stayed out last night, but he was bloody defensive as well. I thought it was just because he'd postponed dinner because of his totty, but I wonder if it was guilt. I would be really, really mad if he was screwing Pandora as well as not-screwing the niece. Anyway, how do you know all this?'

'Just doing another bit of spying. And if he did screw her it was a quickie, because, and get this, about an hour later Pandora walked into Zanzibar with another man, and you'll never guess who that was, to meet someone else.'

It was rather bewildering for someone who'd spent an evening and night enjoying uncomplicated, friendly sex with a couple of her husband's employees. Although she was interested to know how Josh had found all this out, Yasmin wasn't sure it was really relevant to her situation.

'Josh, do I care who this man was?'

'Only if you think it's a bit odd that Pandora should be spending an evening with Milo.'

'Oh. That is a bit odd.' She had a nasty feeling that all was not as well as it had seemed the night before.

'Yes. And another thing. Milo had what he called a "quiet word" with me yesterday. He says he's concerned about you, feels you're not firing on all cylinders, seems to know your personal life's up the spout and wonders if the series would be better if you were replaced.'

'Bastard!'

'Indeed.'

The last piece of information was the worst. Yasmin felt incredibly tired all of a sudden. She had guessed, from Briony's admission that U had gone to Holland Park, that he had been summoned by Amelia, and the fact that he had had a talk with Pandora was not particularly surprising or worrying. And though she couldn't imagine what Milo and Pandora would have in common, the fact that Milo seemed to want to get rid of her reeked of conspiracy.

She threw her coffee cup in the bin. 'So Pandora's niece is wrecking my marriage, U had a chat with Pandora last night and then she went out with Milo, who incidentally is trying to get me fired. So call me paranoid.'

'Quite.' Josh's face was grim. 'Milo was quite nice about it, by the way. He's coming over all concerned about you rather than griping about your work, which is an improvement on his position last week.

'I don't think he suspects I know anything about your private life, though he was obviously fishing. Of course I acted totally innocent about the whole thing, but he said that he'd heard rumours that things weren't all that good with your personal life and he was afraid it was affecting your work.'

Yasmin laughed bitterly. 'I don't know about you, Josh, but I do get sick and tired of soap producers going on as though we were bloody Shakespeare. God knows any idiot could write this stuff.'

'Yeah, yeah. I actually think I'm a cut above your average idiot. But the point is, it's not the writing he's talking about, is it? He wants you out – and it's got to be something to do with Pandora.'

'Christ.' Yasmin stared at him. 'I don't know which way to turn.'

'There's something else,' said Josh hesitantly. 'You know I reckon all this stuff about U intuiting things is a load of bullshit, but something really odd is definitely going on. I got Sandy to show me the next storyline yesterday.'

'Well?' said Yasmin. She was only half listening, still preoccupied with Milo's treachery.

'In the next episode Lisanne is supposed to have a reconciliation dinner with Johnny. Which he cancels to go and see Imelda.'

'Oh, fuck. That's not funny.' She suddenly felt cold inside. 'How did anyone know that was going to happen with me and U?'

'Nobody could, could they? It's not possible. Beth and Gerard won't be in on any of this, will they? And even if they knew U was having a thing with Amelia, they would have to know that she was going to ask him to go over there last night and make him cancel your dinner.'

'No, it's not possible. So why do I feel sick?' She looked helplessly at Josh. 'You've got to be right. They can't know. Unless – unless Milo told Pandora to tell Amelia to get him to go over there to fit in with the story.'

'Absolutely.' Josh was looking grim. 'Yesterday afternoon I thought it was all a very weird coincidence. Then last night when I saw Milo and Pandora together, I thought it could be more than that.'

'This is ridiculous!' said Yasmin fiercely. 'Look, Lisanne and Johnny are having a bit of marital difficulty. U and I are, too. It's not unusual for couples in that situation to try to have a reconciliation dinner.'

'Or for the girlfriend to sabotage it?' sniffed Josh. 'Well, I've got another little snippet of information about the storyline, but first of all I want to know what you did last night.'

'I didn't know you cared that much.' Yasmin grinned, her memory of the night before eclipsing her worry about the sinister goings-on in her life. 'Actually, I'd quite like to tell you when we can be a bit more personal, if you know what I mean. I'm sure you'd like to know all about it. For the time being, suffice it to say I was an unpaid soft-porn model.'

Josh smiled. 'That sounds good. And nothing to do with the storyline, thank God. For a minute I was afraid that I would have to start believing in the supernatural. So tell me a bit more about your modelling.'

His obvious relief made Yasmin feel happier. 'You know the other day in the kitchen with Euan I was thinking how great it would be to make a porn film, well, a few days later I end up screwing both a guy and a vibrator for the camera, would you believe. It was all about the G-spot. Funny, I was sure I'd found it before, but it's never been like it was last night.'

'Wow. I'd like to see the pictures.'

She winked at him. 'That was the main event. Before that I was photographed being felt up by this guy Kip while two others looked on. I think I should add I'd had a couple of absinthes first.'

'Good Lord. You decadent thing, you. But how on earth did you get involved in it? Is this something you do on the side, like bored suburban housewives doing the odd bit of prostitution just for kicks?'

'Oh, like they really do! That was a French film, dear,' sniffed Yasmin. 'Actually, having tried it, I wouldn't mind the odd spot of modelling. But to answer your question, it was my first time and an amazing coincidence. I went to *Slice* to pick up U, only to find he wasn't there and not likely to be back for a while. In the meantime the star photographer was having a row with some girlfriend on the phone who was supposed to be posing for him for this G-spot session, so I just volunteered.'

Josh shook his head. 'You really are unique, Yasmin. Like most women would find out their husband had stood them up and instead decide to become a porn star.'

'Marvellous, aren't I?' She beamed at him, happy that he was impressed by her evident insouciance rather than shocked by her casual embrace of the world of soft core. 'Knew you'd like it. As I said, I'll tell you the details later.'

Josh looked at his watch. 'Yeah, we haven't got time now anyway, the script conference is in two minutes – I can't wait, can you?'

'Not sarcasm, surely,' mocked Yasmin, getting to her feet.

'Just one thing,' he said hesitantly. 'Though I don't really want to push this conspiracy thing, you don't think that somehow U engineered it that this photographer should be there at that time, needing a model?'

'No, I'm totally sure he didn't,' said Yasmin emphatically. 'For one thing the girl who let him down only phoned the minute I walked into reception.'

'So you were told,' observed Josh. 'How do you know it wasn't U on the phone pretending to cancel just as you walked in the door?'

'Because I do,' she said impatiently. 'Honestly, Josh, you're getting too carried away. Thanks for all you've found out – there's definitely something strange going on with Milo and Pandora, isn't there? But I think that's the extent of the problem.'

'Yeah, I guess I'm just getting paranoid on your behalf,' he conceded. 'After all, it seems laughable to me that Lisanne is going to see these two gay guys and ends up having sex with them.'

Yasmin sat down again heavily. The sick feeling returned to her.

'That's the plot?'

'Yeah, daft, isn't it? I knew it was, but I just had an awful feeling you were going to say you went to see a couple of gay friends – thank goodness you went for a sleazy photo shoot instead.'

She couldn't answer. Josh was right, there was something extremely weird going on. He seemed so relieved at her account of the previous evening that she almost couldn't bear to tell him that Kip and Stevenson could be described as a gay couple, even though she'd found out they liked to dabble in other forms of sexuality.

So whoever came up with the plot had foreshadowed her evening of abandonment by her husband and sex with a couple of guys – well, with Kip at least – who were supposed to be gay. Was it conspiracy or was it, as Josh had said, something supernatural?

'Are you OK?'

She couldn't tell him, not yet. There wasn't time, and anyway she would hear the story herself at the meeting.

'Sorry, Josh, it's all a bit much.' She shook her head to clear her mind. 'Come on, let's get the bloody meeting over with.'

Like a lamb to the slaughter, she thought as they entered the conference room. Still, at least Josh was on her side, and at least if there was anything scary going on she had him to help her. God knows she needed a friend more than ever.

'Whoever wrote this storyline doesn't live in the real world,' said Josh bluntly. 'Lisanne's gay friends end up screwing her out of sympathy because she tells them Johnny's having an affair? Spare me!'

'Josh, love, the whole basis of *49* is adult entertainment,' said Milo, enunciating every word as though to a child. 'I thought we all realised that we are talking explicit sex here. And in every variety. We want to have the whole nation hooked. Surely you remember the classic moments of soaps? Deirdre Barlow's affair with Mike Baldwin? The lesbian kiss on *Brookside*? This is what attracts the viewers, love, whatever anyone may say. Sex is the seller here.'

'I know that,' said Josh, separating each word in imitation of Milo's speech. 'And I'm quite happy for a storyline featuring gays, believe me. The only thing I find totally preposterous is that the gay characters, who've featured as a happy couple so far, suddenly open their arms and their bed to a woman. It's total bollocks.'

'Well, if you'll actually let Beth go on, you'll find out that they're not totally gay at all, but bi. The viewer is just finding out, at the same time as Lisanne, that they're only actually living together out of convenience, and that though they do have a sexual relationship it doesn't mean they don't like women as well.'

'Excuse me, I'm not feeling too good.'

Josh looked concerned as Yasmin, who was in fact looking extremely pale, bolted out of the room as though she were about to be sick.

'What's the matter with her now?' asked Milo petulantly.

Josh stared at him. 'What do you mean, *now*?' he snapped. 'There's nothing the matter with her, except that obviously right now she's not feeling well.'

'Oh, come on, Josh, you know she's not herself at all lately. I thought we had all this out yesterday.'

'Actually, it was only you saying yesterday that she's

169

not been herself. As far as I'm concerned she's as normal, and as nice, as ever.' He surveyed the rest of the table. 'Anyone else got any input into that?'

Hugh, one of the other writers, shrugged. 'She seems the same as usual to me. Mind you she looked like she was going to chuck up just now. Don't suppose she's up the duff?'

'Well, there's a thought,' said Milo, looking maliciously at Josh. 'That would explain it. Hormones, you know.'

'Oh, can it, Milo,' said Josh with exasperation. Beth and Sandy were making delighted faces at each other at the thought that Yasmin could be pregnant, and he wished Hugh had kept his little comment to himself. She had enough to worry about without rumours flying round that she was having a baby.

He was tempted to say that the problem with Yasmin was obviously Milo's carping, and the fact that he'd been seen out with U's mistress's aunt the night before hadn't added to her well-being. However, he guessed that Yasmin didn't want the world to know about U's infidelity and he wanted to challenge Milo in private about his connection with Pandora. It would have to wait till after the script conference.

'Well, I think that as you're working together with Yasmin we can carry on without her,' said Milo sniffily. 'So, Beth, that's the Lisanne storyline for the next episode. What about the developments in the attempts by the national hotel chain to take over 49?'

Josh listened to the rest of the plot with half an ear, more concerned with how Yasmin was feeling than with the next episode. Part of him was wishing he'd taken the previous job that was offered to him, writing for a children's series based on Norse myths, which would undoubtedly have been a delight to work on, though not very lucrative. This job was the best paid he'd ever had, but he was beginning to question whether it was worth it. Money rules, he thought bitterly, but you pay in other ways.

Although the conference dragged on for another hour, Yasmin didn't return. At least Milo refrained from making any more sarcastic comments, and Josh thankfully packed up his papers at the end and went in search of her – but in vain.

'Sandy, you wouldn't do me a favour and see if Yasmin's in the ladies, would you?' he asked. 'I think she's gone, but I'd hate to think she was sick and alone.'

'Of course, Josh,' said Sandy, patting his arm. He realised she must have a soft spot for him. After all, she'd let him see the storyline the previous day, and was obviously touched by his concern for Yasmin.

'Not there,' she said, back almost as soon as he'd asked her to go and look. 'Do you want me to call her for you?'

He shook his head. 'No, let her be. She's actually had a bit of a shock, though don't tell anyone else.'

Her eyes widened. 'She's not really pregnant, is she?'

'No way,' he laughed. 'It's something else. Hey, can you take a lunch break, or are you too busy? I fancy a glass of wine – do you want to come with me?'

Did Sandy blush, or was it a trick of the light? Josh felt almost guilty. He'd used Amelia and Pandora in his attempt to help Yasmin, and now he was buttering up Sandy. But then did James Bond ever have any qualms about using women? And of course, they always loved it – didn't they?

He also had to admit to himself that he was getting an enormous kick out of what seemed to be his sudden attraction to the opposite sex. Maybe it was just that he had finally got over Veronica – thanks in part to Yasmin and Amelia – and was paying attention to women again, and receiving it back. Or maybe his role as a spy gave him an indefinable mysteriousness that women just couldn't help picking up on. But, he told himself, that was pure fantasy.

Vino's was packed, but they found a tiny table next to the kitchen. The swing doors kept opening and closing, giving them snatches of shouting in Italian, a ferociously loud extractor fan and a noisy dishwasher every couple of minutes, but they were comfortable enough with a bottle of house Chianti and a toasted mozzarella and tomato panini. Josh kept the conversation general for the first glass, but halfway down the second went for the kill.

'I am really worried about Yasmin,' he said confidingly. 'Can you keep a secret, Sandy?'

'Oh, absolutely,' she said earnestly.

'Well, her husband's having an affair,' he said, watching her closely to see how she would react. It was as he'd guessed – she acted shocked, but he could tell she wasn't really surprised. She knew, all right.

'And that's not all,' he added. 'Milo's out to get her. He wants her off the project, he told me so himself yesterday. Now, Sandy, please don't tell me that you don't know anything about this, because I won't believe you.'

Her face was a picture of confusion; she didn't know whether to show her loyalty to him, or to her boss. Josh fixed her with his most sympathetic, but slightly stern, gaze, and won.

'I know,' she admitted finally. 'Sorry, Josh. I just told you I could keep a secret, and then you ask me to break Milo's confidence. I don't want to be the sort of person everyone thinks can't keep their mouth shut about anything.'

'Don't worry, I know you're not,' he said consolingly, patting her hand sympathetically. 'The thing is, Sandy, it seems that everyone's out to get Yasmin, and I don't like it, and as a woman I don't suppose you do either.'

'No, I don't!' she said stoutly. 'Milo's a pain in the arse, and I know he's being really horrible to Yasmin, but it's not really his fault. He's been told to have a go at her.'

Josh felt his pulse quicken at the news. 'Been told to? By whom?'

Sandy took a deep breath and exhaled loudly. 'Josh, please do not tell anyone I told you this or I'll be for the chop. It's all right for you, it's just another contract, but for me it won't be so easy to find another job — especially if they find out that I gave out confidential information.'

'They won't,' he said quickly. 'So who's pulling the strings? Is it Pandora?'

Sandy looked puzzled. 'Who's Pandora?'

'Sorry, go on.' So that was a red herring.

'It's top level. Milo's under orders from the board of New Order to destabilise Yasmin's position.'

'What? That doesn't make sense. How on earth can anyone on the board give a toss about one of the scriptwriters on one of the TV shows?'

Josh's bewilderment was total. New Order was the parent company of On the Edge productions, a large media conglomerate based in New York. He was surprised that anyone on the board would even know that there was a new soap opera being made in the UK, never mind have it in for one of the writers.

'I know, it's bizarre, isn't it?' Sandy looked at him

earnestly. 'That's what I said to Milo. He said it's none of our business, but what the board wanted they were going to get and that was the end of it.'

'I'm sure,' said Josh drily. 'I suppose this little project is why Milo's here in the first place. I thought he'd risen too far up the ladder of the entertainment industry to produce a little UK soap.'

'I don't know,' shrugged Sandy. 'But if this all started in the beginning, I don't see why they wanted Yasmin in the first place – they could have turned her down, Milo needn't have come on the job, Bernie would have been in charge and everything would have been OK.'

'Mmm.' Josh's mind was racing in different directions. 'You really don't know why they're out to get Yasmin?'

Sandy shook her head. 'No. All I know is that Danny DiGeronimo, who's a mighty big shot, is in London and met Milo last night.'

'Ah. Ahahaha. I'm beginning to see the light. So the Wicked Witch *is* involved!' said Josh excitedly. 'Danny DiGeronimo – Christ, it sounds like a mafia plot.'

Sandy giggled. 'More like a Nazi one. The code name for this business is "Project U-boat".'

'Oh, my God. Sandy, you've got it. You don't know Yasmin's husband, obviously.'

She shook her head, a bewildered look on her face. 'No, why should I?'

'So you don't know his name is U?'

She stared at him. 'U? As in letter U? As in U-boat?'

Josh nodded. 'The same. So, Holmes, it's not hard to work out, is it? For some reason, something to do with Yasmin's husband, they want to upset, sack or otherwise destabilise Yasmin. And if I'm not mistaken it's got to be something to do with his magazine. God, I wonder who owns that? Or who owns *Black Box*?'

Sandy looked helpful but confused.

'Don't worry,' said Josh, planting a finger kiss on her nose. 'It's going to be all downhill from here. I promise I won't tell anyone you told me anything, Sandy. Thanks a lot.'

'That's OK.' She was definitely blushing. 'I trust you, Josh.'

'You're a sweetie,' he said. 'Now, I think I'd better get on the phone and see if I can find out where Yasmin is. For one thing, I'd better tell her to watch out or everyone's going to start asking her when it's due, but more importantly I think she might be pleased to know that this seems to be about U, not about her.'

'Just make sure she doesn't confront Milo with it,' said Sandy anxiously. 'I trust you, but she might not realise that she'd be landing me in it if she said anything.'

'Don't worry, with what you've told me I know how to find out what's really going on, and that's not from Milo,' Josh reassured her. 'And I think it's down to me to do a bit of serious spying.'

Sandy laughed. 'I suppose that's what you've been doing with me.'

Josh realised her voice sounded a little disappointed, as though she guessed he'd just been using her.

'Yes and no,' he said slowly, looking at her thoughtfully. Her purple-framed glasses and magenta-streaked hair were standard-issue media secretary, but her face was sweet and her lips plump and attractively parted beneath it. He wouldn't climb over her to get to Pandora, that was for sure.

'Sandy, I've got a couple of things to take care of at the moment,' he said softly. 'But when they're done – maybe we could get together for dinner or something?'

'You don't have to say that because I've helped you,' she said nobly.

Josh laughed. 'I don't do anything any more because I think I have to,' he told her. 'I meant it. OK?'

She did have a lovely smile. 'OK,' she said happily.

He walked her back to the office and kissed her briefly on the lips outside the door. 'Let's hope Milo doesn't see us and put two and two together,' he said mischievously. 'Otherwise it'll be Operation Josh next. I'll see you soon.'

He guessed she was looking after him as he went up the street. God, you lady killer, he told himself. There was just one more move he could make to try to sort the muddle out, and that was to try to get Pandora to tell him what was really going on. As long as his cover wasn't blown, he reckoned he was in with a chance.

An hour later he was at home listening to the Diabelli Variations, which was on his mind at the moment for some reason. He had tracked down Yasmin, whose phone was now fully functional, at home. She explained that she had been spooked by the fact that the photographer she had been with the previous night also had a sexual relationship with his male friend. It was odd, Josh had to admit, but then again, as he had said to her earlier, maybe U's intuitiveness wasn't such a load of rubbish after all. Anyway, they agreed that whatever happened it probably wasn't part of the conspiracy – but that the conspiracy could probably best be unravelled by Pandora.

Josh called her to try to make a date. First she was furious with him for seeing Amelia the previous night but he talked her round and she agreed to see him the next evening. He phoned Yasmin back to tell her everything was in place, then settled down for a quiet night in. God knows after the previous night he needed one.

Amelia had proved a dab hand at Thai cooking. She had also looked very appealing as she chopped, stirred and fried wearing nothing but her stockings and suspender belt, and been most amenable to being penetrated as she bent over the worktop with knife in hand and, despite having already laid the table to his orders, obligingly lay on it – the cutlery must have been digging into her back – while he decided he'd just have to come before she started frying.

After dinner Josh had realised he hadn't exactly carried out his previous promises of bondage and anticipation, and had belatedly tied her to the bedhead with shoelaces and stood behind her with his cock through the bars of the headboard for her to suck him till he was hard again. It took quite a long time but there was no hurry. He wondered whether to fuck her again but decided to keep her waiting, and instead gave her just enough attention with his own mouth and tongue to start her moaning, then stopped and allowed her to resume her attentions on him. He came in her mouth, and then sent her home wet and wanting. She was happy, he knew, waiting for him till the next time. Though after his date with Pandora the following evening God knows what would come to light, or who would be talking to whom.

'Gorgeous girl. I've been worried about you.'

'You must be psychic,' said Yasmin wryly, sick and tired of the very idea of any psychic vibrations whatsoever. 'How are you, Euan?'

'Fine as usual. How's U? Oh, sorry, couldn't resist it.'

'Yeah, yeah. Actually, I'm not great. Things aren't going very well, quite honestly. Josh has done another brilliant spying job, but at the end of it I don't really know if we're getting anywhere. U's affair all seems to have been set up by Pandora but God knows why, and it all seems to be linked with me having trouble at work. It's a bit of a mystery.'

'Bummer. Look, Cody thought she might try to see Amelia again, to see if she can find out what's going on. What do you think?'

'I don't know. If she wants to – I guess you'll want to be there in the audience, as it were?'

Euan chuckled. 'You know me so well already. And maybe not just as part of the audience. I thought I'd check with you though before she made any plans.'

'Thanks. I can't believe how nice everyone is being. You, Josh, and now Kip and Stevenson –'

'Oh?' Euan's voice was interested. 'Not another pair of spies?'

'Not really – but an evening you'll be interested in hearing about. Meanwhile someone at work reckons I must be pregnant because the whole thing made me feel sick today and I walked out – now that'd be a turn up.'

'It wasn't me, honest! I always took precautions, miss.'

'Sod off. Let me know if anything happens.'

'Take care. Especially in your condition . . .'

Yasmin laughed as she put down the phone. Everyone was so solicitous, it was almost as though she were pregnant, or even ill. All in all things weren't so bad, really. She had been totally spooked by the fact that the story of 49 seemed to be identical to her own life, but had recovered. After all, coincidences did happen. It was silly to be upset by one.

She wondered if Amelia would be seduced by Cody's invitation. If so, U wouldn't be seeing her that night. She rather suspected anyway that he would be at home, hoping they could have a reasonable evening. It was almost laughable, given that she'd spent the previous night being photographed in various compromising positions, and he'd jettisoned their anniversary dinner to be with his teenage mistress, followed by a – drink? chat? or more? – with his ex-lover. Still, should they decide to play truth or dare, it would be interesting. To say the least.

Amelia realised that she had only accepted Cody's invitation for a drink because she didn't want to face Pandora after rushing off to meet Josh the night before. She'd been so against him last time, despite using him for a quickie on the sofa, and it was almost inevitable that U would have told her why she'd left in such a hurry.

Pandora had been in bed by the time she'd got back home just after two in the morning, still hyped up from Josh's attentions. They had had great sex in the kitchen but then he had aroused her again and refused to satisfy her. Tied to the bed, obediently sucking him, revelling in his lips and fingers on her sex and waiting for the moment of climax, only to have him move away again and use her mouth – he really had used it, fucking it almost impersonally while she lay helplessly bound. Not that she had any complaints about that; her sex had pulsed and she couldn't help pushing it up for attention as he used her, her excitement compounded by his amused observations on her obvious desperation for satisfaction. Eventually he had come in her mouth, telling her to swallow and sound like she was enjoying it, then pulling out to make sure some of his semen ran over her face.

She had expected him then to return to paying her back with his mouth and hands, but he had left the room. The next thing she heard was the shower running, and Josh whistling a snatch from the Diabelli Variations while he washed. He came out of the bathroom with a towel around him and, without a word to her, picked up the phone and ordered a cab for Holland Park.

'Josh, that is so unfair!' she had moaned.

He raised a shaggy eyebrow as he untied her bonds.

'Do you know what the time is? One thirty in the morning. I have a –' he hesitated '– a meeting tomorrow morning. You can presumably sleep in for as long as you like, so you can bugger off home, satisfy yourself as you told me you prefer to do, and then go to bed till you wake.

'Anyway, get a move on and get dressed. The cab's going to be here in ten minutes.'

Oddly, she hadn't felt like masturbating when she got home. She had suddenly lost the taste for solitary sex. Instead she lay awake thinking about Josh, his refusal to allow her satisfaction, the way he had almost jeered at her pushing her sex forward for him, and the horrible, thrilling, selfish, exciting way he had taken just what he wanted from her, leaving her wanting him more than ever.

Realistically, she couldn't expect to see him for a few days – he would want her desperate for him. And cynically she gauged that Cody – she didn't even remember exchanging names with her, let alone phone numbers – owed her a hand job, at least. They were meeting in some Scottish bar in Soho. The drink in the ultra cool bar last night followed by her meek and shivering compliance with Josh's desires would be a world away from a few beers in what was presumably some rowdy drinking den, with the evening rounded off by a woman's hand or mouth to satisfy her. Variety's the spice of life, she reminded herself. Anyway, it would get her out of Pandora's way.

'Golden Promise?'

Amelia nodded mutely, not knowing what it was and hoping it had nothing in common with a golden shower. Cody looked as off the wall as the last time they'd met, now wearing a turquoise crop top and ra-ra skirt, with sixties white leather boots over white lace tights, the whole thing topped off by an outra-geously large pewter Celtic cross and chain.

It was a beer, a large bottle of which Cody drank out of while providing Amelia with a glass.

'It's too big to drink straight from the bottle – unless you're used to getting one at the end of a hot and sweaty shift when you're not even given the choice of a glass,' she explained as she took another swig. 'I reckon it's good for the biceps as well.'

Amelia nodded, feeling she was being treated like a dainty girlie who wasn't strong enough to pick up a beer bottle. Still, if Cody wanted her meek and femi-nine, she had no complaint. After all, she'd had enough practice at it with Josh the night before.

'So what do you do on a hot and sweaty shift?'

'I'm a chef. Here.' Cody waved her arm around the bar.

'Wow. And you spend your night off here, too?'

'Not always. As you know, I also go to the opera.' She gave Amelia a sidelong look. 'Actually the head chef here was very interested when I told him about you. I remembered you said you liked guys too, so I thought maybe after a few drinks he won't be so busy – if you like, that is.'

Things were looking up, Amelia thought. Although

she'd more or less decided to give up random acts of sexual kindness, this really wasn't the same. Cody had asked her on a date – it was almost like she was the one being seduced. Kind of nice, she thought. Depending on what this guy looked like.

Cody finished her beer with bewildering speed, but demurred when Amelia offered another, saying she'd wait for her to catch up. Not really being a beer drinker, Amelia struggled womanfully and managed to down the bottle within a few minutes. She wasn't allowed to get her round in, though, as Cody told her it was on the house. A huge, kilted red-headed man brought over the next drinks, sat down at their table and introduced himself as Willie.

'I hear you give terrific hand jobs,' were his first words to Amelia.

'Yes,' she answered shortly. 'Only when I feel like it, though.'

He chuckled. 'Don't worry, pet, I wasn't after one for myself. I'm a happily co-habiting man. After all, someone's got to be in this place. All the barmen are gay and the kitchen staff fuck like rabbits.'

'Shove off, Willie,' said Cody fondly. 'You'll frighten Amelia from going into the kitchen.'

Willie sighed. 'Oh, not another one. I'm afraid this kitchen's getting a reputation for strange women invading it and throwing themselves at the chefs.'

'Well, I won't be,' said Amelia tartly. 'I'm just here for a drink with Cody.'

He scrutinised her intently, so much that she felt uncomfortable. What was he trying to gauge from her face? Or was he really just getting a load of her tits, which Cody had presumably told him all about?

'You carry on, pet. Just let me know when you need another drink.'

'Actually, Willie, a wee whisky chaser wouldn't be a bad idea,' interjected Cody.

He heaved his bulk out of the chair. 'Coming up, ladies.'

'I don't drink whisky,' said Amelia sulkily, as he trundled back to the bar. 'I didn't like the way he was looking at me.'

'Don't worry, Amelia. He's a sweetie, really. It's his bar, and he lets us have free drinks on nights off, not to mention the odd bottle of beer after service. He's just a big old bear looking out for us, that's why he was looking at you. And in all honesty your transparent blouses do really ask for attention.'

'OK,' said Amelia, mollified. She had been worried about wearing her usual clothing in the bar, expecting it to be full of drunks shouting football chants, but hadn't wanted to disappoint Cody by covering up. As in fact it turned out to be a perfectly civilised café bar full of normal people eating and drinking, she would have felt a real baby if she'd wimped out.

She sipped at the next beer. Maybe she was just being a big soft girl as far as drink was concerned, preferring vodka or white wine – it could be time to get to grips with this guys' stuff.

The whisky appeared, but in a bottle with a couple of shot glasses rather than the discrete measure she had been expecting. This time it was brought by a sulky-looking dark-haired waiter, also kilted.

'Don't you have anything with it?' she asked Cody, who poured two generous slugs into the glasses.

'It's great for sex,' said Cody slyly, avoiding the question and putting one glass into Amelia's hand. 'Cheers.'

Amelia grimaced as she sipped, while Cody downed hers in one.

'Wimp.' She grinned.

'Oh, fuck it,' Amelia said crossly and threw the whisky down her throat. It stung her entire mouth and she felt it burning as it went down inside her, right down to her belly, where it spread a sudden warmth that reached right down to her toes.

She realised Cody was laughing at her. 'See? Warms the cockles of your heart, doesn't it?'

Amelia giggled, realising her brain felt slightly anaesthetised. 'I know exactly what you mean,' she said in an undertone. 'So what's the plan? You want to go to the ladies?'

Cody tutted at her. 'Patience, little Amelia. For one thing I need a couple more drinks, and for another, while I was quite happy to feel your tits up in the Coliseum's toilet, it was necessity rather than desire. While I can't say I haven't had sex in toilets before, if there's an option I'll take it. Like on a staircase, for instance.'

Amelia looked round. 'There aren't many options here.' She picked up the glass where Cody had poured her another whisky.

'There are in the kitchen. The prep room, the cold room, just outside the back door – mostly Euan likes to have women on the prep tables, but I'm a bit fed up with stainless steel.'

'Euan?'

'Don't just knock the whisky back, you're supposed to alternate it with your beer,' said Cody humorously as she watched Amelia getting to grips with whisky. 'Euan's the head chef I told you about.'

She looked at her watch. 'He'll be mostly finishing off in half an hour or so. We'll hang on here till then.'

'Don't *you* want me?'

Amelia realised with dismay that her voice sounded slightly desperate. What had gotten into her? And was it U's fault? Or Josh's? Or Pandora's?

Cody had laughed at her spontaneous exclamation, then put her hand out over the table and lightly tweaked one of Amelia's nipples.

'Of course I do. How can I not, with those on show? But as I just said, we need to get into the kitchen. Hey, do you want something to eat first?'

Amelia nodded. She'd forgotten about food in her deliberations over dressing and her anxiety to be out of the house before Pandora came in. Since her Thai meal the night before she'd had nothing but a bowl of muesli and some fruit.

Cody disappeared for a few minutes and came back with two plates of sandwiches. 'I thought you weren't really a haggis kind of girl,' she said, putting one plate down in front of Amelia. 'There's Aberdeen Angus steak as well, or venison and blueberry casserole, but I thought you might prefer something a bit lighter. It's great beef. Now tell me you're a vegetarian!'

Amelia shook her head and launched into one of the rare beef sandwiches. They were liberally spread with mustard which assaulted her taste buds and successfully competed with the taste of whisky. Cody ordered another beer apiece to wash them down with, and it wasn't long before Amelia realised that she had a pressing desire to go to the toilet.

Cody cocked her head on one side as Amelia asked her where the ladies was.

'I know I said I didn't fancy sex in the toilet, but perhaps I'll just come and watch – if that's all right?'

It was only when she stood that Amelia realised she'd definitely had too much to drink. But she didn't care; she felt marvellously light-headed and loose-limbed, and was looking forward to Cody watching her – or whatever else she had planned.

'Come through here to the staff toilets,' said Cody, pushing her towards the back of the bar. 'We'll be able to take as long as we like.'

Behind the door marked 'Staff Only' were two further doors with male and female toilet signs on. As Cody pushed the door to the ladies, a man – obviously a chef, in white top and checked trousers – came out of the men's toilet.

'Well, here she is,' he said with a grin. Amelia was immediately taken by his open, handsome face, the obvious good nature of him and his curly hair. 'I was hoping Cody was going to bring you here. I've been looking forward to seeing your tits, and I'm not disappointed.'

'This is Euan, of course,' said Cody drily. 'We're coming through in a minute. Nature calls first.'

He raised his eyebrows. 'And you're going in there together? Isn't this something I should be watching?'

'I just need to pee at the moment,' said Amelia, feeling desperate. 'If you'll excuse me –'

She lunged for the door of the ladies, only to be followed first by Cody and then by Euan.

'I didn't invite you,' said Cody firmly.

He ignored her. 'I love watching women pee. Go on, if you're desperate.'

Amelia had no choice. Euan held the door to the cubicle open and stood smiling at her. 'Go on, you'll wet your pants.'

'I don't wear any,' said Amelia. Wearing a pencil skirt had obviously been a mistake, but she had no choice but to raise it almost to her waist before sitting on the toilet seat and mercifully letting the golden stream flood out of her.

'Oh, man!' breathed Euan. Cody merely whistled. Amelia closed her eyes, knowing they were both focused on the shaven bareness of her pubis.

She had drunk a lot of beer and it took a while to expel it. Well before she had finished, Euan suddenly said, 'Can you do that thing of tensing your muscles and stopping it?'

'Of course I can,' she said almost indignantly, instantly stopping the flow. 'I always exercise my muscles. It's good for sex.'

'Yes, I know,' said Euan, moving towards her. 'Can you keep them like that for a bit?'

'Yes – why?'

In reply his hand shot out and gently stroked her clit. Amelia moaned.

'Because,' he went on, steadily rotating his finger over her suddenly hard bud, 'I wondered what it was like if you came while your muscles were like that. Would you come really hard? Would you pee as you came? Just an experiment.'

'I don't know,' whispered Amelia, aware that if she relaxed her muscles now she would pee all over his hand, which might put him off. It could result in her most definitely not coming, which suddenly seemed the most important thing in the world.

'This is really supposed to be my gig,' said Cody almost crossly from outside the cubicle. 'Kneel down, Euan, I want a feel.'

Although Josh had treated her almost like an unpaid hooker, it was nothing compared to the humiliation of being fingered and grabbed by Euan and Cody almost as though they were feeling up a particularly plump piece of Aberdeen Angus. It was weird and it was brilliant. Amelia gave herself up to the sensation of Cody's rough hands on her breasts, feeling her undo the buttons of her high-necked blouse and pull it aside so she could squeeze the warm flesh rather than the cold polyester. Meanwhile Euan's finger circled her harder and she clenched her muscles as tight as she could and suddenly she couldn't control them any more – she came with a paroxysm of pulsating muscle and warm pee and she could still feel the mercilessly moving finger and the hands roughly rubbing her nipples. Her head was still fuzzy from the whisky and she felt totally and wonderfully out of control as her body shuddered helplessly and convulsively.

'I was right, it was pretty good – wasn't it?' observed Euan with a beatific smile.

'Extremely,' she admitted, still breathing shallowly.

'Good. My turn next. But I reckon we could all do with a drink.'

'I don't think I need any more beer,' said Amelia, giggling at the thought of the amount of urine she'd just expelled.

'I'll grab our bottle and we'll come through to the kitchen, if you're ready,' said Cody.

'I don't think I can manage any more whisky either.' Amelia thought she'd had enough to drink for the night. She pulled at the toilet paper as Cody disappeared, but Euan moved her hand.

'I think you need more than a quick wipe,' he said, going towards the hand basin and running some water. 'I'll give you a little wash instead.'

He rubbed the soap between his hands and motioned for her to stand. Like a baby she stood still while his hand rubbed between her legs. The harsh lather was uncomfortable after she had been so comprehensively rubbed by his fingers, and she was also shamefully aware of the smell of pee that came from her.

'Turn round,' he told her, rubbing her arse with his soapy hands. 'Lovely bareness. Was that your idea?'

'Yes,' she whispered as he rinsed the soap from his hands and cupped them to rinse her off too. She knew it wouldn't be easy to get rid of the lather and that it would chafe her, but she didn't care. Euan made a total mess of the floor as he rinsed her.

'I just wondered, seeing as Cody saw you with some old guy the other week, whether he liked you like that, sort of schoolgirl fantasy stuff.'

'That is so sick!' cried Amelia. 'He had nothing to do with it. I just decided on it myself.'

'Sorry,' said Euan, though there was a malicious light in his eyes. 'I said it was probably your dad, anyway.' He dried Amelia with paper towels; she was sure he must have seen her wince, but ignored it.

'He's my lover,' she said sulkily, aware that the amount of lovemaking she'd done with U was even less than the fingering she'd just received from Euan. 'And he's not that old. He's only forty-two.'

'*Only?*'

'You know what young guys look like? Still spotty, shrouded in beanies and parkas? That is so not my scene.'

Euan shrugged and gave her a friendly slap on the bottom. 'Never mind. Come and see my little empire. You don't need to pull your skirt down, there's another way into the kitchen.'

'Very funny,' she snorted, pulling the tight skirt back down to her knees and rebuttoning her blouse. She'd thought that Cody would have been turned on by the sexy secretary look, but hadn't really given enough thought as to the impracticality of the tight skirt.

She followed Euan through yet a different door into a warm, noisy corridor which led into the stifling heat of the kitchen. Cody was already sitting on a steel table drinking, and two other glasses of whisky were waiting.

'Cheers.' Euan raised his glass to Amelia's. She didn't want any more – she already felt drunk enough – but couldn't refuse to toast him. They clinked glasses, then with Cody, and she swallowed it quickly.

'I was just telling Amelia that a shaved pussy gives a guy all sorts of decadent ideas,' Euan observed. 'Like quite fancying seeing your mouth round it, C. What do you think?'

'As a prelude to your cock inside it, I presume?' said Cody drily.

'But of course. After all, she's given you a hand job, I've just sorted her, so I reckon I deserve a little sorting myself – don't you?'

After the last drink Amelia felt that she would happily do anything to anybody. Her body felt like rubber and her head like cotton wool. She was aware that her glass still seemed to have whisky in it – or was it more whisky? She didn't know or care, and drank.

'I can't be arsed with being the bloody spectacle again,' Euan was saying. 'Come on, Amelia, let's go outside. We probably all need a breath of air.'

They walked through the kitchen and out of the back door. A couple of men also in whites were lounging on a wooden bench, smoking.

'Back in,' Euan ordered. 'Get the kitchen tidied up, for goodness' sake.'

They grumbled and threw their cigarettes down and went back into the kitchen.

Amelia realised they were in the bar's backyard, a bare paved enclosure which was tidy enough but spoilt by the smell coming from the huge dustbins which were the yard's only furniture apart from the bench. The outside light was bright but seemed muted after the fluorescent lights of the kitchen. She knew what was expected of her, and lifted her skirt again and lay down on the bench, letting her legs fall either side of it.

'Wow, that's fantastic. One word and she's there, right in position,' said Euan. 'I guess you know yours too, C.'

It was a shame that as Cody's mouth touched her clit Amelia almost immediately began to feel slightly nauseous, but she decided it was better to keep quiet and concentrate on the sensations. Unfortunately the penetrating stench of the rubbish added to her nausea and won over the lips on her sex.

'You know, I don't feel very well,' she said quietly.

'You'll be fine after Cody's finished with you,' said Euan, his eyes on Cody's fingers spreading open the lips of Amelia's naked pussy. 'Where were we, anyway? Oh yes, your forty-two-year-old boyfriend. Do you always go for older men?'

Amelia shook her head, and wished she hadn't. 'No. Look, I really don't feel great.'

'Shh. Just concentrate on her mouth,' soothed Euan, stroking Amelia's breasts through the blouse. 'How did you get together with a guy like that? I mean, you didn't bump into him in a club, or a bar, did you?'

'No,' said Amelia, closing her eyes. 'My aunt fixed us up together.'

'Really?'

She really wished he'd fuck her, get it over with and then she could sit up and stop feeling sick.

'Yes. I always quite fancied him, 'cos he used to be her boyfriend, but she asked him over and then pretended she couldn't go to a concert so he had to take me.'

Euan had a soft laugh. 'Sounds like an arranged marriage, old guy getting niece of ex-lover.'

'No, he's already married,' said Amelia abstractedly, trying to focus on Cody's lips, which were doing quite a good job on hers. She was starting to feel a bit better.

'Married? You mean your aunt set you up deliberately with a married man? That's bizarre.'

'I guess,' she mumbled. Cody's tongue was sweeping up and down her sex. 'She really wanted me to have him, then she got all ratty when I wouldn't have proper sex with him, and now she'll be even rattier because I went out with Josh last night.'

Euan lifted her shoulders so that she was sitting on the bench, still with Cody's tongue on her. He sat behind her and she felt his cock, thick and warm on her back, and then his strong hands lifted her and sat her down on it. His arms then pulled her back into a prone position, lying on top of him, while his hands gently moved her hips back and forth.

'Nice tongue, C,' he said breathlessly. 'Go on, Amelia. Why did your aunt set you up with this guy?'

'I don't really know. Except it's something to do with her magazine. It's being taken over, but what that's got to do with me I really don't know. Or with U.'

It was probably a good thing that Amelia had had too much to drink or she would have noticed the absence of Euan's asking what on earth it had to do with him. Even so it would have probably been eclipsed by Cody suddenly insinuating her body on top of hers, fitting her pubic mound on top of hers and pressing her tits on hers. Amelia was the filling in the sandwich as Cody ground hard against her and Euan jerked inside her. She heard Euan breathe 'Nice one' into her ear but it wasn't for her, because Cody's mouth, also around her left ear, said 'Yeah' and then Cody and Euan were kissing on the mouth, as though they were screwing each other and she had nothing to do with it. And that was just what was happening, as Amelia lost her rhythm and her inclination to come, and allowed herself to be fucked by one and rubbed off on by the other, a mere instrument of their pleasure.

8

'I thought we could have an anniversary dinner at home, since last night was such a disaster.'

Yasmin had gambled on U being home and rustled up a special meal: lobster salad, beef Wellington and crème brûlée. Not that it was much of a loss if he'd not been around, as there was at least three days before the sell-by date on the packets.

'That's nice,' he said gravely. 'I'm sorry about all the mix-up. If you'd just waited –'

She raised her hand. 'No, U, we're not going to do that if stuff. Except I'll just say that if you hadn't postponed twice, not to mention getting a cab to Holland Park so I knew exactly who you were with, then I would have waited.'

He had the grace to look ashamed. 'Briony wasn't supposed to tell you where I was.'

'I forced her. She didn't exactly tell me where you were, just that you asked her to get you a cab, and I twisted her arm to tell me where to. She looked very worried about it, I can tell you.'

'Yes, I know. She was very apologetic.'

'Basically, U, if you're going to dump on your wife you just shouldn't get anyone else involved. And that's the last word. Let's have a civilised evening. I've been slaving away at a hot checkout for the last ten minutes getting dinner, so why don't I put the oven on and have a bath and get changed.'

Part of her hoped rather wistfully that U would

follow her into the bathroom, but he just used the opportunity to slip upstairs to the meditation room. Yasmin watched him in exasperation. He'd been meditating for almost half of his life and what on earth had it achieved? It certainly wasn't going to help the evening ahead of them. If instead he'd come into the bathroom while she was lying in the silky water and quietly and intimately started washing her back it would do a lot more for their relationship than a quick ten minutes communing with his inner self.

'I forgot to say this morning, I like having your real hair back.'

U had put his head round the bathroom door after all, just as she'd got into the water. Dammit, she thought, he really is psychic.

'Thanks. You want to wash my back?'

Yasmin had considered how much she should tell U. He had no idea that Josh was spying for her, and she didn't want to risk him storming off so that they were even farther apart than ever. She half wished she'd stuck it out at the script conference – at least she might have had some precognition of what was going to happen in her own life, as it seemed to be shadowing the plot of the soap so closely.

'I did come home, you know, in case you were here,' he said quietly as he soaped her back. 'I would have made the restaurant if you hadn't left that message.'

'Well, another offer came along and I guessed I ought to take it, just in case you didn't make it. Then I would have sincerely hated you for dumping me on our anniversary for her. That could have been the end.'

'Yasmin, I was never going to let you down. I know it doesn't seem much like it at the moment, but you're still fundamentally the most important thing in my life.'

She turned and looked at him over her shoulder. 'Fundamentally isn't going to hack it, U. I don't want to be the solid foundation of your life unless I'm also the icing on your cake, if you see what I mean.'

He nodded. 'Of course. You know things aren't going too well with Amelia at the moment –'

'Don't tell me. I don't want to know about that. All I want to know about that is, hopefully sooner rather than later, it's over. And I think we could actually have quite a nice evening talking about something else.'

He kissed her soapy shoulder lightly. 'Just talking?'

She hesitated. It would be so nice, so comforting and so anniversary-like to rise out of the bath and make love with U. But then again, it would be a sham. Until she'd fought off the wretched Amelia, it just wasn't going to happen.

Besides, she felt quite sore from the combined attentions of Kip and the vibrator.

'You say you're not actually fucking her, so I guess I'll just have to say we'll stick to talking. I don't want to have an unfair advantage over her.'

U winced. 'Clever. I must admire your determination to fight fair.'

Yasmin thought of innocent Amelia, probably getting ready right now to meet Cody and Euan, her spies, after a night spent with Josh, another of her spies, and felt just a bit guilty at being complimented on being fair, but hey. Whose husband was he anyway?

'Thank you. Now why don't you go and choose some wine for the beef Wellington? I got a cold bottle of Riesling for the lobster – actually I wouldn't mind a small glass of that now.'

'Sure.' He got halfway out of the door and then turned back. 'Yasmin – you are so beautiful.'

'Yeah. Probably even better than when I was nineteen.'

He didn't reply but stayed at the door for a silent minute, then she heard his bare feet padding up the hall to check on the wine. She almost had a tearful moment, but thought better of it. It had been a fraught day, and it would be far better to keep her emotions in neutral for the time being. It would be nice just to have a reasonably civilised evening with U. After all, she did so much miss his company.

She couldn't help dressing to kill, though, in a black dress slashed down to the waist at the front and slit up to the thigh at the side. It was a shame she couldn't wear the outfit she'd planned for the anniversary dinner, but then U had seen it when she'd got home that morning, and besides it seemed to have an absinthe stain, not visible but smelling slightly of aniseed, on the skirt. It would have to be dry-cleaned, or maybe she would take a leaf out of Monica Lewinsky's book and keep it stained, as a souvenir.

Sitting opposite her at Jalabert's, Josh had plenty of time to study Pandora. The last time they had met he had been under the impression she was at least fifteen years younger than her age, and Yasmin's bombshell that she was in fact eligible for her old-age pension had caused him a few qualms. But as Yasmin had pointed out, ageism was just so tabloid, and he tried to feel like a super-cool pioneer of sex between the generations. It was just a pity that to a curious stranger they probably looked more like mother and son, or even worse, client and escort.

She definitely looked no older than fifty, he decided. Her face was almost flawless, and though she might indeed be lifted and Botoxed, as Yasmin had described her, she was obviously blessed with good skin in the first place. Her hair was doubtless dyed, but so what? He had known quite a few women who coloured their hair red for effect, not to hide any grey. Her hands were white and free of the brown spots he associated with the elderly, and her figure – though it was too thin, that was for sure – was once again proudly on display, her bra-less tits high and firm in her halter-neck black dress.

He also had to admit that apart from her looks she was decidedly amusing, albeit in a bitchy way. Not a particularly nice person, he decided, but fun. She knew everybody on the London scene and regaled him with discreet and not-so-discreet anecdotes about many people in the fashion world. She liked to talk and to amuse, which was fine by him because he certainly couldn't give out much information about his own professional field without blowing his cover.

'How did you get to run your own magazine?' he asked idly as they put down their knives and forks after a most satisfactory main course – ravioli of lobster topped with caviar for her, and braised guinea fowl with pickled lemons and olives for him.

'Bloody hard work and a lot of conniving,' she said bluntly, smiling her catlike smile. 'I started off as a secretary on a weekly women's magazine and worked really hard at it, but I just couldn't seem to get promoted on to the editorial side. After a couple of years the penny dropped – the girls who did get moved on to the fun bits of the job rather than the routine ones were the ones who were basically not very good at coping with the routine. I thought by slaving away and being the perfect secretary I'd end up moving on, but I was too valuable. So I got a secretarial job at another, younger and trendier magazine, and made a point of screwing up every so often while also coming up with bright ideas for features. Within six months I was an editorial assistant.

'I kept plaguing the fashion editor with ideas and dressed ultra stylishly until I became her assistant. Once in I networked like mad and made a point of being incredibly nice to everyone in the business thinking I'd need to move yet again to get to be fashion editor myself. That was hard because to be perfectly honest, Josh, I'm not a naturally nice person, believe it or not.'

He merely smiled and nodded. The little gems of gossip she had already confided in him had made that obvious.

'Anyway, I got an unexpected break. The fashion editor went sick and was signed off for three months. I'm afraid to say that there was no reason at all why she shouldn't have made a full recovery and come back to carry on with the job, but that was no use to me. I convinced the editor she wasn't going to be fit enough to cope when she came back.' She gave him a sidelong glance. 'The editor was a man, so you can guess how I managed to persuade him.'

'The casting-couch touch, I suppose?' Josh was really quite shocked.

'Naturally. So there I was, the youngest fashion editor in the country at the time. But you know, once you've attained your goal, you just set yourself another one.'

'Not all of us are that ambitious,' he demurred.

She smiled dismissively. 'I haven't got any time for people who aren't.'

'I'm not.' He regarded her steadily and her eyes softened into a sexual sparkle.

'I should have said, except as a sexual playmate.'

'Playmate of the month?' he enquired ironically.

Pandora laughed throatily. 'You might last longer than that, if you want to. Anyway, to cut a long story short I met a rather rich playmate during my fashion editor days. He had more money than he knew what to do with, so he decided – with just a little encouragement from me – that he'd start a magazine.'

'*Black Box*, I presume.'

'Yes. It was going to be Pandora's Box, of course, but I told him I might not be the editor for ever. There were lots of plane crashes at the time and black boxes were always being looked for. They held the key to what was happening, just like my magazine did – and still does.'

'Good name,' said Josh gravely. 'So it's still owned by this rich guy?'

He was finally getting to the heart of the matter, which meant of course that fate intervened so that the conversation took a completely different turn. The chef-proprietor, Maurice Jalabert, appeared at their table with effusive greetings for Pandora.

'Darling Maurice, it was just too divine,' she gushed after their protracted air kisses. 'The ravioli were absolutely fantastic. Your pasta is to die for.'

'Thank you, Pandora. I hope you got my little note after your very kind review last month?'

'Yes, I did indeed, my dear, and it was greatly appreciated. I'm so pleased it's going well.'

Josh was amused that she didn't bother to introduce him, a little reminder that his role was merely that of playmate of the month. Not that he cared. The chef politely asked him if his meal had also been to his liking, which he confirmed.

'Now you must allow me to give you a little trio of

desserts,' the chef said graciously, and Josh just as graciously accepted. The bill was going to be an arm and a leg as it was, and unlike a regular spy he didn't have an expense account.

Unfortunately the conversation stayed on food and restaurants after that, with Pandora commenting acerbically on many of the topical celebrity chefs. Josh realised it would be not just gauche but also rather pointed to draw the conversation back to *Black Box* and the state of play of its owners, so went with the flow for the time being. It could do for pillow talk; there was certainly no doubt that they would be hitting the metaphorical sack, if not the pillow, and once he'd managed to make Pandora relaxed and mellow, who knows what she might let slip.

'A lovely meal. I'm so glad you chose Jalabert's – what made you? You obviously hadn't been there before. Was it the review in *Black Box*?'

'No, a friend recommended it,' Josh replied, smiling inwardly at what Pandora would say if he told her that the friend was Yasmin. 'I don't always take restaurant recommendations seriously, but she's a woman of impeccable taste.'

'A lover?'

Pandora flashed him a lascivious glance.

'Sometimes. Why?'

'Well, I happen to like hearing about other people's experiences. I know last time we had a functional fuck, but assuming you're not rushing off too quickly after you take me home, we'll have a little time. You can tell me a story or two, or if you haven't got any I've got quite a library – you could read to me.'

The taxi jerked to a halt as it failed to get through the traffic lights before they turned red, and Josh seized the opportunity the lack of motion afforded to put a hand on Pandora's black-silk-clad knee.

'I don't know which I prefer. Maybe I could tell you a little tale of my own. Do you want me to start now?'

'No,' she said emphatically, opening her thighs slightly to allow his hand to slide up her leg. 'Sex in cabs reminds me of Amelia. Who, by the way, is out, so you won't have to confront her.'

'Good,' said Josh sincerely. He wondered if he had the nerve to relate to Pandora his last sexual experience with Amelia, casting someone else in her role. He certainly couldn't ascribe his first time with her niece to anyone else, at least not unless he pretended to make a habit of chasing after female violinists.

He hadn't taken a great deal of notice of Pandora telling him she had a library of erotica – after all, it wasn't so unusual. It was all the more surprising then when he entered her bedroom.

Like many rooms, it was hung with pictures, but they were quite unlike the tasteful botanical prints or soothing watercolours that usually appeared in bedrooms. They were all framed photographs, and, although they ranged from the subtle to the outrageously graphic, they were all erotic.

'My God.' Josh's eyes moved from one picture to the next. A black and white photo of a dark girl being felt up by an unshaven macho man while a laughing friend looked on could have been taken in a barrio of Mexico City, while a series of coloured prints of a blonde girl strapped to a table and being massaged, stroked and penetrated by another woman in a nurse's uniform could have come from anywhere. Some of the pictures were straightforward poses by women in conventional erotic dress such as suspenders and corsets, while some were of pierced and erect penises. The variety – and the quality of the prints – was amazing.

'This is just incredible,' he said, absorbed in the pictures. 'How have you managed to amass such a collection?'

Pandora laughed. 'Being a magazine editor means that pictures come through the post every day – not all suitable, of course, but from the few that are I've managed to build up enough contacts among photographers to keep them coming. This turned up today, for example.'

She pulled a colour photo from a folder on her desk and handed it to Josh. He had to stifle an exclamation, hoping to God he hadn't betrayed himself. It was a woman lying submissively and ashamedly while a man touched her up while talking to friends who were looking on lewdly and enviously. And the woman was Yasmin.

'That's pretty good,' he observed as blandly as he could.

'Yes. They're from a photographer from a rival magazine – he wants to move to *Black Box*.'

'Wow. Surely that's not the sort of thing you'll be featuring in the magazine?'

Pandora laughed shortly. 'No way. He's apparently heard of my little collection from someone else in the know, and thought I might be influenced by these. He used to work in the porno photo business in Thailand years ago, and he sent me these as a taster. I must say I wouldn't mind seeing his photos of Thai girls together.'

Josh desperately wanted to see the other pictures in the folder, which were presumably of the session Yasmin had briefly described to him, but was as equally afraid of arousing Pandora's suspicions as he was keen to arouse himself by seeing the luscious Yasmin being screwed by another man.

'This is fantastic.' His eyes alighted on the bookshelf. 'And this is your library?'

He'd heard of many of the titles, which spanned the generations of erotica from the *Kama Sutra* through *Moll Flanders* to *The Well of Loneliness*, up to the twentieth century with Anaïs Nin and *The Story of O*, plus several score of other modern novels encompassing every aspect of sex, from S&M to bondage to gay and lesbian, even encompassing mainstream male porno.

Pandora was stripping off for him, sexily but briskly. She wore nothing under her dress but stockings and suspenders.

'Always?' he asked, indicating them.

'Oh, yes,' she replied flirtatiously. 'Always stockings, and always black.'

The thought came unbidden into his mind that the black stockings probably had a use other than arousal, in that they might be covering up a sixty-two-year-old's varicose veins, but he vehemently pushed it to the back of his mind. After all, he was going to perform and perform well, and reminding himself of her age wasn't going to help in the slightest.

Although she had no reason to hide her breasts she opened a drawer and pulled out a black silk camisole and put it on. One of the thin straps immediately fell off her shoulder, and she left the ribbon at the low neckline unfastened so that most of her breasts could be seen. Josh realised that it was true that there was nothing quite as seductive as a little clothing, rather than total nudity. Age just didn't come into it. She was lovely, and he was ready for her.

'Come on,' she said huskily as she snapped light switches so that a rosy glow was cast over the red velvet of the bedspread and a choice few of the pictures were highlighted.

He didn't need any further invitation. Quickly shedding his clothes he took her in his arms and kissed the sweetness of her mouth which was redolent of a mixture of the almond, peach and raspberry flavours of their puddings, plus the brandy they had taken with their coffee. Her body, too, had a sensual perfume which he remembered from their last encounter. He was already hard from looking at the erotic photographs and pressed his cock against her to show his excitement.

From her request for stories he knew exactly what she wanted, and he picked her up in his arms and put her in the centre of the bed. Under the warm light she looked younger and more beautiful than ever, and although he was only in her bed for dubious intelligence gathering he knew he would enjoy the experience and, more importantly, he would make sure she would enjoy it too.

He kissed her again, then moved his mouth down to her breasts, tantalisingly half revealed by the camisole, and then down her body to the sweet spot of her clit. His finger rubbed at her sex lightly and curiously, to gauge how wet she was, and found out that she had started to get excited herself. He lapped gently at her hardening bud for a few seconds, but it was mainly to give it plenty of lubrication. He knew she didn't want his mouth engaged on her body, but rather put to use in exciting her mind.

Lying on his side he propped his head on one arm while the other stroked softly along her sex, and started on his story.

'I started off working as a journalist on a local newspaper, which didn't suit me at all. Golden weddings, 100th birthday celebrations, local school fund-raising activities – it just wasn't me. I wanted to be a proper writer, but the novel in the desk drawer wasn't going anywhere while I was working full time. I saved up and packed in my job and went off to live on a Greek island to write.

'Every Greek island has an expatriate community and this one was no exception. Artists, writers, musicians, bar owners – I'd imagined living like a hermit with no one to talk to, seeing as I hadn't bothered to learn Greek, but I had as full a social life as I'd had in Oxford.

'One of the guys I got particularly friendly with was a musician. He was from the States and was working on his own songs. The lyrics were beautiful, more like poetry than songs, though the music was slightly ethereal. I guess he was influenced by Leonard Cohen, though he didn't have his simplicity of musical form, which meant that he basically wasn't going to hit the dizzy heights. So what – he was from a wealthy family, so money was no object.

'He lived alone in what I assumed was a monastic state until one night when he invited me round for a drink – we all drank loads of Greek brandy, because as you probably know it's dirt cheap. There was a girl there, who I recognised from one of the village shops.

'She was gorgeous, skin like toasted almonds, wild black curls cascading down her back and eyes the colour of wild violets. Her face could have been perfect if it hadn't been for a slightly high bridge to her nose. Her voice had a slight huskiness which sounded extremely sexy, though what she said was totally unintelligible – she spoke no English at all.'

Josh was pleased with his substitution of Yasmin for the Arianna of his memory, and wondered if Pandora would think he was inspired by the picture she had showed him.

'I wondered why on earth Lance bothered with her as they had no conversation, until I found out during the course of the evening that he had taught her a few words of English. The first was "strip".

'She laughed as she removed her clothes, her eyes flashing with delight at our attention. The odd thing was that she did it as though she'd been trained by an expert, teasing us with little peeks at her breasts and arse before finally removing her clothes.

'Lance was pleased with my reaction – well, my eyes were out on stalks. I was young and still fairly naïve, my sexual experience being limited to quickies with girls from school and one rather boring relationship with another reporter. I'd only seen one stripper in my life and she'd been a bored brassy blonde, not a truly gorgeous nineteen-year-old.'

Too late he realised he had borrowed Amelia's age as well as Yasmin's looks, but Pandora didn't seem to notice, only nodding as though impatient. Josh realised he had better get on with the action. His finger continued to stroke her, and now her sex was weeping copiously.

'The next word he said was "suck" and pointed to me. She came up and knelt in front of me, opened my flies, got my dick out and gave it the most amazing blow job. I'd say the best one I'd had in my life, but I'd only had a couple before and they were miserable compared to her; it was as though she was really making love to my cock. I tried not to come, but I couldn't help it – she obviously wasn't going to stop until she was told. I came in her mouth and she swallowed it as though she liked it, which was certainly a first for me.

'I was still groaning and her mouth was still sucking gently on the head of my cock when Lance said "down". I was shocked at first – it was as though he was ordering a dog, and in fact she immediately dropped her hands to the floor and pushed her arse in the air ready to be fucked doggy-fashion, which Lance started to do. As he was pumping into her, he talked to me about her.

'She loved it, he said, and she loved every new trick he taught her. To prove it he said, mid-stroke, "sit", and she promptly turned round and sat on him, bouncing up and down energetically.

'Then Lance told me he'd been screwing her for about six months, just like this, but he had never caressed her in any way. That really shocked me – but God, it turned me on. I guess it's every man's dream, just having a woman to attend to his every need without having to worry if it's all right for her. Just a beautiful female living doll, one who makes no demands, one who can't make any because she can't even communicate.'

Pandora moaned softly, and Josh realised he'd guessed correctly just what she'd like. Most powerful women had that fantasy, of being submissive and used, although they wouldn't dream of actually living like it.

'Halfway through telling me he interjected "back", and Arianna immediately turned on to her back and obligingly lifted her legs. He turned to me and laughed, and again I felt it was awful because he was laughing at her, made worse by the fact that she didn't know it. In fact she laughed back at him as he pushed inside her again.

'Then he told me he'd asked me over that night

because he'd decided it was time to teach her about orgasm. He pulled out of her at that point and ordered her to "stay". She just lay there smiling, and he opened her legs and pushed his fingers inside her.

'Then with the wetness of her sex on his fingers he started stroking her clit, and for the first time she cried out with pleasure. God knows I would have thought she would have felt pleasure from pressure on her clit before, but presumably she just didn't connect sex with pleasure for women.

'He continued to touch her and she started moaning more urgently. Then he said, "come". She didn't, but he said it again and again. Then he put her own fingers on her clit and rubbed them over her bud while he kept saying "come".

'Lance lay down on the floor and said "sit" again. Arianna sat on him and he then added "come". She looked puzzled and looked to him for approval before touching herself again, and he shook his head, which in Greece means yes. So as she moved up and down on him she continued to finger herself and moan louder in pleasure, and just when he gauged she was about to climax Lance said "come!" really urgently – and she did.'

Pandora's moans had increased in volume and he wondered how ready she was to come, but he reckoned she wanted more storytelling.

'Lance came at the same time, quite vociferously too. When he had finished groaning, he started laughing.

'"Look, the silly bitch is still going!" he said. "Christ, Arianna, don't tell me you're still coming!"

'She just laughed, and he said "finish" – she understood that one too, and stopped straight away, but she was still panting and moaning and I wondered if she'd come and stopped but just obediently kept rubbing herself, or whether she'd managed to make her orgasm last that long. Whatever, I couldn't ask her and she couldn't tell me.

'We had a few drinks and Lance told me to keep quiet about her role in his life. As far as her family knew she went over to his house once a week to do housework. He paid them about fifty pence a week for her services. She must have been the cheapest whore in Greece, especially as I guessed I wasn't the first visitor he'd invited over to share her charms.

'She just watched us while we drank, and then Lance said "come", and she got down on the floor and started playing with herself again. God, I felt like a complete shit but I was so turned on by her. I asked Lance if I could screw her and he just asked me how I wanted her. I said from behind and he called out "down" and I entered her. But I wanted to make her come, so I started fingering her while I fucked her, and when I felt like I was about to shoot my load I said "come" and right on cue she came.'

From the rising and falling of her breasts and the way she was moving her sex Josh guessed that Pandora too was ready.

'Come,' he said commandingly, putting her in Arianna's place. He increased the pressure on her and moved his hand faster. 'Come, bitch. Come, you fucking bitch.'

'Christ!' moaned Pandora, now bucking wildly against his hand. 'Oh Christ, you bastard, you shit, you – oh, God help me!'

Josh smiled to himself as he pulled on the rubber he'd left on the pillow, and murmured 'back' as he pushed his distended cock into her extremely wet and still-pulsating pussy. Like the Josh and Lance in the somewhat embroidered story, he took his own pleasure without needing to worry about hers, and came more quickly than he had intended, having turned himself on as well.

'OK?' he asked, kissing her softly as he slowly subsided, still inside her.

Pandora opened her eyes and smiled hazily. 'Yes, very good. True? No, don't tell me, it's not important.'

'Quite,' agreed Josh, breaking away from her and lying on his side, face to face. 'As long as we both enjoyed it. And I certainly did.'

'Me too,' she said simply.

The post-coital Pandora seemed a different person from the cynical, wittily acerbic bitch who had entertained him at dinner. Now she seemed small and vulnerable. But then again, she was a complex person. He'd never met anyone else who blatantly decked their bedroom out with erotic images and literature, at least not anyone who wasn't a professional.

'Do you mind me asking – how did you get the taste for this?' He indicated the pictures and the bookshelf.

Pandora laughed. 'Well, that's a story in itself. I used to have a close relationship with a guy who was very rich and very busy, and he hadn't really bothered much with relationships for a long time, preferring instead to use hookers when he wanted sex. Despite his wealth it wasn't always convenient to even fit in a prostitute, so he started collecting pornographic literature and pictures.

'When I met him he told me he took it upon himself to show me the most shocking pictures he had and told me to imagine myself in the picture. Now, I'd had lots of sex but most of it was fairly straightforward. I'd certainly never had sex with a woman, and thought the idea repugnant. That was a challenge to him, and he kept showing me pictures of women together and telling me I was one of them and going into detail of what the other woman was doing to me. Soon I started to get really turned on by his voice telling me about it. He'd show me pictures of three men with a woman, each with his penis in a different orifice, and make up a scenario where I was that woman.

'I got hooked on his voice talking to me. He would sometimes call me when I was in the office and tell me one of his stories, and when he was near the end he would tell me to touch myself and tell him when I came, which always amused him because I was so turned on by his stories that it took me no time at all to come. I almost started wondering if I could come without a touch, it excited me so much.

'We stopped having sex after a few years because he got married, though that was purely for business reasons: his wife was the widow of his former business partner and it was the only way he could get total control of their partnership. As I said, he liked sex to be convenient, so of course it was more convenient to transfer his sexual relationship to his wife and abandon me.

'I was busy too, and so I decided that if he wasn't there to talk to me I'd have to talk to myself, and that's when I started to build my collection. Of course I soon had other lovers, but I couldn't lose the taste for erotica.'

She smiled at him, almost mischievously. 'And I'll tell you something, too. They say a woman loses her desire as she gets older, but thanks to all this I've never for a moment not felt like sex. And of course just like my former lover, if I can't be bothered with a man, I can just do it myself.'

Josh felt almost touched by her admission that she was getting older, but realised she had unwittingly paved the way back into the conversation that had been interrupted in the restaurant.

'This guy – was he the one you were telling me about, the one who started the magazine?' he asked.

'Well remembered – you should be a detective,' she said lightly, causing a shiver to go through him.

'Yes, that was Quentin. He wasn't purely a hard businessman – he didn't expect it to make any money, but did it as a favour to me. Although it turned out to be a good investment after all.'

'So he's still the owner?' asked Josh, trying to sound only casually interested.

'He still owns half. He gave the other half to me when we started making money.'

'Nice one,' said Josh. 'So his new wife didn't mind about his continuing relationship with you, even though it was only a business one?'

Pandora laughed. 'I doubt she knows anything about it. She probably doesn't even know he has any interest in *Black Box* at all. He's got so many interests he's not even sure himself what they are any more – his investment manager looks after all that.'

'So, you both do well out of it.'

'Yes. Although we may do even better soon – I'm in talks with a big American media multinational about a takeover.'

'Ah!' That's wrong, thought Josh. His exclamation sounded more like a eureka-type 'ah' than a politely interested, oh-you-don't-say-type 'ah'.

'That must be exciting,' he said hastily. 'But if you're taken over you'll lose your half of the business – and presumably your control over it.'

'God, no. That is definitely not on the cards,' she said dismissively. 'They're only getting Quentin's share and half of mine, and a watertight contract that gives me total international editorial control.'

'I'm sorry, I didn't even know you were international,' said Josh apologetically, though at the same time pretty sure that *Black Box* was a uniquely British publication.

'We're not – yet. That's part of the deal – they want to launch an American edition, which suits me just fine.'

'So you'll be going to the States?' Josh felt that finally he was getting somewhere.

'No way, I couldn't live in New York.' She yawned. 'God, I'm tired. Do you want to stay, or are you going home?'

He couldn't give up this near to solving the riddle, even though it might look like he was being overly persistent.

'Not sure – so, how near are you to finalising this takeover?'

'Almost there. We've had a few meetings this week. There's just one thing that I haven't broached yet – that's getting the person New Order want to edit the US edition. But I've got irons in the fire as far as that's concerned, and if it all works out it'll not only close this deal but ensure there's not much competition in the UK either.'

She yawned again. 'That's enough talking for tonight. Now make your mind up, but I warn you, there won't be a replay. I want my sleep and I hate sex in the morning.'

'In that case I'll go,' said Josh, now desperate to get out and call Yasmin with the news. 'If that doesn't make me sound too single-minded.'

Pandora gave a tinkling laugh. 'We're both in this for one reason only, aren't we?' she said philosophically.

No, we're not, said Josh to himself as he dressed. Sorry, Pandora, but you've been had. I got two things out of tonight, and I'm afraid the sex was the least important.

She wished him goodnight sleepily as he left. He hoped she was right about Amelia being out, feeling almost superstitiously that if he bumped into her then everything would somehow go disastrously wrong. His fears were unfounded, however, and he let himself out of the house, breathing a sigh of relief. He waited, though, till he was at the end of the road before leaping in the air and shouting 'Yes!'

All right, he hadn't got her to admit to plotting to get U to take the job in New York, but it was pretty obvious that she'd attempted to undermine his marriage and, in case that hadn't worked, to wreck Yasmin's job so that if he stayed with her she'd have no regrets about leaving England either. He couldn't wait to tell her.

9

Yasmin sat cross-legged on the divan in the meditation room gazing out at Clapham Common, its grass fresh and green after an early shower that had washed the sky to the palest blue. Small white clouds scudded across the sky, just as a battery of thoughts were hurtling across her mind.

She was tired. After what was after all a good evening, apart from the moments when U's infidelity was mentioned, they had gone to bed early, as friends. However, Yasmin was woken up just an hour later when a triumphant Josh called her to tell her that he'd managed to find out what was really going on.

Strangely enough the news wasn't that surprising. Obviously some high-level plotting was at work, and it was almost with relief that she found out exactly what she was up against. In an ideal world she would have thanked Josh briefly, gone back to sleep and had the full details from him the next morning, but he insisted on giving her a blow by blow account of the evening, from what they'd had to eat through to Pandora's predilection for the erotic and finally on to her soporific 'confession'. The only detail he spared her was the actual sex, saying that he'd rather tell her in person – not that she was surprised by that.

It was almost one when she got off the phone and back to bed, only to have another call at three. Euan, totally off his face, in some club with Cody, with the revelation that Pandora had put Amelia up to seducing

U, and that her magazine was being taken over. Despite her tiredness Yasmin tried to break it gently to him that Josh had beaten him to the winning post with an even fuller account of the plot against her, but he was too far gone to even listen. He was full of remorse for not calling sooner, but said Amelia got completely rat-arsed and had to be sent home, and he and Cody had gone out to celebrate and forgot to call her.

After that it took ages for her to get back to sleep, finally dozing off just before U rose as usual at six to meditate for an hour before going out for his morning walk on the common. As he went out, she decided she might as well get up and think things through properly rather than lie in bed and let the thoughts swirl round her mind randomly.

She felt better after a shower and so she dressed in her white silk meditation pyjamas and went up to the meditation room. Chanting helped settle her mind a little, and she sat for another few minutes concentrating on her breath before allowing her brain to sift through the myriad thoughts, reactions and ideas that were inevitably occupying it.

U had to be told what was going on, but it would be so easy to make a complete hash of it. Unless she told him in front of Pandora, who would be unable to deny the conspiracy, it was only too likely that he would find the whole thing ludicrous and accuse her of paranoid invention. Obviously time would prove her right, but she didn't want an ugly scene with him. That was not part of the plan at all.

She would take him to Jalabert's; that was where it had all begun, at least as far as she was concerned, and that was hopefully where it would all end. As to how they were going to fight Pandora, she was going to sit there for another half hour and wait for the right solution to drift into her mind.

U arrived at the office in a better mood than he had for some time. The last two weeks had been hell, and he knew it was his fault. His stupid Aryan rectitude had made him confess his affair to Yasmin, and it had caused unhappiness. However, they had made tentative moves towards a reconciliation the night before and during his morning walk he felt a new hope inside him, or maybe it was just in the air, literally and psychically. It had rained at dawn and the air seemed washed clean, and that freshness and purity communicated itself to U as well. On his return Yasmin had suggested dinner at Jalabert's to have a proper talk on neutral ground, and he was even more encouraged that she was happy to return to the place where it had, as far as she was concerned, all started.

'A friend of mine went there the other night, and apparently his date said the lobster ravioli was absolutely to die for,' she told him. 'Although after lobster last night –'

'You can never have too much lobster,' said U.

'Indeed,' said Yasmin gravely. 'That's how I feel at the moment; in fact I feel in rather a shellfish mood.'

He had smiled weakly at her joke – the English sense of humour still sometimes eluded him even after all these years. Anyway, she had cracked a joke and made a dinner date, and that was good enough for him.

Until Briony brought the post in.

A large brown cardboard envelope, the type that photographs are sent in, was the last thing he opened. It was addressed to him and marked 'Personal', though there was nothing personal about the white printed address label. He guessed it was yet another photographer trying to get a job. Too bad, he thought good humouredly as he slit the envelope open with his onyx paper knife. Stevenson's the best in the business, and he's already here.

Except that the photographs were obviously taken by his own chief photographer. The angles were distinctive, and even more so was one of the participants – Kip. And it was of course only the other day that U had instructed Stevenson to take a series of erotic photographs. 'G-Spot Tornado' had been suggested, and if he wasn't mistaken the vibrator being used on the woman was one he'd seen on a TV programme about the best way to reach the G-spot. All of which would have been fine, if the woman hadn't been Yasmin.

He leafed through the photos. What on earth was she doing, posing like this? It wasn't erotic, it was downright pornographic. Stevenson knew only too well that the erect penis couldn't be legally featured in a UK magazine. But how the hell, and why, had he got his editor's wife to pose for him like this?

The final pictures were of a slightly different scene. Two men watched, lascivious and laughing, and Kip explored Yasmin, blatantly exposing her sex to the camera, while she looked embarrassed.

It was too much. That the photographer should have put his wife in that position was just inexcusable. He might be the best, but he'd have to go.

'Just two things, Stevenson,' said U, trying to appear composed. 'First, why did you send me these –' he flicked the photographs across the desk contemptuously '– and why and by what means did you get my wife to act as your model?'

A faint look of surprise came over Stevenson's aristocratic face, though he soon returned it to his usual disdainful expression.

'Easy to answer, U,' he replied urbanely. 'First, I didn't send them to you. Secondly, your wife overheard Kip and I discussing the non-appearance of our model and volunteered to step in.'

'Don't fuck with me,' said U calmly. 'If you didn't send them, who did? Kip? Yasmin?'

The photographer gave a wintry smile. 'No, I expect it was Pandora Fairchild. I sent them to her – I know she has a taste for the erotic. I must admit I didn't expect her to send them to you – I rather thought she would appreciate them herself.'

U's controlled facade was beginning to fray at the edges. 'And you seriously expect me to believe that Yasmin knew what she was letting herself in for?'

'You can ask Briony if you don't believe me,' said Stevenson uninterestedly. 'It was when Yasmin came to pick you up for your anniversary dinner and you weren't here. You may remember you'd left a couple of messages that she decided meant cancellation, and Briony said you'd gone off to see your mistress; I mean, Briony said you'd gone to wherever it is she lives. We showed her the G-spot vibrator before she even mentioned wanting to volunteer.'

'Like I believe you,' jeered U. 'Look at her face in this picture. She's overwhelmed with embarrassment. You must have forced her.'

'On the contrary,' replied the photographer. 'She actually suggested this scenario. Apparently it's based on a story by Anaïs Nin – I don't know it myself, but Yasmin told us how to act it out.'

That was a blow. U knew the story only too well.

Pandora had introduced him to the explicitly erotic short stories, and he had read them to Yasmin himself.

'And in fact if you study her face in the subsequent pictures, she's rather overwhelmed with joy,' added Stevenson tartly. 'Now, is that all?'

'No, it's fucking well not,' said U furiously. 'I don't care how Yasmin came to be in these pictures, you had no right sending them to Pandora Fairchild, or anyone else.'

'Why on earth not?' asked Stevenson, his tone astonished. 'After all, we live in a new age of sexuality – don't we? The whole business of taking erotic photographs was your idea. I really don't see what difference it makes if it's your wife or my friend who acts out the part.'

'Like hell you don't,' shouted U. 'You can just get out of here. You're finished, Stevenson. And if I have anything to do with it, you won't be working in the magazine business again.'

The photographer laughed brusquely. 'Wrong again, U. Pandora called me the minute she got these pictures and offered me a job. Which I have to say I was most delighted to accept.'

He rose languidly. 'I'm very sorry this has had to happen, because this was where I wanted to work, and you were the person I wanted to work for. But if I can speak bluntly, and as you've just fired me and/or I've resigned I believe I might as well, quite honestly I have to say that you've lost it. This sex business will be a complete embarrassment to anyone associated with *Slice*, which is why I decided I had to leave. *Slice*, frankly, is toast.'

U was still telling him to fuck off as the photographer left the office.

God, what have I done? he thought, looking at the photographs again, leafing through them compulsively. Was Stevenson right? If he really believed in the new sexuality, what was the problem with Yasmin being plastered all over the magazine with strange men's hands on her, and obviously enjoying a strange cock inside her?

He had no choice but to believe Stevenson's account of the way in which Yasmin had stepped in as his model. For one thing, he knew that the photographer was a man of scrupulous honesty, and for another there was no way he would have asserted that Briony could be called upon as a witness if it were untrue. U wasn't going to embarrass himself further by getting Briony to admit it. Yasmin was wearing the outfit she'd bought for their anniversary dinner, the one she had stayed out all night in when he had postponed their date.

But if Briony knew, how many other people in the *Slice* office were in on it? Maybe the entire staff were laughing at him behind his back?

It was impossible. For the first time he fully regretted ever getting involved with Amelia. She had convinced him totally about her sexual philosophy, but it seemed as though he was the only one to be seduced by it, rather than by her. He had to admit that none of the magazine's staff had been keen on it and, as Stevenson said, he himself appeared to have reservations about it when it involved his wife.

U had always scorned hypocrisy, and now it appeared he was in fact practising it. Not only was he not really behind the new sex, but now it appeared that Amelia wasn't either.

Had he really lost it? Would the new sex issue make him a laughing stock of the entire business, the entire country, never mind already being openly cuckolded before his staff?

He steepled his hands in front of his face and gazed unseeingly at Yasmin flaunting herself. It was also a mystery as to why Pandora had sent him the pictures. Surely not just to force his hand in the choice between Yasmin and Amelia? He could hardly believe that they'd had sex just the other night – she must have sent the photographs the next day. What was she up to?

The day had started so well and was now in tatters. His optimism about the evening ahead also left him. In a black mood of despair he continued to sit at his desk with his wife's body exposed in front of him. He didn't have the energy to do anything, or even think about anything. If he could be so wrong about the next big thing, had he really lost it completely? In which case his career was over – and if his career was over, his life was also over.

Outside the door the office hummed and ticked over as usual, but U stayed closeted inside, ignoring phone calls and messages. He didn't have a clue as to what his next move must be, except that he had to be honest with Yasmin that evening. Which also had to include his interlude with Pandora. It wasn't just his career that was on the line.

'Yasmin, you don't seem to be actually doing very much work on this script,' said Bernie, rather nervously, she noted.

'I'm sorry, Bernie. I have to tell you, well I know that Milo at least knows this, but I've had marital problems. However, it's all being resolved now.'

'Too late in my view, darling,' snorted Milo. 'I've asked for your contract to be rescinded. You've technically broken it by not producing the next episode, anyway.'

'Excuse me, but I believe I just handed over the next episode,' interrupted Josh indignantly. 'We're working as a team, remember? Yasmin worked on that too.'

'I don't think she really gave sufficient input,' said Milo, smiling shark-like. 'You're not working for the Civil Service, dear. You can't just take a few days off and not put out when you've got a little personal trauma.'

'I see,' said Yasmin, nodding rather vaguely. 'So you're rescinding my contract – I presume there has to be a pay-off?'

'I haven't got the faintest idea,' snapped Milo. 'Why don't you give contracts a call?'

'Why don't you go fuck yourself?' returned Yasmin, smiling equably. 'You're a complete arsehole, Milo. I've always thought so and now I've got proof, which you'll doubtless hear about in the fullness of time.'

'Can't we all calm down?' said Bernie weakly. 'Look, let's not have any talk about breaking contracts. Let's just get on with the next episode, shall we?'

'Sorry, Bernie, you're overruled,' said Milo rudely. 'I'm the producer here and I say she goes.'

'Actually, you might as well say that I go too,' suggested Josh.

Milo laughed contemptuously. 'Sorry, dear, but you have a contract too. I'm afraid you stay.'

Josh stood and walked towards the producer and stood over him. 'I'm afraid I go, Milo. As Yasmin said, we have proof of your behaviour. Not to mention your meeting with Pandora Fairchild and Danny Di-Geronimo. Very silly, really, because if it all comes out New Order will distance themselves both from you and from On the Edge, so you'll probably end up on the scrapheap and *49 Madison Avenue* will be the soap that never was. So think on, lad, as we say up north. And goodbye.'

They made a reasonably dignified exit from the conference room.

'I didn't know you were from up north,' said Yasmin with interest.

Josh snorted. 'Of course I'm not. Trust you to pick up on the most irrelevant piece of information. Did you see his face when I mentioned Pandora and Danny DiGeronimo?'

'Classic. Will he get the push?'

'I doubt it. After all, we're not going to really hit the headlines with this, are we?'

Yasmin laughed. 'Do you really think anyone would care? Anyway, sod them. I'm really pleased to be free of this gig. I've had it with soaps, Josh. I'm going into something else next.'

'Oh, really?' he asked with interest. 'What? Porn modelling?'

'Discount no possibility,' she said gravely. 'What about you?'

He sighed. 'I'm suppose I might get the odd episode of *EastEnders* again if I keep badgering them. But what the hell. Maybe I'll see if I can get into the children's series, even though it's a bit late. Still, worth a try.'

Yasmin pressed his hand. 'You didn't have to quit because of me, you know.'

'Bollocks,' he said roundly. 'There's no way I could carry on kowtowing to Milo after all that I found out. Especially not after he sacked you.'

'Talking of finding things out, I almost forgot. What's the next stage of the story?'

'You should care! But actually, it's rather relevant, though I don't want you getting the creeps about it again. The hotel's being taken over by an American multinational.'

'Are you kidding me?'

'I'm afraid not. And they want Johnny to move to New York, which is why Imelda's been put on the spot to seduce him away from wife and business.'

Yasmin stopped walking and looked gravely at Josh. 'Seriously, are you kidding?'

Josh laughed. 'Does it matter?'

She didn't know, and anyway didn't have a chance to find out at that moment because Josh had stopped at Sandy's desk to write a note.

'Your new belle?' asked Yasmin acidly.

'Why, are you jealous?'

She shook her head, laughing. 'How can I be? Thanks to me you've had Amelia and Pandora, both twice – a real score draw. Anyway, I'm going to be concentrating on my marriage from now on.'

'Really?' Josh raised an eyebrow. 'Haven't you forgotten you promised me that whatever I did with Pandora I could do with you?'

Yasmin pouted at him. 'I thought you'd never ask. Where exactly is it you live?'

'Exactly ten minutes' cab ride from here,' he said with a grin, as they headed down the stairs. 'Shall I start now?'

'Pandora may be a nasty, ambitious, scheming bitch, but she's definitely got taste,' sighed Yasmin contentedly as she swallowed the first mouthful of lobster ravioli.

U looked up startled. 'What, you mean me?'

She regarded him affectionately. 'Well, of course I mean you, that goes without saying. But I was really referring to the lobster ravioli.'

He had put down his fork, which was a pity as the slow-roasted belly of pork with Chinese spices and braised pak choi looked extremely succulent, and definitely as though it ought to be eaten hot.

'And Josh, of course,' added Yasmin.

Why was it, she wondered, that even having bagged the coolest, most stylish, intelligent and razor-sharp guy in the world, she couldn't help realising that like all men he was just a little boy at heart? Are women not to be spared any illusions about the opposite sex?

'Do close your mouth, U,' she said quietly. It was still hanging open in shock. 'I have a little story to tell you.'

Between exquisite mouthfuls of the flavoursome lobster and tender pasta, not to mention odd forkfuls of meltingly tender pork, which U seemed to have lost his appetite for, she told him everything.

'I'm sorry,' she added finally, as she scooped up a stray pearl of caviar on her finger and sucked every atom of flavour out of it. 'I'm afraid you really have been had.'

U was still looking shell-shocked.

'I'm sorry too,' he said after a long pause. 'I have to tell you something, too.'

He explained that he already knew about the photographs, thanks to Pandora's duplicity.

Yasmin could see he was struggling with himself and kept silent, waiting.

'And the final thing. I – I had sex with Pandora the other night.'

'Oh.'

The bastard. She had thought she had the whole royal flush in her hand but he produced this jack from up his sleeve.

'I really am sorry,' he repeated. 'Yasmin, I've been a fool. I realised when I saw your photos that Amelia's philosophy just doesn't work, and I'm afraid Stevenson's right when he said it would make the magazine a laughing stock.'

'Well, I'm glad that's sorted,' she said with relief. 'After all, you don't want to hand Pandora the magazine on a plate with disastrous circulation figures.'

'God, I was such a fool,' moaned U. 'Amelia – she's a sweet girl, but what did I think I was doing with her?'

Yasmin gave a wry smile. 'It was pretty hard to work out, seeing as you weren't even shagging her.'

U winced, as usual, at the 's' word.

'If it wasn't for you I could have blown it completely,' he said. 'Yasmin, I told you right from the start I loved you and didn't want anything to come between us, and I meant it.'

'Don't get carried away, U, just because you've had the courage to be honest with me,' she said waspishly. 'You can't just say you loved me all along, so everything's all right.'

'I didn't mean that,' he protested. 'Though I did.'

'OK,' she said, patting his hand affectionately. 'Now, Maurice Jalabert's walking this way. This is a test of how highly *Slice* is regarded, U. Pandora was offered a plateful of puds on the house – will you get the same treatment?'

She regretted her teasing comment at the look of alarm that crossed his face. Poor old U, he really was going through a crisis of confidence. Luckily the chef-proprietor fawned over him as much as he could have wanted, and indeed the delicious desserts were ceremoniously placed on the table, which Yasmin thought was just as well as U had seemed to have lost his appetite before.

'So, Bear, we have to decide what we're going to do,'

she said once they had finished the gorgeous mouthfuls.

'What do you mean?' he asked, bewildered.

'Why, I mean what we're going to do,' she repeated brightly. 'I guess you're going to have to decide what to do about Amelia –'

'Yasmin, I can't believe that you're saying that. Of course I'm going to finish with her.'

She held up her hands in protest at his indignation. 'OK, OK! I didn't want to presume, that's all. So, we have to decide how and when to confront Pandora. And that's not all we have to do.'

They ordered coffee, and Yasmin remembered that it was just after they had ordered coffee on their previous visit to the restaurant that U had made his dramatic announcement about his affair with Amelia.

Well, I won, she thought with satisfaction. But it wasn't over yet and, unlike the last time when she had been totally wrong-footed, this time she had the upper hand. U had to believe that they were a team again, but she was the one with the whip hand and she was determined that things were going to go her way.

When the coffee arrived Yasmin ordered an Armagnac for old times' sake and put her head close to U's and outlined her ideas. At first he argued with her, but slowly she persuaded him that she was right. It took three coffees before he finally agreed with her, but that didn't matter, because she wasn't planning on trying to get to sleep for a couple of hours, at least.

'You've got to tell me about Pandora first.'

U stopped mid-strip in front of the window. Yasmin always loved the thought that anyone wandering on the common at night might just be able to make out his athletic figure high up in the dimly lit meditation room, though conceded to herself it was probably pure fantasy.

'Why? It wasn't that thrilling.'

'I mean it, U. Did it start with a story?'

He laughed ruefully as he took off his trousers. 'Your friend Josh really did tell you everything, didn't he?'

'Oh yes,' she said softly, 'Everything. Which you are going to do as well. So?'

He sighed and took her in his arms. She was wearing a brief white satin bra, which barely covered her big brown nipples, and matching frilled knickers. U held her tight, then pulled the knickers off.

'I suppose it really started when she stripped her dress off and I buried my face in her breasts, but from there it continued the usual way. With Pandora, there always has to be a story. And if you know that, you know why I've taken your knickers off.'

She nodded breathlessly, suddenly wanting so much to know what story he had told her.

'She would have lain down on the bed like this,' said Yasmin, lowering herself to the divan. 'And you would have been beside her.'

'Just like this,' said U, resting next to her, his face towards her. 'I kissed her lips, and ran my hands over her breasts, but that wasn't what she wanted.'

'She wanted to feel your fingers on her – just like that,' moaned Yasmin, as U's index finger settled lightly on her clit. 'And then you had to start.'

'Yes,' said U with a sigh. 'And I'm afraid I chose the easiest option. I told her a story that had just a few minutes before been related to me.'

His finger moved up and down, scooping up the moisture that seemed to be welling out of her.

'What do you mean?' she asked with breathless anticipation.

'This seems tacky in the re-telling,' U said with a frown. 'But Pandora didn't think so – at least, it was obvious who I was telling her about, but she didn't care. Amelia had just told me about her encounter with Josh, where he had used her violin on her – I told Pandora.'

'Oh God.' Yasmin was partly appalled and partly strangely excited.

'I didn't name names, of course,' said U hastily. 'I started off by telling her that I'd heard a story about a man who took a female violinist home and made her play for him.'

'But she knew who you were talking about?' breathed Yasmin, fascinated.

'Of course. I waited to see if she would object, but she didn't, so I told her the next part, that while she was playing the man stripped her but ordered her to keep playing.'

'And did Pandora get excited?' asked Yasmin, whose own excitement was in no doubt.

'God, yes. I guess it was because she was picturing Josh doing it to her. The thing with her is that she just puts herself in the place of the woman in the story you're telling, so the fact that it was Amelia wasn't as sordid as it seems.'

'OK,' said Yasmin. 'Anyway, I know the story. He brought her off with her violin.'

'It was a bit more than that,' said U, amused. 'He actually ended up just holding the violin and making her rub herself on it – he didn't actually move it.'

'Yeah, yeah, yeah. What else did she tell you?' she asked, her excitement intensifying as U's fingers started to move fractionally faster.

'Well, she confessed that though she'd occasionally had moments of degradation while fucking strangers, that was the ultimate humiliation. And of course when I told Pandora, she put herself in the frame of being totally humiliated. That's what she wants, you see.'

'Yes. So that was enough to make her come?'

'It would have been,' said U, his fingers exploring more of her before returning to the smooth hard pearl that in their brief absence had already started to ache for their attention. 'But I stopped touching her. She was totally nonplussed – that's not in her usual script. Then I told her that she was that girl, and she had to do it for herself too.'

'What, you mean you got Amelia's violin?' asked Yasmin, rather hoping not. It was one thing having your own sex juices on your violin, but your aunt's – that was too gross.

'No, of course not. I made my hand into a fist and put it next to her sex and told her she knew what she had to do. I've never seen her so excited. She rubbed herself against my hand, but I saw her eyes flicker open and look at me. You see, she really likes the sound of someone talking to her as she comes.

'I told her to say please, and she did, so I carried on talking as she rubbed on my fist, telling her that she was obviously desperate and making her agree. Just as I reckoned she seemed about to come, I stopped talking and moved my fist, to just in front of my face, and told her that if she wanted to come she had to ask me if I would allow her to move so that she could carry on.'

His fingers still moved but his voice faltered. 'Yasmin, this makes me sound like a complete bastard, I know. But if you knew Pandora, you'd know that this is just what she likes.'

'It's OK,' she said impatiently, but her voice was

strange and remote to her and, she guessed, to him. 'Go on, I like it. What happened?'

U's fingers moved faster still. 'She begged me, she crawled to her knees and knelt with her sex just touching my fist, and said I could do anything I liked to her, she knew she deserved to be called all the humiliating names under the sun for her desperation, but please would I let her come.'

'And you did? What did you do to her?'

'I just told her that I was going to make a video of her begging me, saying I could do anything to her and then rubbing herself like a bitch on heat against my hand. She took that as permission and started rubbing herself off on my hand again, and I grabbed her wrists in my other hand and held them tight while she did it.'

'And what names did you call her? Did she come? Did she . . .'

Yasmin didn't even hear what names he called her as she exploded into orgasm. She felt herself degraded by her excitement at Pandora's humiliation and that in itself was even more thrilling.

Finally her body returned itself to normal. She almost wished she could turn over and go to sleep, but she knew what happened next.

'Then you screwed her,' she said simply, opening her legs just like Josh said Pandora did, and taking U to her. It was so good to feel him inside her again, and although he'd already given her satisfaction she moved against him and whispered encouragement to him for his sake rather than her own.

And indeed, although she wasn't going to climax again, no way, that beautiful tanned face, those corn-flower blue eyes, looking down at her in that vague lack of focus eyes take on when the body is about to orgasm, turned her on again, and she realised that she really was glad to have him back, and that despite the rather too many sexual encounters she'd had recently, he was the one who really did it for her. Then he came, calling her name, almost sobbing, and she held him tenderly, like a precious object, which was what he was to her.

'I can't get over what a complete idiot I've been.'

They were at the breakfast table, Yasmin with a croissant and a deep bowl of latte – after all, she had no work to hurry in to – and U with his usual antioxidant-rich white Chinese tea and papaya and banana salad topped with non-dairy yogurt and pumpkin seeds.

She licked the buttery flakes from her fingers. 'Please, U, just stop this self-recrimination. We've decided on our future, and there's no point in looking back at the past. You of all people have always said that.'

'I know,' he sighed. 'But I don't understand how I got sidetracked down this new sex road. When I was walking round the common yesterday morning, I knew something else was dawning, but it wasn't clear what it was. Yasmin, we're heading for a new era for sure, but it's nothing to do with sex.'

'Oh, no?' she said, almost politely. 'So what is it?'

'There's a mood change against the harsh multinational capitalism that's dominated society for so long,' he explained. 'A new caring ethos is abroad. Even the big conglomerates will have to toe the line, or they'll lose their business.'

Yasmin stared at him incredulously. 'U, doesn't this have everything to do with you being shafted by a US multinational, and not much to do with vibes you picked up on Clapham Common?'

'No, no,' he insisted. 'I noticed subconsciously, though I didn't pick up on it at the time, that things were changing. People aren't wearing so many logos any more, you know. Even the joggers weren't wearing brand-name trainers. We're heading for an age of caring, of acceptance of what is real rather than a culture of selfish brand-buying.'

She couldn't laugh, because really she did love him. I must, mustn't I, she thought, otherwise why have I been fighting so ferociously for him?

It wasn't exactly a road-to-Damascus moment, because his adoption of Amelia's sexual philosophy had shaken her faith in his precognitive abilities, but she felt that a few more scales had dropped from her eyes. But then again, he was still hers, and he was what she wanted – and, more importantly, was also going to do what she wanted.

'Well, go and change your plans for the next issue then,' she said good-humouredly. 'You'll have your work cut out, changing everything from sex to world peace in three weeks.'

'I didn't say world peace, I said –'

'Yeah, yeah.' She kissed him on the forehead. 'Now, can I ask you something? Will you call Pandora and try to see her now? Because, if you don't mind, I want to go to see Amelia and tell her it's over between you. And that would be a lot easier if I knew that Pandora was on her way to your office.'

U hesitated, then nodded. 'Sure. I suppose it's a bit hard on Amelia if I don't tell her myself, though.'

Yasmin shook her head. 'I'll be gentle with her. And we're agreed as to how you're going to handle Pandora?'

'Of course.' He leant over the table and kissed her. 'Yasmin, things are going to be fantastic, you'll see.'

'I hope so, Bear,' she said seriously.

He rose and went to the study to get his briefcase for work.

I do hope so, Yasmin thought. After all, I'm the one who's decided what we're going to do next, so if it all goes disastrously wrong I'll only have myself to blame.

On the other hand, she reasoned, maybe I could just blame fate, which was probably what U would do. In any event, first she had to see Amelia. She wanted her to be absolutely clear as to who'd won the fight for U. Then she had some more planning to do. The least she could do was to have a celebration with the friends who'd helped her win U back.

10

'Hi, you don't know me but don't hang up, I'm not trying to sell you anything. A friend of mine told me to call you – that *is* Amelia, right?'

'Sure,' said in a bored tone. 'What's it about?' She reached over to the bedside table for her coffee, knocking her magazine – *Slice* – on the floor as she did so. 'Oh, shit.'

'Sorry?'

'Nothing. So, who are you?'

'It's kind of hard to explain. My name's Alexandra, and I'm a friend of Cody's – you remember Cody, don't you?'

'Oh, yeah.' How could I forget, she thought, still feeling rather sour about the way Cody and Euan had seemed to ignore her apart from using her body as a buffer zone. Still, she couldn't really blame them. It had been stupid of her to drink so much.

'Well, Cody gave me your number. She said – oh God, I feel really embarrassed about this – but I'm having a lot of trouble with my sex life, and I can only really get off on the phone. None of my friends are speaking to me any more, and Cody said I should call you, because you give great sex and she's sure you'd be able to give me great phone sex.'

Amelia held the phone away from her ear and looked at the number – it wasn't anyone she knew. She wasn't in the mood for practical jokes.

'Is this serious?'

'Absolutely,' reassured the voice. It was actually quite a nice, warm voice, Amelia thought. Well, hell, she didn't have much to do today except practise, so why not. If she could help this woman out, she could maybe have a little play with herself at the same time. It could be fun.

'OK. So what do you want from me?'

'Can you tell me what you're wearing? I mean, as long as it's something sexy.'

Looking down at her nude body Amelia reckoned it was sexy enough, but obviously not what the caller wanted. She would have to improvise, and hope that Cody hadn't explained that she didn't go in for sexy underwear.

'It's sexy all right. In fact you got me just at the right moment. I'm in the middle of getting dressed, and so far I've got nothing else on but a bra and a thong in red satin. The bra's a really tiny quarter-cup one, because I like my nipples to show through my clothes.'

The voice murmured appreciation. 'How big are your tits?'

'Very. Well, not massive, not vulgar or anything, but just nice and round and bouncy.'

'What about your nipples? Have you got big nipples?'

'Sure,' said Amelia reassuringly. 'In fact, they're starting to get hard from talking to you. You've got a really sexy voice.'

'Oh, my God, is that right? Can you play with your nipples for me?'

'My pleasure,' said Amelia, smiling and giving one nipple a perfunctory tweak. 'Hey, Alexandra, why don't you tell me what you've got on?'

'Me? Oh, well, I dressed up to call you. I've got a

little camisole on with lots of ribbons, though it's undone so I can play with my tits while I'm talking to you, and some French knickers. They're black, you know, matching.'

'That sounds great. I'd love to see you. Are you touching your tits, too?'

'Yeah,' breathed the voice. 'I'm looking in the mirror, too. Have you got a mirror you can look in?'

'Well, I have, but I'd have to get off the bed. And I'd really like to picture you rather than see myself,' said Amelia, feeling quite pleased with herself for thinking that one up.

'You're right! I'm not looking any more. I'm getting on the bed, and I'm lying on my back. I want to put my hand down my knickers.'

'I'd like to be there to put my hand down your knickers,' replied Amelia, lowering and softening her voice. 'Why don't you do it, and imagine it's me?'

She just heard breathing on the other end of the line. 'So, are you touching yourself?'

The voice moaned. 'No, it's you, isn't it? It's your hand I can feel. You're just gently stroking my clit, and probing up inside me with another finger to make it all nice and wet.'

'That's me,' Amelia confirmed, smiling as her own hand went down to her sex. 'You're amazingly wet, Alexandra. Do you always get this wet?'

'No, it's just for you,' said the woman, sounding almost delirious. 'That is incredible. God, your hand knows just what to do.'

'That's right,' confirmed Amelia as her hand moved exactly as she wanted it to do. How much better could this get? It was a real turn-on, reminding her of when she and Melinda Sue used to masturbate together while recounting each other's random sex acts. 'Alexandra? I think I'd like to give you some head, if that's OK?'

'Oh, my God,' the other woman squealed. 'I can't believe this. God, your hair brushing against my thighs, oh, your mouth against me – this is so amazing!'

'Mmm, you taste really good,' said Amelia, as though coming up for air. 'I'm going to get my head down to taste some more of your sweet juice, Alexandra.' She realised that her role as phone sex goddess was somewhat limited while her mouth was supposedly in action, so made yummy noises instead.

'You know just what to do,' breathed Alexandra. 'Have you had sex with lots of women, Amelia?'

'Loads,' she boasted. 'I know, they always say I give great head. Do you want to come yet? Or shall we go on as we are – oh, shit.'

The doorbell pealed loud and clear.

'What's that?' said the voice on the end of the phone.

'It's the door. I'll ignore it, and we can carry on.'

'No, don't ignore it,' Alexandra urged. 'Just say you go to the door dressed like that and it's some really sexy meter-reading guy or something? He can play with us, too.'

'Very likely,' laughed Amelia. 'It'll either be the postman, who'll die of fright at the sight of a young girl in the nude, or someone trying to get me to change the gas to electricity or vice versa.'

The bell rang again.

'Sod it, I'll have to go,' said Amelia in exasperation. 'Just hang on, I won't be a minute.'

Throwing the phone on the bed she shrugged on her ancient tartan dressing-gown and padded out to the door. Opening it, she found neither a man nor anyone who looked remotely like someone who was interested in where her energy came from, unless it were her sexual energy. A quite beautiful woman with long black curly hair, a white suit and a phone to her ear stood there.

'Amelia, I presume,' she said.

Amelia nodded co-operatively, and then took in fully the fact that the woman was talking into her phone rather than at her. A second passed and she realised.

'Oh, God, you must be Alexandra. Come in.'

'Thanks.' The woman turned off the phone. 'Not much need for that now.'

'You said you were lying on your bed,' said Amelia accusingly.

Alexandra pushed the tartan robe aside. The hastily tied belt quickly disentangled itself to show Amelia's naked body.

'You said you were wearing a red satin bra and thong, so we're about even,' returned the woman.

'So what's going on? It's not phone sex you're after, is it?'

The other woman, who definitely didn't look like the type who needed to get sex from a stranger over the phone, smiled and sat down on the sofa. 'No, dear. It's not sex at all. And it's not Alexandra, it's Yasmin. We have met, but it's probably about five years ago, and you've certainly changed so maybe I have.'

'Oh, my God. What a disaster.' Amelia felt completely nonplussed. 'What on earth – why on earth did Cody give you my number?'

Yasmin gave a brittle laugh and instead of replying looked appraisingly at the furniture.

'I guess this is the sofa Josh fucked Pandora on?' she enquired politely.

Amelia stared at her in amazement. 'How do you know that?'

Yasmin shrugged, smiling. 'I know lots of stuff, my dear. Don't you hate it when your lover screws your aunt?'

'Sure,' said Amelia like a sulky child. She really didn't know how to react.

'I suppose you don't even know that she had U after you rushed out to meet Josh the other night,' Yasmin added.

Amelia stared. 'That is so not true. I don't believe you. Pandora really wanted me and U to make a go of it.'

'Oh yes, obviously. Though did it never occur to you to ask yourself why?' said Yasmin.

Never mind that, Amelia thought, what about this tale of Pandora and U?

'Tell me that's not true, about him and her.'

Yasmin shook her head slowly. 'I'm sorry. He told me himself last night. I don't know how much you know about your aunt's rather odd sexual habits, but you've seen her bedroom so I guess you know she's into erotica in a big way. Well, one of her favourite turn-ons is to have her lover tell her a story first. U couldn't really think of one, which isn't that surprising as he's screwed Pandora so many times in the past it's probably hard to think of an original scenario. However, you'd just told him a rather titillating tale about Josh and your child-hood violin, so he made do with that.'

Amelia stared at her. 'No, surely not. Surely he wouldn't tell her that?'

The other woman laughed shortly. 'Well, you might think that's shocking. Personally I think it's a lot more distasteful that your aunt actually got off on being told about your degradation.'

The words hung in the air for a moment, a moment which started with Amelia unable to believe what she had just heard, but ended with the realisation that what she was being told was actually true. Amelia let out an anguished sob. She couldn't believe the double betrayal. But as much as she tried to tell herself that Yasmin was lying out of some nasty revenge, she knew that it was true. It was just too horrible for anyone to invent.

'I'm sorry,' Yasmin was saying. 'I know this must be a shock to you. But I'm afraid I have another one. U's finished with you, dear. You don't have to believe me, but he only took up with you because Pandora threw you together, and she had her own rather nasty reasons for doing that.'

Amelia couldn't help the tears from coming. She wanted to be sassy and cool and dignified, either telling Yasmin she really had got a little tired of U anyway or just throwing her out imperiously and refusing to believe her little game, but she just couldn't manage it. Not for the first time since she'd been involved in Pandora's world, she felt like a lost little girl.

She was more than surprised when Yasmin put her arm around her and stroked her back.

'I'm sorry to be so blunt. We've only just found out exactly what's been going on, and we had a long talk last night and we've decided to make a go of it. I'm afraid we can't really fit you into the equation.'

'What makes you think I'd want to fit in with you?' demanded Amelia fiercely between her slowly lessening sobs.

'I'm just telling you the way it is. If you want to carry on fighting for him, I can't stop you but I can tell you that you're not going to win. You have absolutely no chance.'

'So what? Maybe I don't even care any more. I have my own life. I was doing just fine until I met U.'

'Sure,' soothed Yasmin. 'I understand you're a very good musician, and you could have a great future ahead of you. But if you're going to continue to live with Pandora, you'd better know what she's been scheming.'

Amelia could hardly believe what Yasmin related. She thought Pandora had betrayed her by having sex with U but it was far worse – she had merely used her to destroy the serenity of U's life.

'I wish I could say I didn't believe it,' she said slowly. 'But I know how ambitious she is. That's everything to her. Sometimes mum reckoned that it was just compensation because she wasn't any good at relationships. Maybe I should feel sorry for her rather than hate her.'

'I shouldn't bother with hating,' offered Yasmin. 'Life's a bit too short for that. On the other hand, I shouldn't feel sorry for her either. If Pandora was more interested in relationships than her magazine, she would have gone full-on for them instead. She's a single-minded woman, and you have to have a certain admiration for her.' She smiled. 'God, I can't believe I said that. I used to think she was a real old harpy, but I have to say you have to admire a woman who really goes for it, regardless of how abhorrent you think her ideas are.'

'Like Margaret Thatcher?' suggested Amelia.

Yasmin frowned. 'That's taking the analogy too far. Anyway, don't hate her. Just see her for what she is. Christ, I'm sounding wise. It must be time to go.'

It was bizarre but Amelia didn't want her to go. Yasmin was nice, and kind, and hadn't been too hard on Amelia, which was pretty good considering she'd just done her best to screw Yasmin's marriage up. More importantly, Amelia's female friends were all at home or in New York and she really felt like having someone to talk to, even though it was a woman who had every reason to hate her.

'You know I never actually had penetrative sex with U,' she said shyly. 'I don't know if he told you.'

Yasmin nodded. 'Oh yes, that reminds me. If you don't mind a little advice, and although I hate to say it you must admit I'm just about old enough to be your mother, your sexual philosophy is all about going nowhere. It could have destroyed *Slice*, you know, if U had used it as the basis for the next issue.'

'Hang on, that was nothing to do with me.' Amelia felt stronger in her indignation. 'I was totally surprised when he told me. It was never meant to be a nation-wide movement, just something my friend invented.'

'A little nineteen-year-old's rebellion?' said Yasmin kindly.

'Not exactly. I think as far as she was concerned it was a way to stand out in the crowd – this was in New York, where everyone wants to stand out – but for me it was just –' Amelia looked at Yasmin helplessly, knowing she was going to confide in her without really knowing why '– it was just because I'd had a really bad time before I left England, and it was a way to stop that happening again.'

Yasmin sat down on the sofa. 'What happened? Go on, tell me. I won't tell anyone else.'

Amelia sighed. 'Please don't tell U. Not that there's much to tell. About a year ago, just after I finished my A levels and before I went to summer school, I was volunteering at the local music festival where I met a guy doing the same thing. I really fell for him. We had music in common but that was about all – he was twenty-six, I was eighteen, he was a computer geek and I was about to go to music college. But I fell for him totally. I suppose so far I'd just hung out with guys from school or music lessons who were about my age, maybe a couple of years older, but really just boys. Rob was a really together guy, and he was so nice looking. It sounds stupid because there was nothing that special about him, but I guess that's what love's all about. I was in love, or I thought I was, and at the time – I know this is so immature, but I thought we'd be together for ever.'

Yasmin smiled sadly. 'First love, yeah, I remember. We all do. So what happened?'

'Well – nothing! We had a great time at first, doing lots of crazy things and lots of ordinary things, well, just the things lovers do, I suppose. The sex was fantastic, right from the first time. He played music in his flat all the time, and every time we screwed it was to music.' She smiled at Yasmin ruefully. 'I think I can remember everything we made love to, from the 'Ride of the Valkyrie' to Purcell to 'Carmina Burana'. Every time I saw him I was ready for sex, it was unbelievable. I almost felt I could come the minute I walked through the flat door.

'But suddenly, though I didn't feel any different towards him – I was really totally besotted, quite honestly – I realised he had moved away from me, emotionally. One week we were having this incredibly close, warm, *loving* relationship, and the next week his mind, heart, whatever you like to call it, was in another place. We were getting on OK, but it was all superficial. Do you know what I mean?'

'Only too well,' said Yasmin sympathetically. 'When it goes, it goes.'

'I wish I'd just accepted that,' said Amelia bitterly. 'But I didn't. I clung on, thinking that it would get better, and then one night I just pushed him. I suppose

I thought that if I threatened to end it, he'd come to his senses and realise how much he loved me, and everything would be OK from then on.'

'Don't tell me, you threatened to end it and he said, fine.'

'Ten out of ten. He said we seemed to be getting on OK but if that was the way I felt, so be it. I told him OK wasn't enough, that I wanted more, but he just said he wasn't really ready for commitment. He was happy to carry on being friends and having great sex, but that was all.'

'And you didn't want that.'

'No way! So we split.' Amelia looked down at her hands. 'I know, you're going to say that this happens to every woman, and that it'll never be as bad again, and look, I've got over it now, et cetera.'

'I wasn't, actually,' said Yasmin. 'I was just going to say that something I've only recently learnt is that there's really nothing quite like being friends and having great sex.'

'With U?' said Amelia in a small voice.

Yasmin laughed. 'No, although I guess that's true too. During the last couple of weeks I've been looked after by good friends, with whom I've also had great sex, and it's been an eye opener. Don't dismiss it. So what happened after you split? Did you see him again?'

'No. I cried for a week. Mum was really worried about me. To make matters worse we broke up just about a week before my birthday. I hadn't made any plans – I just assumed Rob and I would be going out somewhere. Mum dragged me out to a concert, but my heart wasn't in it. I even wore black in mourning for him.' She giggled. 'Hey, that really was childish. I think I am getting over him now. So, just to finish up, Mum decided I needed a distraction before I went to music college, otherwise I just wouldn't be able to concentrate, so I managed to put my course off for a year and Pandora pulled some strings and got me a year's tuition at the Juilliard School in New York. And there I met Melinda Sue, the inventor of random acts of sexual kindness. Having been thrown over by someone who wanted a good friend to have sex with, the idea of sex being completely segregated from relationships seemed a very sound idea.'

'Sure.' Yasmin looked at her quizzically. 'And with U, did you feel the same way you felt about this guy Rob?'

Amelia shook her head. 'Oh no, it was completely different. For a start, we didn't have sex, well not properly. And he was so much more sophisticated, and older, and stuff.'

'So you weren't in love with him?' pounced Yasmin.

'Well, I thought I was, but – oh, shit, I can't really get over him screwing Pandora. Especially after telling her about me and Josh.' Amelia suddenly felt overwhelmingly desolate. 'Maybe this is the way life's going to be for me, falling for men who don't really want me.'

'Don't be daft,' said Yasmin bluntly. 'You've had two serious relationships which have failed, well, believe me, that's nothing. Especially considering the first one was with a commitment phobe and the second with an older married man. You're not so immature that you really think that's set a pattern.'

Amelia suddenly felt surprisingly mature. 'Hey, you're right. What is it Mum always says, two swallows don't make a summer? I suppose two relationships with the wrong guys doesn't make me a failure.'

'No,' said Yasmin softly. 'Not at all. You'll be fine.'

'I know. Look, thanks a lot for listening to me. I

never really talked to anyone about it much. Mum just said I was being silly, which was right but the last thing I needed to hear at the time, and Melinda Sue just dismissed it as relationship shit that was bound to happen. I suppose I need more friends, really.'

'Ones you have sex with?' said Yasmin teasingly.

Amelia laughed. 'Maybe both!'

They looked at each other with something that couldn't really be described as affection, Amelia thought, but was perhaps just a little bit like understanding.

'You get yourself some friends,' said Yasmin. 'I used to have some close girlfriends, but you move around, change jobs, they emigrate – I only just realised I'm not so hot on mates either. That's something I'm going to sort out, too.'

She put her hand on Amelia's arm. 'Take care. I don't suppose we'll see each other again. It really would be better if you didn't see U either.'

Deep down Amelia wished she could see U, just to say goodbye, but knew that Yasmin's generosity of spirit was conditional upon her backing off.

'No. Thanks.'

'Have a nice life.'

Amelia walked Yasmin to the door and watched her as she walked purposefully up the road, her rear view provocatively swaying in her high-heeled shoes, her arse defined by the tight white skirt, her wild and sexy hair tumbling over her shoulders. At least, she thought, I've lost to someone worth losing to.

Going back to her bedroom she thought about Yasmin's advice. She was right about friends. Once college started she'd make lots of them. Some might be guys who she'd have great sex with – just like the relationship she could have had with Rob.

Thinking of friends and sex sent her thoughts to

Melinda Sue. It was eleven o'clock – seven in New York. Throwing off the tartan robe she snuggled up in the duvet and picked up her phone. Yasmin's ruse had been a bit of fun. She'd wake Melinda Sue for a little phone sex before getting on with her new life.

'Right, people! Hey, Kip, just shut up for five minutes, please! I just want to propose a toast and say a few words.'

'Oh, my God, it's like a sodding wedding,' said Kip, turning away from his new friend Cody. 'Go on, bitch. Get it over with.'

'Thanks.' Yasmin nodded to Willie, who motioned one of his interchangeable barmen to bring over a couple of bottles of champagne.

'Well, first of all you know why you're here. I just want to say jointly and communally thanks to all of you for being great mates at a time of extreme need.'

U shifted uncomfortably in his chair, and she smiled at him mischievously. 'Except U, of course, who has been – and will be again, I'm sure – a great mate in all sorts of times, but obviously not recent weeks. However, it seemed only right that he should be here today as guest of honour.'

'You mean like if it hadn't been for him, we wouldn't all have got to know you – or maybe not in the same way,' said the irrepressible Kip.

'Something like that,' said Yasmin vaguely. U certainly knew how Kip and Stevenson had helped her, and he probably guessed it wasn't them she stayed with on the first night of their troubles, but it wasn't really necessary to go into details about the others. They'd wiped the slate clean, and as long as he wasn't going to go on about Amelia she didn't see the need to flaunt her own little infidelities either.

'First of all, thanks to Willie and Euan, who were here for me on a very unhappy night, and made me feel a lot better. Secondly to Cody, who I'm sure would have been there on that night if she hadn't been on holiday, but who gave me her friendship later.'

'More than friendship, I bet,' said Kip in an undertone, winking slyly at Cody. Yasmin heard him but ignored him.

'Then Kip and Stevenson, who happened to be around on another fateful evening. Thanks for everything, guys. Apart from calling me Yas.

'And lastly, thanks to Josh, who put up with me at work day after day, and has been the best friend a girl could have. It's just a shame that we're no longer working together.' She looked at him with more than affection. 'I miss you already.'

'Me too,' he said wistfully.

'So cheers, guys. Thanks to you all again.' She lifted her now full glass. 'To the best friends a girl could have.'

'Well, I'll drink to the best girl a friend could have,' said Euan, raising his and gazing fondly at Yasmin. 'Good luck, gorgeous girl.'

'Hear, hear,' said the others, all drinking.

'There's something else,' she said after they'd all started talking again. 'I didn't only arrange this evening to thank you. There's something I want to tell you.'

'If you are, it's not me,' said Euan, obviously remembering the pregnancy rumour.

'Shut it,' she said equably. 'No, it's about U and I. You know that we're going to seriously make a go of our relationship. Obviously, or he wouldn't be here.'

'You're not going to tell us that you really are going to try for a baby,' said Willie disbelievingly.

'Don't be dense, Willie. Just let me finish. You all know as well the part the Wicked Witch of the West, as Josh calls her, played in all of this, and why.'

'The cow,' sniffed Kip. 'Not only did she try to wreck your life, but she's taken my little playmate away from me.'

'Let's face it, Kip, we spend too much time at home together as it is. Things'll be much better when we're not together all day as well.'

'Can't you take him back, U?' said Kip imploringly. 'Now you're not going to make us a laughing stock and all that. You know he's the best.'

'Kip, just shut up a moment,' said Yasmin severely. 'As I was saying, you know why Pandora did what she did.'

She looked round the expectant faces at the table. 'This may come as a bit of a shock to you, but we've decided that U's going to take the job of launching *Black Box* in New York. Which means that the take-over's going ahead, *Slice* is going to get a new editor, and we're emigrating, or at least moving across the Atlantic for a couple of years, within the next month.'

There was a stunned silence. Even Kip couldn't find anything to say.

'I guessed you'd be surprised,' said Yasmin lamely.

'Surprised? I'd say appalled,' said Josh bitterly. 'You thank us for helping you to fight for U, and now you're more or less giving in and doing exactly what she wanted all along!'

'This is terrible!' said Willie tragically. 'How can you just play into her hands, Yasmin? If it wasn't for her you wouldn't have had all this trauma. I'd like to strangle the conniving old cow, right enough!'

'I know how it sounds,' she said placatingly. 'If someone had suggested it to me a few days ago I would have told them that they'd lost their marbles. But when I sat down and thought about our future, I realised that it wasn't enough for U and I to make a new start in the same old life.

'I'm fed up with writing soap operas,' she continued, looking round the table thinking that she was actually giving a boardroom speech like someone out of *The Brothers*, the first soap she remembered from her childhood. She wondered incidentally if she'd ever stop comparing her life to a scene from a TV show.

'U's been editing *Slice* for ever. If we stayed in London we'd carry on doing the same old things. We're a bit too used to luxury to backpack round the world, and anyway both of us really like to work.

'When I turned over in my mind alternatives for a proper fresh start, I decided I wanted to live somewhere else. I've lived in London all my adult life, but then where else do you live if you're a media professional?'

'New York,' said Josh, nodding. 'Of course. But did you have to go with Pandora?'

'I know, it seems bizarre,' said Yasmin almost apologetically. 'But I knew that U would love the challenge of setting up a new magazine. I also knew that Pandora wanted this so much that she'd make it very attractive financially. It was an offer too good to refuse.'

'I still think you're barmy,' said Josh bluntly. 'So you'll be working for those arseholes who tried to shaft you. It doesn't make sense.'

'Well, I won't be working for them,' explained Yasmin. 'In fact, I won't be working at all, at least not for anyone else.'

'So what are you going to do?' Josh asked.

'Oh, Josh, surely you can guess. The same thing that all us media hacks end up doing – or rather trying to do,' she answered.

'Oh, fuck. Not the bloody novel,' he groaned. 'Spare me!'

'I'm afraid so,' she said, laughing. 'And what better place to do it! A new city, the most vibrant in the world, with plenty of time on my hands to explore and get inspiration –'

'Or blown up,' said Cody darkly. 'I wouldn't fancy it.'

'You've got to live a little on the edge,' said Yasmin. 'At least, every so often. And now U's got over the shock of me suggesting it, he's quite keen too – aren't you?'

He nodded as she turned to him, and they both started smiling at each other, and Yasmin felt she wasn't ever going to stop.

'And let's face it, the story's already been written. U was meant to have an affair, I was meant to take my revenge and find some new friends, the magazine was meant to be taken over and we were meant to move to the States.'

'What in God's name are you talking about?' asked Willie, obviously bewildered.

'Oh, my God. Don't tell me you're following the plot,' groaned Josh disbelievingly. 'This is ridiculous.'

'Ridiculous or sinister?' riposted Yasmin. 'For those of you who don't know, the new soap Josh and I were working on has a plot that mirrored my life – the affair which was set up because of the imminent takeover.'

'But, Yasmin, you can't believe you have to follow the plot,' said Euan slowly.

'No. But the more I thought about it, the more I realised that it was the right move,' she said. 'What I can't explain is why our lives have followed the same storyline as the series.'

'I suppose U thinks the plot's floating about in the

great blue yonder, unconsciously influencing what everyone's been doing,' said Josh sarcastically.

'Something like that,' laughed Yasmin. 'Whatever, it's fairly bizarre. I was pretty frightened a couple of times, thinking that the storyliners were somehow controlling our whole lives, but now I think it's just coincidence.'

'Synchronicity,' supplied U.

'Fucking stupid,' growled Josh.

'So that's our news. Now, is anyone going to propose a good luck toast?'

'Rather reluctantly, seeing as you'll be going out of our lives,' said Willie. 'Well, if you're sure it's what you want, good luck, darling girl. Take an awful lot of care, and if you need me, or I should say us, we're all at the other end of the phone.' He raised his glass. 'To your new life together. Yasmin and U!'

The others echoed his words and they all drank the toast.

'I said it was like a wedding,' observed Kip. 'Don't suppose there's any cake.'

'No, but there's a choice of desserts,' said Euan, looking directly at Yasmin. 'I particularly recommend the poached peaches – do you remember them, gorgeous?'

She felt a slight flush come to her cheeks. 'Of course. It was absolutely fantastic.'

And that wasn't all that had been fantastic, she thought wistfully as she watched her friends talk animatedly about the respective merits of fruit or cake. Despite all the misery she'd had over the last couple of weeks, she'd had some marvellous, memorable moments.

In fact, she reflected, probably enough marvellous

moments to fill a novel – though she'd have to publish under an assumed name, of course.

She felt U's eyes on her and turned to kiss him. Dear U. He was worth it, after all. At least she hoped so. The only thing she hadn't told him was that he was seriously on probation for the next year or two. Temptations were going to abound in New York, but then again not just for him. As she'd already said, she'd have to do a bit of research for the novel. Which could be rather fun.

Visit the Black Lace website at
www.blacklace-books.co.uk

BLACKLACE

FIND OUT THE LATEST INFORMATION AND TAKE
ADVANTAGE OF OUR FANTASTIC FREE BOOK OFFER!
ALSO VISIT THE SITE FOR . . .

- All Black Lace titles currently available
  and how to order online

- Great new offers

- Writers' guidelines

- Author interviews

- An erotica newsletter

- Features

- Cool links

**BLACK LACE – THE LEADING IMPRINT
OF WOMEN'S SEXY FICTION**

**TAKING YOUR EROTIC READING
PLEASURE TO NEW HORIZONS**

LOOK OUT FOR THE ALL-NEW BLACK LACE BOOKS – AVAILABLE NOW!

All books priced £6.99 in the UK. Please note publication dates apply to the UK only. For other territories, please contact your retailer.

DRIVEN BY DESIRE
Savannah Smythe
ISBN 0 352 33799 0

When Rachel's husband abandons both her and his taxi-cab business and flees the country, she is left to pick up the pieces. However, this is a blessing in disguise as Rachel, along with her friend Sharma, transforms his business into an exclusive chauffeur service for discerning gentlemen – with all the perks that offers. What Rachel doesn't know is that two of her regular clients are jewel thieves with exotic tastes in sexual experimentation. As Rachel is lured into an underworld lifestyle of champagne, diamonds and lustful indulgence, she finds a familiar face is involved in some very shady activity! **Another cracking story of strong women and sexy double dealing from Savannah Smythe.**

THE LION LOVER
Mercedes Kelly
ISBN 0 352 33162 3

Settling into life in 1930s Kenya, Mathilde Valentine finds herself sent to a harem where the Sultan, his sadistic brother and adolescent son all make sexual demands on her. Meanwhile, Olensky – the rugged game hunter and 'lion lover' – plots her escape, but will she want to be rescued? **A wonderful exploration of 'White Mischief' goings on in 1930s Africa.**

Coming in July

COUNTRY PLEASURES
Primula Bond
ISBN 0 352 33810 5

Janie and Sally escape to the countryside hoping to get some sun and relaxation. When the weather turns nasty, the two women find themselves confined to their remote cottage with little to do except eat, drink and talk about men. They soon become the focus of attention for the lusty farmers in the area who are well-built, down-to-earth and very different from the boys they have been dating in town. **Lust-filled pursuits in the English countryside.**

THE RELUCTANT PRINCESS
Patty Glenn
ISBN 0 532 33809 0

Martha's a rich valley girl who's living on the wrong side of the tracks and hanging out with Hollywood hustlers. Things were OK when her bodyguard Gus was looking after her, but now he's in hospital Martha's gone back to her bad old ways. When she meets mean, moody and magnificent private investigator Joaquin Lee, the sexual attraction between them is instant and intense. If Martha can keep herself on the straight and narrow for a year, her family will let her have access to her inheritance. Lee reckons he can help out while pocketing a cut for himself. **A dynamic battle of wills between two very stubborn, very sexy characters.**

ARIA APPASSIONATA
Juliet Hastings
ISBN 0 352 33056 2

Tess Challoner has made it. She is going to play Carmen in a new production of the opera that promises to be as raunchy and explicit as it is intelligent. But Tess needs to learn a lot about passion and desire before the opening night. Tony Varguez, the handsome but jealous Spanish tenor, takes on the task of her education. When Tess finds herself drawn to a desirable new member of the cast, she knows she's playing with fire. **Life imitating art – with dramatically sexual consequences.**

Coming in August

WILD IN THE COUNTRY
Monica Belle
ISBN 0 352 33824 5

When Juliet Eden is sacked for having sex with a sous-chef, she leaves the prestigious London kitchen where she's been working and heads for the country. Alone in her inherited cottage, boredom soon sets in – until she discovers the rural delights of poaching, and of the muscular young gamekeeper who works the estate. When the local landowner falls for her, things are looking better still, but threaten to turn sour when her ex-boss, Gabriel, makes an unexpected appearance. **City vs country in Monica Belle's latest story of rustic retreats and sumptuous feasts!**

THE TUTOR
Portia Da Costa
ISBN 0 352 32946 7

When Rosalind Howard becomes Julian Hadey's private librarian, she soon finds herself attracted by his persuasive charms and distinguished appearance. He is an unashamed sensualist who, together with his wife, Celeste, has hatched an intriguing challenge for their new employee. As well as cataloguing their collection of erotica, Rosie is expected to educate Celeste's young and beautiful cousin David in the arts of erotic love. **A long-overdue reprint of this arousing tale of erotic initiation written by a pioneer of women's sex fiction.**

Black Lace Booklist

Information is correct at time of printing. To avoid disappointment check availability before ordering. Go to www.blacklace-books.co.uk. All books are priced £6.99 unless another price is given.

BLACK LACE BOOKS WITH A CONTEMPORARY SETTING

☐ IN THE FLESH Emma Holly	ISBN 0 352 33498 3	£5.99
☐ SHAMELESS Stella Black	ISBN 0 352 33485 1	£5.99
☐ INTENSE BLUE Lyn Wood	ISBN 0 352 33496 7	£5.99
☐ THE NAKED TRUTH Natasha Rostova	ISBN 0 352 33497 5	£5.99
☐ A SPORTING CHANCE Susie Raymond	ISBN 0 352 33501 7	£5.99
☐ TAKING LIBERTIES Susie Raymond	ISBN 0 352 33357 X	£5.99
☐ A SCANDALOUS AFFAIR Holly Graham	ISBN 0 352 33523 8	£5.99
☐ THE NAKED FLAME Crystalle Valentino	ISBN 0 352 33528 9	£5.99
☐ ON THE EDGE Laura Hamilton	ISBN 0 352 33534 3	£5.99
☐ LURED BY LUST Tania Picarda	ISBN 0 352 33533 5	£5.99
☐ THE HOTTEST PLACE Tabitha Flyte	ISBN 0 352 33536 X	£5.99
☐ THE NINETY DAYS OF GENEVIEVE Lucinda Carrington	ISBN 0 352 33070 8	£5.99
☐ DREAMING SPIRES Juliet Hastings	ISBN 0 352 33584 X	
☐ THE TRANSFORMATION Natasha Rostova	ISBN 0 352 33311 1	
☐ STELLA DOES HOLLYWOOD Stella Black	ISBN 0 352 33588 2	
☐ SIN.NET Helena Ravenscroft	ISBN 0 352 33598 X	
☐ TWO WEEKS IN TANGIER Annabel Lee	ISBN 0 352 33599 8	
☐ HIGHLAND FLING Jane Justine	ISBN 0 352 33616 1	
☐ PLAYING HARD Tina Troy	ISBN 0 352 33617 X	
☐ SYMPHONY X Jasmine Stone	ISBN 0 352 33629 3	
☐ SUMMER FEVER Anna Ricci	ISBN 0 352 33625 0	
☐ CONTINUUM Portia Da Costa	ISBN 0 352 33120 8	
☐ OPENING ACTS Suki Cunningham	ISBN 0 352 33630 7	
☐ FULL STEAM AHEAD Tabitha Flyte	ISBN 0 352 33637 4	
☐ A SECRET PLACE Ella Broussard	ISBN 0 352 33307 3	
☐ GAME FOR ANYTHING Lyn Wood	ISBN 0 352 33639 0	
☐ FORBIDDEN FRUIT Susie Raymond	ISBN 0 352 33306 5	

To find out the latest information about Black Lace titles, check out the website: www.blacklace-books.co.uk or send for a booklist with complete synopses by writing to:

Black Lace Booklist, Virgin Books Ltd
Thames Wharf Studios
Rainville Road
London W6 9HA

Please include an SAE of decent size. Please note only British stamps are valid.

Our privacy policy
We will not disclose information you supply us to any other parties. We will not disclose any information which identifies you personally to any person without your express consent.

From time to time we may send out information about Black Lace books and special offers. Please tick here if you do <u>not</u> wish to receive Black Lace information. ❏

Please send me the books I have ticked above.

Name ....

Address ....

....

....

....

Post Code ....

Send to: Cash Sales, Black Lace Books, Thames Wharf Studios, Rainville Road, London W6 9HA.

US customers: for prices and details of how to order books for delivery by mail, call 1-800-343-4499.

Please enclose a cheque or postal order, made payable to Virgin Books Ltd, to the value of the books you have ordered plus postage and packing costs as follows:

UK and BFPO – £1.00 for the first book, 50p for each subsequent book.

Overseas (including Republic of Ireland) – £2.00 for the first book, £1.00 for each subsequent book.

If you would prefer to pay by VISA, ACCESS/MASTERCARD, DINERS CLUB, AMEX or SWITCH, please write your card number and expiry date here:

....

Signature ....

Please allow up to 28 days for delivery.